Advance Praise for
Love, Sometimes

"This is the funniest and most honest book I have read about inside Hollywood, ageism, and love. If you want a good laugh and an education pick this book up!"

—Mo'Nique, *actor*

"*Love, Sometimes* is a scream about ageism in the Hollywood Industry and a poignant love story about an unconventional love!"

—Marissa Winokur, *actor, singer*

"At last a writer is writing the truth about ageism, Hollywood, creativity, and true love and sexuality! Love it! Couldn't put it down!"

—Paula Abdul, *dancer, choreographer, actor*

"Barbara Rose Brooker is a hoot! This book is funny, and deeply serious and interesting. Love the book!"

—Kathie Lee Gifford, *TV host, singer, author, actor*

"Barbara Rose Brooker, author of *The Viagra Diaries*, does it again! Her latest book, *Love, Sometimes*, delivers the honest truth about ageism in the Hollywood networks and her struggles trying to figure where she fits in until she falls in love with a fifty-one-year-old! Barbara's brutally accurate, often funny observations about still trying to matter after sixty is spot on, thought provoking and honest! A great read!"

—Cristina Ferrare, *author, TV host*

"This book breaks all boundaries, speaks the truth about ageism in the networks, love and sex with a younger, bi-racial gay man. It's funny, and true and smart!"

—Miss J, *TV host*

Love,
Sometimes

Love, Sometimes

A Novel About
Risk, Hollywood,
and Controversial Love

Barbara Rose Brooker

A POST HILL PRESS BOOK

Love, Sometimes:
A Novel About Risk, Hollywood, and Controversial Love

ISBN: 978-1-64293-412-0
ISBN (eBook): 978-1-64293-413-7

Cover art by Cody Corcoran
Interior design and composition, Greg Johnson, Textbook Perfect

Post Hill Press
New York • Nashville
posthillpress.com

Published in the United States of America

To my late father Barney Rose,
who taught me perseverance.

1

You never know with fate. Just when you think your dreams have fallen apart, something fantastic happens.

After all the years I've been writing books that went nowhere, my agent Edwina Miller calls and informs me that WC Network wants to option my novel *The Viagra Diaries*. "Straight to series," she says exuberantly. Excitedly she informs me that Joshua Bitterman, the head of WC Network, wants to meet me "pronto," that he's setting up a lunch in two days, and that she wants me in LA the next day so we can have a meeting first. I'm beyond thrilled, but apprehensive. So far *The Viagra Diaries* has had two former options on it and the network writers turned my sixty-five-year-old protagonist into a twenty-something moron and the options fell apart. "This time it will work," Edwina promises. Her new assistant Amen will text me the flight details, and they'll send a car to pick me up at the airport.

By now, it's near twilight. Feeling ecstatic and wanting to process the good news, I stand by the window, admiring the mist of fog floating on the San Francisco hills like gray lace. God, it's something. The city's beauty never ceases to amaze me. Still, it's hard to believe this is happening. One never knows with this business. Thirty years I've been writing, dreaming of writing a bestseller, fame, fortune, and a legacy for my two daughters. But things have been hard—teaching writing workshops to adults for little money, writing columns, and then I had writer's block. Until several years ago when I'd written *The Viagra Diaries*, a novel about sex after sixty, but publishers said no one wanted to read about an old lady having sex, so I self-published it. Thank God Edwina liked it and shopped it around. Now finally my daughters will see that all the failed options, ups, downs, and financial hardships were worth it.

Lisa, at thirty-seven, lives in LA with her husband Hank, a robot programmer. For years she was a major talent agent until, sick of the industry, she became a psychologist specializing in agents with anxiety and eating disorders. Nanny is thirty-five, and writes a blog about rescue dogs and lives in the Oakland Hills with her accountant husband Larry.

I call the girls and patch them into a conference call, telling them the good news and that I'll be in LA the next day. Lisa and I make plans for dinner and I promise to call Nanny after the lunch meeting with the network head.

As night falls, I talk to my best friend Myra Saperstein, water my orchid plants, and finish packing. Finally I go to bed, watching the reflections from the moon slide along the ceiling, and slip into a dreamless sleep.

* * *

LA is humid and a grainy dark film sticks to the streets like fallen ash, from the recent fires. As this hot-looking Indian driver wearing a huge turban drives fast, weaving his town car in and out of the lanes along the congested freeway, I think about my father who was a screenwriter for Universal. Mother didn't want to live in LA, so he commuted, and often when I was a teen, he'd take me with him to Los Angeles. At the sets, I'd stood there, watching the actors rehearse, deciding I too wanted to be a writer. I'd been programmed to marry a rich man and write as a hobby but my father had encouraged me to follow my dreams. But then at fifty he'd dropped dead on the set and not one of his scripts ever made it to the screen.

I look out the window at the glaring sun soaking the grimy sky, huge billboards, thin palm trees, and hot cracked streets, as if dreams are stuck under them. Nothing feels real here, but it's where the world of entertainment is and where dreams come true and I love it.

Om, the driver, stops his car in front of a tall marble building. Smoothing my hair, turning frizzy from the humidity, I hurry inside, my high heel platform shoes clicking on the pavement.

I take a small elevator to the tenth floor, keeping my eyes closed, fearing that like in my dreams, the elevator will keep going up and never stop. The doors open and I step into a beige reception area and Edwina's receptionist Heather greets me with a movement of her small lips, as if a kiss. Her purple lipstick matches the streaks in her long black hair. "Edwina is waiting?" says Heather, as if a question.

I follow her down a long hallway, to Edwina's office. "At last we meet," Amen says, placing his long hands under his chin as if homage to a star. No more than twenty, he's dressed in an expensive black silk shirt with a wide black silk tie. "Edwina is off her Zurich call," he says, dramatically waving his hands as if circulating the air. A faint scent of expensive cologne drifts around him like a cloud. "She's *salivating* to see you. Go on in." I pause, smoothing my wrinkled black trousers and jacket, and then I hurry inside Edwina's huge office.

"Honeybun, you look *gorg*," Edwina drawls. She kisses me twice on each cheek, her filler-full red lips barely touching my face. Thin as paper, her expensive black sleeveless dress accentuates her long delicate arms and perfect, size zero body. Her tangerine colored shoulder-length hair flows like silk. Bangs cover her threaded eyebrows, shading her deep-set gray eyes.

I sit on a white leather chair with chrome legs, facing her oval-shaped glass desk covered with piles of color-coded scripts. It's been a while since I've seen her. In her late fifties, she supports not only her mother and sister, but also her much younger husband, a soap opera actor who spends every dime she makes. Still, she works hard and never gives up.

"Coffee? Tea? Wine?"

"A latte would be nice," I reply.

"Amen!" she shrieks to the open door. "Bring Bette a latte. Pronto!" She lights a thin brown cigarette, puffing impatiently, and then jabs the cigarette into a huge glass bowl. In two minutes, Amen appears, carrying a latte. "Amen!" she shouts. "Hold the calls and close the door. Pronto!"

While complaining about the stress of pilot season and the approaching Upfronts, Edwina makes a kale smoothie in her blender. Bottles of coconut water, Alexa, candles, and packages of rice cakes are arranged neatly along her desk.

Sipping the latte, I gush at how thrilled I am about the option. "A dream come true. Finally, Anny Applebaum will be her authentic age."

"...So honeybun," she interrupts with a quick smile, revealing her new veneers. "Joshua Bitterman is taking you to lunch tomorrow at the Soho House. Noon, pronto. Yesterday Zuma Smith, head of story development, will be with him. She's *brilliant.*"

"Great," I murmur, remembering past lunches with story developers.

"Straight to series," she repeats with a smile. "We don't have to go through pilot season and the upfront shit." She blinks, her fake eyelashes dropping shadows on her very high cheekbones.

"Wow. This is amazing. Also, I'm thrilled that WC doesn't want to change Anny's age."

She shrugs, reaches for a cigarette. "Joshua feels...that sixty-five is a bad number..."

"You *promised* Edwina. I don't want to have my character ruined again. Making Anny *younger* spoils the dynamic, defeats the premise–the story, the characterization, and especially Anny's voice. Changing the age is why the options fell apart. If those men in their Armani suits had listened to me *The Viagra Diaries* would have been a hit by now. Soon everyone will be doing over sixty. You mark my words."

"Don't get your panties in a twist," she snaps. "This time I'll have Marci insert a paragraph in the contract that you have *creative* input. Everything can be negotiated. Not to worry. We're good."

She smiles as if the discussion is finished. She drinks the rest of her smoothie, smoking between sips and shouting sudden orders to Amen. Meanwhile I'm struggling not to tell her that once again I smell a rat and thanks, but no deal and that once again she broke her promise. At the same time, I'm assuring myself that I'm fine with it, and definitely when the time is right I'll tell Joshua Bitterman what I think.

"So let's have a *moment*," Edwina says, opening her arms. We hug it out in a squeeze first, then air kiss twice on each cheek. She tells me that I'm to meet Bitterman at noon the next day at the So Ho House and that he's "salivating" about the title.

"Uh huh, great," I murmur, trying to smile.

"Honeybun," she croons. "This is an Emmy. I feel it. Now go. Let me know how the lunch with Bitterman goes."

Later in the evening, I'm at Lisa and Hank's house in the hills. We're sitting on the patio while I'm relating Edwina's every word: "Straight to series she said. Plus, she said Bitterman promised they wouldn't change Anny Applebaum's age."

As I rant about how "screwed" I'd been in the past and how this time it's going to work, Lisa, who knows the business, listens intently, her emerald-color eyes on my face, her Himalayan cat, Spock, on her lap. Her long auburn waves frame her delicate face like a hat. Her catatonic-yet-handsome husband Hank works on his computer while all around him drones are flying and robots are walking around making buzzing sounds.

"WC's shows are about vampires, superheroes, for tiny *teens*," I continue, between sips from my drink. "I hope they break ground with Anny Applebaum's *real* age, at last have a show with a real woman who doesn't play to the age joke. I hope they'll listen to me."

"Stop it. Don't fuck it up," Lisa snaps, her face scrunched up. "Joshua Bitterman is *huge*. Plus, you need money. Stop protecting Anny and let it happen. Think positive."

"Uh huh, get it," I murmur, hating her patronizing tone. But pretending it doesn't bother me, I remind myself that when she was a talent agent, our mother-daughter roles were reversed. I went to her for everything, asking advice, demanding help on setting up meetings with agents and producers.

"Mom, I've put a call into Biggie Delano," she says after a quick silence. "He's a top New York literary agent. He represents bestsellers. I met him when I was at the agency. Not to worry. Once you sign your option contract he'll sell *The Viagra Diaries* to a major publisher."

"Oh thank you," I say happily, feeling relief. "But does he read? All agents read is a log line."

She shrieks. "He *sells*! Agents don't read. They sell!"

"Okay, not to worry," I concede nervously.

"Everything is not about you. I have dreams too," she says, glaring.

"Yes. I understand."

Then there's this angry silence, one we know so well, one that dares us to confront or express what we're really thinking, pretending we're not aware of the other. Not wanting to rattle her up or to push too hard, I remain quiet, wishing I had the nerve to tell her that I hate it when she dismisses me and that I'm sorry I'm a bad parent and that she doesn't understand that everything I'm doing is for her. Instead, I pretend that I'm trying to fish out the olive floating in my drink, feeling like a child in time out.

As if sensing this she says, "You'll see, Mom," she says softly, holding my hand. "Once you get your project on air, something great will happen."

"Like finding love," Hank says, looking up from his computer. He smiles. He has kind, tan eyes behind rimless, round glasses, his silver-specked hair cut very short, like Spock. "Lisa is right. Maybe if you let go of Anny and stop writing about the men in your life, you'll meet the love of your life and live happily ever after."

At dinner, sitting at her pretty glass table set with a vase of pink roses from her garden, avoiding any industry talk, we discuss the news, stuff like that. The dining room faces this humongous pool with sapphire-color water and dotted with plastic pink oversize swans floating softly. Over poached salmon, Lisa tells me about her work and how glad she is that she left the industry, her intense, smart voice relating how she loves her LGBTQ patients and their courage.

"I'm proud of you," I say. "Proud that you love all human beings and not just entitled, privileged white people."

She smiles, her eyes shining. I'm overwhelmed by love for her and suddenly I feel anxious that I won't be able to make up for the years of my indifferent parenting and inability to show love. "Well, maybe my journey will have a happy ending," I say too brightly.

"You need a brand," she says.

"Do I have to release a sex video with some egghead?"

"Mom, don't be defensive. A brand is important. Your column is about ageism, and weird social issues. No one in the industry wants old."

"What I need is a good literary agent. No one buys self-published books."

"Now you expect me to get you a lit agent? Like I have nothing else to do? It's pilot season and I have suicidal agents to take care of and you're hocking. Years I shopped your books."

"I didn't mean...."

"You meant."

Now we're silent. The sounds of drones buzzing, the cats scratching the chairs seem suddenly loud. I pretend that I'm concentrating on my iced tea.

"Not to worry, Mom," she says in a sympathetic tone. "It's all good. You'll see. You always say stay on your path of dreams and good things will happen."

"I want it for you and Nanny," I say quickly. "It's not for me."

"You want it for you, Mom," she says softly. "Which is fine. Your work is fine. It's your...fear of intimacy that bothers me." She pauses, blinking, as if contemplating. "We've been through so much together." She looks reflective. Then, as if figuring something out she takes my hand. "It's amazing that we used to hate each other. Isn't that amazing?"

"I never hated you," I say quickly. "I'm sorry if you thought that. I've only loved you...I just didn't...don't know how to feel it or show it."

She sighs, looking at me curiously, like a parent looks at a child who thinks she knows the answers but doesn't. She hesitates. "...Mom, tomorrow don't wear the black suit with the huge silk flower. It's schmootzy. No rings on every finger. Those thrift store Joan Crawford platform shoes...you need to impress Bitterman."

In the guest room, which is off the kitchen and away from their master bedroom, I'm lying on their fancy Smart bed, so high I'm afraid I'll fall off, watching TV. But then I can't figure out all the complicated buttons on the TV remotes, and all I get are Chinese stations and suddenly these shrill alarms are going wild and Hank, looking panicked, runs in. Wearing Mr. Spock pajamas, he's yelling that I fucked up his $10,000, fifteen-foot TV. After he adjusts it, and with an apologetic tone, explaining which buttons to use and which not to, he goes to bed. After a few moments, I turn it off and try to sleep, thinking about Lisa.

Of course she's right to feel the way she does, I think. All Lisa's life she never had a mother and early on I'd left her to do for herself—making her school lunches, ironing, cooking. When she was barely a teenager, I was writing my Jewish Princess novel, and as she got older I was writing other novels; I was never there for her dreams, only mine. She did everything herself, everything alone. Even a decade ago when she had the eating disorder and checked herself into a facility, and almost died, I wasn't there. No, never there. So I wouldn't feel pain I just kept on writing, assuring her as soon as I made money I'd be there. Ironically, I remember when I was a child and always craving my mother's smile, glance, love, anything.

I shut my eyes tight. Slowly, I exhale deep breaths. I do this when I feel pain, when I don't want to remember.

If only I could climb into Lisa's soul and stay there, breathe back the nourishment I'd stripped her of and the reason she'd had an eating disorder, and if only I could feel my feelings, soak them into my skin.

But now I'll have a TV series, money, and they'll see that I'm successful and then...then everything will be perfect.

I close my eyes and slip into my dream, slowly sinking into the sea, past dark shadows and light filled holes. I float on the bottom, my arms held out. It's still and green and muggy and fish flutter like fans. I love it here. It's peaceful. It's hard to surface up. I live at the bottom and no one can see me but I can look up and see streams of gold bubbles and shadows. I hear my daughter's laughter from above and it's really beautiful here.

I float.

* * *

The next day, dressed to the nines and feeling apprehensive, I'm at lunch. The Soho House is something, it has this shimmering atmosphere as if designed for only successful people; glass walls face LA, and bouquets of white peonies in crystal bud vases sit on every table. Industry people wearing black couture and expensive haircuts talk in whispers, as if any sound will intrude on their power deals.

"I'm *orgasmic* over Anny. I want to marry her," Joshua Bitterman says, clinking his glass on mine. He smiles when he speaks, revealing too-large white veneers, his tanned skin glowing as though it was peeled. His dark hair is puffed perfectly, and his black Tom Ford suit fits his small, athletic body like a wetsuit.

For the past hour, we've been picking at our persimmon salads, gushing about how happy we are to be together, and what a great series *The Viagra Diaries* is going to be, Bitterman smiling and glancing at his gold Apple watch.

"We *salivate*," says Yesterday, in her lyrical South African accent. She's drop-dead gorgeous, with penetrating turquoise eyes and bronze, glowy skin. Intricate loops of braids wrap around her perfectly-shaped head like ropes. Strands of pearls float over her fitted pale gray Chanel suit. But underneath her studied charm, I sense an overly ambitious determination.

"We love your project passionately," Yesterday says, with perfect intensity.

"So happy," I murmur into my second martini shot.

"I hired Kat Zimmerman, an A-list TV writer to write the series," Bitterman says.

"I saw her series, *Rage*," I say hesitantly. "But... she's... twenty-five?"

"She's talented. She *gets* Anny," Yesterday emphasizes. "As you say, age doesn't matter?"

"As long as she keeps my protagonist's age intact," I say.

"I have a call in to Brad," Bitterman says, glancing at his three lit up phones arranged in a row next to him.

"Brad?"

"Pitt," Yesterday finishes with a knowing smile.

"He's perfect for the jazz singer," Bitterman says.

"Jazz singer?" I ask. "My male protagonist is a diamond dealer."

"Diamond dealer, jazz singer—he's fabulous."

"Brad Pitt is too young to play the diamond dealer," I protest.

He glances at an incoming text.

"Kat is already writing six episodes," Yesterday informs me with a patronizing smile. "We want to air it this fall. Not to worry. We're auditioning stars."

"I'd die happy if we got Keaton...Holly Hunter, Sarandon, Angelica Huston, to play Anny Applebaum," I say exuberantly. But then there's this thick silence, and am I imagining that they're exchanging these private looks and doing these knee nudges under the table? At this point I want to warn them about not changing my protagonist's age, but then I feel myself shrinking, feeling the familiar thud of disappointment that no matter what I think or say, they've made up their minds. Picking at my salad and pretending to be thrilled, I want to say, no thanks, this isn't going to work but then I think of the girls, and I feel panic that I won't live long enough to see my dream come true. And I find myself picking at my salad.

As if sensing my distress, Yesterday says, “Honey, we’re *bonded* to Anny Applebaum. Not to worry.”

Bitterman glances at his gold Apple watch, and then, as if to say the meeting is over, he and Yesterday stand. He has to get to the studio. He’s got a pilot he’s shooting. Yesterday has a table read, she emphasizes.

“And you have to get to the airport, Bette,” Bitterman says with another quick smile.

“We’re good to go,” Yesterday says, taking me in her arms. “It’s all good.” They promise to keep Edwina informed, and as soon as Kat finishes writing I’ll be the first to read. As they go along, they’ll Skype me into their meetings.

“You’re *fabulous*. Can’t believe you’re pushing seventy,” Yesterday adds with a sympathetic smile. “I hope I look like you when I grow up. Love the silk flower and feathers—the red platform shoes.”

“Fabulous,” Bitterman says with averted eyes, air kissing me twice on each cheek. “If you need anything, contact Yesterday. Just ask for her.”

I hate flying; it terrifies me. As the plane soars up, my head tilts back and I force myself to look out the window at the clouds and then there’s nothing but blank, solid air. When there’s turbulence, I close my eyes and imagine I’m drifting on a raft along a bumpy sea, holding on tight and trying to keep course.

Squished between two large men, one eating corn chips, I’m writing everything I can remember about the lunch, feeling conflicted about whether or not to call Edwina and tell her I want out of the option and that I don’t like Bitterman, but then I remind myself that based on my bad experiences with my Jewish

Princess novel, and other projects, I have a tendency to be impulsive and to burn bridges.

When my editor complained about my piece on legalizing prostitution, ranting that readers would cancel their subscriptions, I lashed out and told her that her paper was ordinary and that I didn't give a hoot for her conventional readers. She fired me, and it was hard finding work again until a young editor at the *San Francisco Times* hired me to write a lifestyle column. I wrote about everything from dating to ageism, issues I'm interested in, and the column started taking off. Now, Oliver Abbot, an arts editor who owns *The Australian Times,* buys a lot of my pieces and runs them in his paper and I get fan mail from Australia.

As the plane thumps down through the clouds, I assure myself that I'm on a new journey and it may get bumpy but I know the destination.

* * *

Later at home, I settle in for the night. I have a lot of work to do—preparing my column, read manuscripts from the writing workshop I'm currently teaching. But first I call Nanny and tell her about the trip—how fabulous it was, that I'm going to be making a lot of money, "TV money," I say.

"Uh huh. That's what you said the last two times," she says in her husky voice. Dogs are barking in the background.

"Well, this time it's going to work. It's in the fates."

"Enough with the fate. Mom, you're Bette Roseman pushing seventy. You write that weird column, you're broke and celibate and wear those platform fuck-me shoes. Next you'll break a hip and we'll have to take care of you. Stop dreaming about bestsellers and TV shows and find a nice man to take care of you... Be age appropriate."

"Screw age appropriate," I say.

She sighs heavily. "Mom, I love you. Lisa loves you. Lisa said you're frantic. Anyway, we'll talk tomorrow."

As I slip into my dream I find myself walking along the edge of the most beautiful sea you've ever seen, turbulent and dark green with birds flying low. At a small wooden cottage I peek in the window and see myself at my drawing table, my glasses taped on the side and my hair down my back and I want to go inside but I can't move.

2

Things are happening fast. Wow. A few days later, a full-page announcement in *Hollywood Dateline* announces that Joshua Bitterman is developing *The Viagra Diaries* into a TV series based on the book by Bette Roseman. Wow. My picture is there and everything. It's awesome. Lisa posted the article all over Facebook. Friends who'd snubbed me before are now inviting me to memorials, bar mitzvahs, and dinner parties. For the first time in a long time I'm feeling on top of the world and soon I'll have money. For the longest time I've been unable to pay my bills.

To top it, I sign the network contract. Edwina's lawyer—and now my lawyer—Marci Feldstein called and introduced herself. She sounds tough as nails and she rants in a New York accent that she negotiated a humongous deal with the "rats" at WC, and everything is in my power.

"Except there's not a clause that I have *creative input*," I say.

"Don't give me grief!" she shrieks in a voice that could kill a rat. Ranting that she's exhausted from negotiating with the WC morons and dumb authors, she repeats, "I killed myself for you, don't rattle the boat. Be grateful. Go to church or temple or something and thank your lucky stars." She continues ranting how really rotten industry people are and to shut my trap. I'm shaking like a leaf, murmuring how grateful I am and how thrilled I am to be working with her. "Eighteen fucking hours I've worked with these motherfuckers. So don't rattle my cage or sayonara!"

"No, of course not. I'm sorry."

"Don't you people read?" she continues. "*Read* the clause that says you have to be at *all* table reads, that you have creative input! You people don't read!"

"Sure. I didn't see...I have glaucoma and..."

"Get new glasses! The motherfuckers didn't even want to give you that but I scared the balls off Joshua Bitterman who only writes scripts with vampires and idiots."

So again I apologize profusely. I sign the contract online, click the *send* button and God Save the Queen, it's done.

* * *

Dr. T. sits straight in his ergonomic chair, his emotional blue eyes intently on my face. As I rant for forty minutes about how awful my life is, and how horrible the industry is, he writes notes on his clipboard.

"I hate this business. They treat writers like we're idiots." For the past thirty minutes I've been saying to Dr. T. that I've had it with the stupid producers changing my work, talking to me like I'm not there. I take a deep breath. "But I have creative input in the contract. Anyway, everything depends on it."

"Everything?" He stares without blinking.

I nod. "So that my daughters will look at me as a *successful* author. So I'll leave them a legacy...something." I pull a Kleenex from the box next to me, pressing it to my mouth because when I cry my mouth opens funny and my teeth look buck.

"So you think that your daughters will love you if you have TV deals?"

"Fuck yes." I clump the Kleenex into a ball on my lap, praying I don't get another nosebleed. When I'm upset I get nosebleeds. "I have no money, nothing to show for anything, and no man. No love."

He sighs. "All the men in your life end up in your books."

I nod. "I kill them off in my books. The last moron Mel deserved to be in *The Viagra Diaries* and so did Charley, who married me when I was a nineteen-year-old virgin. On our wedding night he refused to touch me and said he made a mistake, took me home and then told everyone I was mentally ill and frigid. He deserves to be in my Jewish Princess novel. No wonder I can only feel when I write or paint." I pause, aware that the session is near the end. "...I have two lives: one I'm living, and one I'm writing about. I...can't connect them. The curse is reliving the past so I can live in the present." I pause, feeling sudden pain, that feeling you get when you don't want to remember something.

He nods, as if affirming what I said. "You give me content, but not a lot about your feelings."

"I hid them. So it's hard to get to them...."

He closes his notebook on his lap. He sighs sympathetically. "Yes, disassociation happened somewhere early in your life when something painful happened. Now, close your eyes, Bette. Let's do our river exercises—imagine your pain is floating in the river."

His lulling voice instructs me how to go into the river and float away with my pain. I half-close my eyes, pretending I'm into it, as he repeats that I'm letting go of my pain, my disappointments floating in this river, imagining a pretty meadow with roses blooming like balloons and my daughters standing by this huge umbrella-like tree, the wind blowing Lisa's long auburn hair and Nanny hugging her dog Fred—

"Time to stop, Bette. Good work. Same time next week."

I open my eyes, feeling slightly disoriented, listening to the inpatient footsteps on the stairs outside. After he sits a second longer, as if in polite reverence, I put on my green bowler hat with the pink silk flower stuck on the side. Shaking out my leg cramps, I stumble to the door, careful not to fall in my Joan Crawford-style platform ankle strap shoes. At the door, I open the double lock and hurry past a pale girl eagerly waiting, and walk into the street.

Later at home when the light is still up, I set my easel next to the window so I can paint the tree across the street. I love this tree. Slightly crooked, it has huge branches like reaching arms, and I know this tree. When the light is on it, the tree turns from dark green to almost yellow, and when the wind is up it barely bends, as if holding on.

I dip my brush into the mound of dark green on my long, glass palette, and then quickly, I draw the tree on the canvas, letting the line drip, and loosely shaping the tree. The tree looks so frail, like it's fighting to stay in its roots. I paint until the light fades.

3

It's several weeks later, and so far the project is going well. Often Edwina calls with updates and assures me that according to Bitterman, Kat Zimmerman is writing up a storm and following my book "to the letter, honeybun." Also, I received option money and paid some bills. In a few weeks Edwina promises that there will be a Skype meeting with Bitterman and the WC team and then I can ask questions. "It's all good honeybun," she says.

Meanwhile I'm teaching my writing workshops and working hard on *Blast,* my column. Though I've never met Oliver Abbot, my editor in Australia, I love working with him. Very rarely does he text suggestions, and often sends emails saying how much he loves my columns and articles. On Google, his bio says before he started at *The Australian Times* as an art critic, he was a ballet dancer. When he stopped dancing, he made films about women artists, and then started the paper. There are no photographs of him but I know he was raised in England and that he's fifty-six years old.

"You need to get out more. Come to our party this Saturday in Sonoma," Nancy Rosenbloom insists on the phone. "Arnold's colleague Martin Kahn wants to meet you. He's read your books. He's a mathematician, and a widower. Very smart. Kitschy."

"Sure, thank you."

"Moo Moo Melman will pick you up."

So wouldn't you know? The one party I accept, I wake up cramping and bleeding. Telling myself that it's probably post-menopause and that I've been working too hard, I stuff toilet paper into my panties. I deck myself out in my black H&M cutout jeans, Joan Crawford shoes, off-the-shoulder black T-shirt, and my favorite pink felt hat with a huge paper flower I made out of newspaper and pinned to the side.

I'm in Moo Moo's new Lexus and while she drives, talking non-stop, this *How To Date At Sixty* tape is blasting from her tape deck. Moo Moo is one of the richest women in the Bay Area. A few years ago, her ugly billionaire husband jumped out of the window and left her skyscrapers all over the state. Decked in this floral kimono with tons of jade necklaces dangling over her huge breasts, a humongous blue Birkin bag next to her on the seat, she's bragging in this tight, entitled voice, how many "eligible" men she's fucking. "They'd die for me," she adds.

"Fabulous," I murmur.

"They say, Moo Moo, you don't look a day over forty. Little does he know I'm sixty-plus. I pay a fortune for this look! My dermatologist Seth knows what he's doing. I paid six thousand dollars to go to a sweat tent in Arizona. For days I was in this hot tent with sweaty people, eating stale rice, but I found my spirituality."

As she continues to describe in detail her latest cosmetic procedure, her sexual conquests, her lips, huge from fillers, barely move. Her short, baby-fine apricot-colored hair puffs like candyfloss. Weaving her Lexus in and out of the lanes, the shrill voice on the tape deck reciting the *do's* and *don'ts* for dating, Moo Moo lectures that women have to be in control. "You can't let these motherfuckers tell you what to do. Most of them either want your money or they're in diapers."

"Uh huh. Get it," I say looking out the window and admiring the fields of grasses.

"...So Bette, everyone is talking...are you a recluse? Or are you seeing those retard men you write about in your column?"

"No one special," I reply, feeling suddenly claustrophobic. I remove a paper bag from my tote, cupping my hands over the top, and blow into it. When I'm nervous I do this. She screams, "Motherfucker!" to the passing car, watching me from her side mirror. "I read *The Viagra Diaries,"* she says in a low voice, like she's telling a forbidden secret.

"Uh huh, great," I say, perking up, waiting for a compliment. I fold the bag and put it back into my purse.

"Everyone bets the diamond dealer is Mel Braverman."

"It's fiction," I reply.

"Like *The Viagra Diaries* is fiction?" She snorts. "Anny is too neurotic! Fucked up! No wonder the diamond dealer left her."

"She realizes she doesn't need a man who doesn't appreciate her and she overcomes..."

"Overcomes *what*?" she shouts. "That the diamond dealer was fucking someone else and left her?"

"Well, Anny overcomes," I insist.

"Bette—everyone says what a shame that your Jewish Princess novel didn't make it."

While she quotes the shit her yenta friends are saying about my books, I'm watching the beautiful cows with their sad eyes grazing on these the green pastures, admiring the poplar trees dropping shadows along the wide, flat road, and assuring myself that as soon as I have a drink, I'll feel better.

"We're here!" she says in a *Here's Johnny* rise of voice, and stops her car next to all these the Tesla cars parked in rows.

On a huge patio surrounding an oval swimming pool, giant, fake lilies float in the pink-colored water. *Saturday Night Fever* is blasting from overhead speakers, and swank-looking fifty-plus couples are shaking their arms and legs like rag dolls. I make a beeline to the bar and this young blonde bartender with spiked hair and attitude makes me vodka up, chilled. I say hello to Nancy, a sweet obese woman who's made a bundle from her company, *Fatty's,* selling tent-size nightgowns to six-hundred-pound women. Her husband Arnold is a tiny man with a large bald head, and when he talks, his eyes squint like slits. All these professorial type men with Einstein-type hair, and schmootzy, outdated clothes, are huddled in groups.

"Hello, you must be Bette. I'm Martin Kahn. Nancy's told me so much about you. I read *Blast.* Love it. Especially your radical views of the world." He pauses. "I also read *The Viagra Diaries* on Amazon."

"Wow, oh great."

He's very tall, thin as an X-ray, and about my age. A puff of salt-and-pepper hair sits like a point on top of his elongated head. He has tiny eyes and a nose the size of an arm. I'm slurping the vodka and ignoring Moo Moo's glares, talking about black holes, time machines, and how much I adore Einstein. "His relativity stuff blows me away," I say, wanting to go home.

"Love your shoes. Thank God for a woman who wears high heels." He pauses. "I love feet."

"Uh huh," I murmur, thinking this guy has a foot fetish.

"Let's dance," he says.

So we slow dance to "Purple Rain." He dances like a klutz, holding me so tight I can hardly breathe, and he sings off-key in my ear. Until, thank God, Nancy blows a whistle and announces dinner through this huge orange megaphone.

Like a herd of cattle everyone runs from table to table, looking for their names on humongous place cards. I'm sitting between Martin and this boring woman named Helen Fishman. On the other side are her husband and two other nerdy-looking couples. Feeling rotten, I pick at my wilted fish salad while Martin is stuffing his mouth and telling stupid Jewish Princess jokes. In a low voice, blowing his fish breath on my face, he confides that he has a wife but that she's in a mental institution. "Poor thing's on Elavil cocktails," he says loudly, his beady eyes feigning sympathy. "She's drooling, can't keep her head up."

"Oh, I'm sorry." I pick at a string bean.

"Are you as sexy as Anny Applebaum?" he asks in a loud voice. "She's hot. Love her multiple orgasms."

"Remember, its fiction," I reply, aware that everyone stopped eating, and they're listening.

"That's what all authors say," lisps Helen Fishman.

"Authors are all liars," says a large man wearing a Hawaiian shirt.

"I read the book," says a small man, his mouth full of potatoes. "At sixty-five, there's no way Anny Applebaum could have those crazy multiple orgasms."

"Over forty you're done," snaps a mousy woman wearing strands of wooden beads the size of marbles.

"You can have good sex at any age," I say, my voice rising above their debate.

"You're hallucinating," they accuse.

Then, like I'm not there, they agree that Anny is nuts.

"A sexual pervert."

"A whore," lisps a woman with puffy silver hair and long, crystal skinny earrings.

"Al, don't stuff your mouth," shouts Helen, slapping her husband's back so hard he spits up. "You'll get sick again."

"So, when are we going to play, Anny?" whispers Martin after a long silence.

"Never," I say removing his clammy hand from my leg. Just then the lights dim and a huge screen drops from the roof. Nancy and Arnold announce that for the next two hours we're going to watch their recent trip to Iran.

"Excuse me. I'm sorry. I'm not feeling well," I say. I make a beeline outside and ask a couple getting into their Tesla if I can hitch a ride to San Francisco. "Sorry. Hope you don't mind."

"We need to do a biopsy," Dr. Joi says the next morning.

I'm on the table, my legs in the stirrups, and as she begins the biopsy, I squeeze my eyes shut, imagining the tree against the purple-streaked sky and the rose bush in front of my apartment building starting to bloom big yellow roses.... Dr. Joi says, "You can sit up now, Bette."

I sit up, dazed and cramping, and relieved it's over. She's young with kind eyes and a doll-like face. "I'll call you as soon as I have the results, Bette. Take a nice warm bath and relax. Not to worry."

From the lobby, relieved that the biopsy is done, I call Myra at the TV station, and tell her about the bleeding. She assures me I'll be fine, that Nancy Blumenthal had the same thing, and it turned out it was post-menopause. "All of us over sixty go through the same shit. Has the doc given you some Botox? You could use it." She pauses. "How was the party?"

"Awful. No more blind dates. He was a moron."

"Honey, most of them are morons. They're swallowing Viagra like candy and still can't get it up. That's why I'm with Mohammed."

"He's twenty-eight, Myra."

"He knows what to do with it."

"He was arrested for being a peeping Tom and he steals your money from your purse while you sleep."

"Honey, most of the oldies only care about a hole. They'll fuck a doughnut. Mohammed will bring you to Nirvana."

"All I got from my affairs were bladder infections. I'm done. I'm sick of the ageism. My cousin Helen is one hundred and seven, wears a bra and makeup, and still hopes to find love. The soul doesn't age. People do."

"Look at poor Linda Jacobson," Myra argues. "She forgot her keys and her ugly, rich husband stuck her in a home, saying she has Alzheimer's. Already he's on Facebook and dating a youngie. These ugly guys with money are ruthless."

The next morning at eight a.m., Dr. Joi's office calls and says she wants to see me ASAP. So I'm sure it's another D&C.

The waiting room is filled with pregnant women, reading or knitting. Dr. Joi's right hand nurse Debbie quickly leads me into Dr. Joi's private office. Petite and beautiful, Dr. Joi sits behind her huge desk, a grim expression on her face.

"Hello," I say cheerfully. "A lovely day isn't it?" I sit on a chair in front of her desk, glad I'm wearing dark glasses.

She pauses, her hands folded officiously. "I'm sorry. You have uterine cancer."

I stare at a sunspot floating on the wall. Stunned, like I slipped off a ledge, falling through space, I hear myself say, "...No one in my family has cancer—are you sure?"

She nods twice. “I’m sorry,” she repeats.

I detach and I’m smiling and watching her lips move as she informs me that I’ll need surgery right away, that she’s calling Dr. John Chan, a gynecological oncologist, and that I must see him tomorrow. “He’s the best, Bette. You’ll like him.” Depending on what stage my cancer is, she further explains, he’ll decide if I need laparoscopic surgery, which requires shorter hospitalization, or the full hysterectomy, which requires a longer recovery. As she explains more about the possible chemotherapy, I feel like I’m in my recurrent nightmare, when my name is called to line up for death. In the dream, I read my name on a grave that is stone and heart-shaped.

She writes Dr. Chan’s name and address on a prescription page. I fold it in my purse. She has patients waiting. At the door, she hugs me. “If you need me Bette, call. I’ll be talking with Doctor Chan today.”

Strangely calm, I walk two blocks to the coffee shop, not feeling my feet, or the wind blowing the leaves like stars along the streets. I sit in the back and order scrambled eggs and coffee. Barely eating, as if in slow motion, I call Nanny and tell her that I have uterine cancer. “But I’ll be okay. She caught it early. I’m seeing Doctor Chan the surgeon, tomorrow.” There’s a long silence and I hear her beloved Fred barking in the background. Then she says in a shaky strained voice that she and Larry will be with me when I go to Dr. Chan’s office. “Not necessary,” I assure her.

“It is necessary!” she shrieks. “You don’t know what to do or say, Mom. You’ll zone out and talk about your book.” I hold the phone tighter. Nanny hocks about how important it is to be paid up on my life insurance, to have my "affairs in order," and I hear the fear in her voice; my hand is shaking.

Not two minutes later, Lisa patches into the call. Tearfully, she asks why I didn't call her first. Hank is on his way to Brazil on business but she'll cancel her patients and be here in the morning.

"No, not necessary."

Ignoring my protest, Lisa and Nanny discuss if my bills are paid, if my apartment is clean, in its usual disarray with books and papers on the floor and what about my laundry? "Mom, Hank said you looked terrible the last time you were in LA—really thin...drawn. We were worried. Mom, don't worry."

Dr. T. is on a vacation, so I spend the rest of the day lying on my couch, zoning out on movies, wondering if I'll die in the hospital on morphine, with family around the bed telling me they love me, apologizing for small slights. Exactly what I did when my poor mother was dying intubated, a morphine bag dripping into her veins, her eyes glazed, her finger wrapped around mine. Frantically, feeling close to death I write letters to my daughters, telling them how much I love them, apologizing for my parenting. Clearly, I know that I've made so many mistakes—given so little emotionally. Inside my dreams I feel emotions that range from hot rage to deep sadness, and I wake shaking and wondering why I can't feel those feelings in real life?

The next day Nanny, Lisa, Larry, and I are in Dr. Chan's office. I really like him. He's young, with intelligent, kind eyes, and with a gentle professional manner. He's drawing diagrams of my uterus on a sheet of grid paper, explaining that the uterus is like a bag and safer than other cancers. “We need to see if some of the cells spread to your cervix.”

“Uh huh. I lean forward, pretending I understand his every word. While Larry takes notes in his yellow lined notebook, Nanny holds my hand, assuring Dr. Chan she will be taking care of me.

“Tomorrow morning, I’ve arranged for an abdominal contrast MRI. Then I’ll know what kind of surgery is needed.”

After we make arrangements for Nanny and Larry to pick me up the next morning, Lisa stays overnight with me.

At my apartment, Lisa is quiet. I ask if she’d like a yogurt bar. “Maybe a peanut butter cracker? You always loved peanut butter crackers. Fresh towels are in the bathroom.”

“Mom, I’m fine. Stop it,” she says softly.

“Or maybe a hot bath? Try the new lilac bubble bath I bought…it’s…”

“Mom, I’m exhausted. I want to go to bed. You need your rest.”

“Have you heard from Biggie Delano?” I ask after another long silence.

“I told you I sent him the book three weeks ago. On your deathbed and you’re hocking. Stop worrying Mom,” she says in a baby voice. “Let’s go to sleep. I’m exhausted. I have to leave at six to get to my office by nine.”

Because my leather couch is too short, Lisa and I sleep in my low Japanese-style IKEA bed together, her long thin body pressed close to mine. As she sleeps I lie awake, my past coming over me like a fast tide, and telling myself that I can’t die, not yet, that I have a lot to say to the girls. I slip into one of my dark, scary dreams, trying to find my way out of a dark street but there's only ocean, no streets, and I awake with a jolt, my body shaking. A strand of dawn light struggles along the room.

Cancer, I have cancer, I repeat to myself. Am I going to die soon? Death feels close, like something you know is there but hiding. My eyes shut tight, I listen to Lisa's soft breathing, to the creaking sounds from the old elevator in the hallway, sirens outside, a dog barking—listening to life, to life, to life, tears flooding my face. As if my body is separated, I feel myself get up and kneel by Lisa, watching her sleep. But is she sleeping?

I whisper, "Lisa. Lisa! Listen to me. It's Mom. I'm sorry. So sorry I didn't show you love. Didn't give you dolls, hold your hand when you were sick, wasn't at your college graduation. I'm sorry, sorry, sorry. Forgive me. No wonder you didn't want children. But know before I die that I love you so much. Admire you. I didn't get close to you, because I was afraid you'd breathe in my anger and become like me. Please believe that even though I can't feel everything I'm saying, I know you mean more than my books. Everything I've done is for you. For you and Nanny. I think I'm going to make money now Lisa...have success. I want us to be close before it's too late."

Slowly she opens her eyes, blinking at the expanding light.

"You're already successful, Mom. You're my mom. You don't need to make money. I already love you."

Tears flood her pale, lovely face and in the half dark, I lie next to her until it's time to get up and dress.

* * *

On a dark rainy morning, I'm in surgery. Several doctors are around the table. The lights are blaring above and I'm very drugged; in a moment I will go to sleep, the doctor says. Is this what dying is, a slipping away into another place? I feel suddenly homesick for my children, sad that I won't be with them when they slip into another place and that I didn't leave them that legacy. Then I feel a hot tingling along my body and I hear a nurse say just think of a white beach and a quick flash of sand as white as pearls surrounds me and then there's nothing.

In recovery I wake and for a second I'm dizzy and confused by all the lights and noise. "I got it all out. You won't need chemotherapy," Dr. Chan assures me. When I'm wheeled on a gurney into my room, and see Hank, Nanny, Larry, and Lisa holding a pot of yellow roses and a card, my heart soars. *Family is my legacy,* I say to myself. *This is what it's about.* Lisa gives me a card with the roses. "Read the card later, Mom." When she returns to Los Angeles, I read the card. *I heard you. I love you too, Lisa.*

I'm so happy to be alive. I want to touch the roses in bloom, the clouds hovering like layers of foam—oh life, no matter what your problems, living life is magical. Was the sun always like sprays of yellow? The late daylight full of butterflies? Dusk, so mauve?

Suddenly my dreams of fame and fortune seem so small, and the world so big and the soul is so full of feelings, art, and truths. No matter how much I stumble, I must go deeper within myself, face who I am, what I want, and begin the journey of loving.

Proust said that true paradise is the paradises we have lost.

As the days pass, my dreams are full of memories: my grandmother at her sewing machine, making costumes for the opera; Mother pruning her roses, a meadow with sprays of forget-me-nots, lilacs; Lisa sewing ribbons on her pointe shoes; Nanny doing cartwheels, her long legs spinning, spinning, and the air suddenly dim....

The days following my surgery, Nanny stays with me. Myra brings flowers, age crèmes, books and magazines. Edwina sends white roses, my favorite flowers. Nanny makes chicken soup, banana breads, writes lists what I should eat, and shouldn't eat, folds laundry, and puts it away. Anyway, my laptop on my lap, I'm writing my next column about how homeless people should have the access to Medicare and hospital care, remembering the poor homeless man who every day sits on the corner singing special songs, ill from cancer and unable to get the proper care he deserves. I write fast now, enjoying the sound of the keys clicking in the silence. Nanny is cleaning out my fridge, carefully stacking what to keep and what to throw out. She's very tall, at least five feet ten, with long gorgeous legs. She wears red shorts, red leather ankle boots with four-inch heels, her long black satiny ponytail swinging as she works. She loves to clean and I recall the years when she was a teenager, cleaning a socialite's house, until the socialite's husband tried to rape her. Poor Nanny. Her drunken father abandoned her, and unlike Lisa who'd had a scholarship to NYU, Nanny stayed home, gone to night college, and then worked in an investment firm downtown, until she'd met Larry and married.

"Filthy, your place is filthy," Nanny says, as if to no one. "Mom, no wonder you got cancer. Mildew shit on the mayo and cheese. Crap. You eat crap."

"Uh huh." I write faster.

"Do you hear me?"

"Yes, I agree," I say, typing.

"Agree what?" she yells. "That you have shit in your fridge? God knows what's growing."

She dumps everything from my fridge then calls Whole Foods and officiously orders fresh fruits and vegetables. As I watch her I'm remembering Nanny at eleven standing on a box and baking banana breads in coffee cans and Lisa nearby ironing, a Walkman over her head. As she cleans and folds my laundry, the afternoon is shadowed with dusk. Nanny neatly arranges the box of cleaning supplies in my kitchen closet, removes her apron, and carefully hangs it on the hook next to the stove.

"Mom, I have to get home to take Fred for a walk." She places her bulging red backpack around her shoulders.

"Again Nanny, I can't thank you enough. I...love having you here all day. I love you, Nanny."

She looks at me intently, her almond-shaped eyes narrowed as if evaluating what I said and then from her backpack, slowly, she removes a white cardboard box wound with a thin red rubber band. "...I want to give you this. It's my manuscript."

"You finished your novel?"

She nods slowly.

"I always knew you would. Knew that you're talented. All your teachers said you were. Now you'll be published."

"I don't want to fucking publish," she yells, her face turning red. "Don't hock!"

"Oh, I understand. Just saying..."

"To go through what you've gone through. No thank you."

"Sure, I get it."

The expression on her face softens. "Just read it, Mom. It's for you. I wanted you to have it."

On the front of the box, in bold print, is the title: *Two Moons Away*, by Nanny Zuckerman. I hold the box close to my heart. "I'll read it tonight. I'm so proud of you."

As soon as she leaves I get up and turn on the light next to my small leather chair by the window. My hands shaking, I roll the rubber band from Nanny's manuscript and begin reading. Slowly turning the pages, I'm marveling not only at the beauty of her poetic prose, but the control of her story—about a girl wanting to write, but afraid if she does, she'll suffer like her neurotic writer mother. I read: "*As I watch my mother at her typewriter, I want to hug her. Her interesting face is sad, and her back is hunched as she leans over her pages. I move closer and she doesn't look up or hear me even when I say Mother, I'm sick. Mother, do you hear me?*"

I have to stop for a moment. I'm feeling suddenly sad, remembering Nanny with her hula-hoop around her thick waist, watching me at the kitchen table, typing my Jewish Princess novel.

After a moment, I resume reading, turning the pages slowly, in awe again of her magnificent prose, her talent, and her absolute ability to go into her protagonist's interior thoughts. So this is my legacy, I think. Somewhere she got my father's genes, or before him, as he came from a family of musicians and writers.

The night spreads into early dawn and I read until the end, feeling guilty, ashamed of my parenting, and at the same time, feeling great pride at her talent. So vividly she characterized me, even my '*numbing out*,' as she calls it. She writes: "*Mom had a blankness in her eyes and sometimes I don't think she knew I was there.*"

Stunned that I'd been so removed and unloving to my daughters, I'm remembering Nanny at thirteen, when she went missing. I'd gone on typing, assuring myself she'd be back, until two days later when the police had called. She ran away to Mexico for a weekend with an older man named Carlos.

I place the rubber band around the manuscript, deeply shocked and saddened by my indifferent parenting. But you can't obliterate the past. Who you were. All you can do is face your emotional crimes and move ahead. I vow to go deeper into my subconscious and face my past, and only there will I know who I really am.

Dawn is straggling into the room. In bed, I close my eyes and sleep and prepare for the long journey ahead.

I dream that Nanny is twelve years old and she's sprawled on the floor, watching *I Love Lucy* on our small television and her hair flows around her broad shoulders like a cape. Lisa is fourteen. She wears her ballet leotards and is at the kitchen table doing her homework. She wears braces with heavy headgear, and rubber bands stretch along her protruding teeth. I'm on the other side of the table, typing a short story for my graduate class in creative writing. My hair straggles long and my thick glasses are bent on one side... I'm crying in the dream and I want to leave it but I can't and why is the camel in the dream and it has walnut colored eyes and a bird flies by—

5

Biggie Delano calls. In a slow, smart, literary voice, he informs me that he loves *The Viagra Diaries* and sent it to the big publishing houses in New York and in Europe. "Let's get this baby global."

"For sure. Wow. I'm excited."

He lets out an enervated sigh. "It's tough to sell *old.* Your protagonist is pushing seventy but she sounds young. I told the publishers you're an age activist. This will be your brand."

"I *am* an age activist and I don't believe in numbers."

"Age is in," he continues. "Trump, Hillary, Pelosi—they're all old farts," he says with a nasty chuckle. He complains that self-published books are hard to sell and that they're shopped like old whores. He snorts. "However, with a hot TV series announced, I'll sell it."

"Do you think you'll really sell it?"

"I sell everything I want to sell," he snaps. "Don't call me. I'll call you."

A week later on a November rain-filled afternoon, I'm home writing *Blast* when my cell phone rings. When I see Biggie's name, I quickly answer it.

"Mom, Biggie and I are on conference call. He has something to tell you."

I hold the phone tight, bracing for the news.

"One hundred K. Avalon Publishers bid the highest," Biggie says with a heavy sigh. "Three houses bid but I took the highest bidder. A three-book deal and with each book, the advance will go up—subsidiary rights—audio, eleven countries—the whole schmere." He chuckles.

"My God, oh Biggie thank you, I'm excited, beyond thrilled... and..."

"Let him talk," Lisa interrupts.

"Avalon wants a rewrite," he explains, casually in his low, staccato voice.

I feel the thud of disappointment. "...It took four years to write *The Viagra Diaries.* I hope you don't mind but I'd rather not rewrite."

"I *mind*!" he snaps. "The other houses offered bubkas. You have no sales figures on your former books. What I've been through to get you this deal and you have the fucking nerve to complain? You're not a household name yet. You'll be working with Emily Marino, the best editor at Avalon."

"Mom is very excited," Lisa interjects in a warning tone. "...Aren't we Mom?"

"Yes, yes, of course," I say, thinking I can negotiate with the editor. But once again I'm not standing up for myself, am afraid that if I do he'll back off and everything will once again dissolve. For a second, I can't breathe.

"Emily Marino will call you in a few days to go over her suggestions."

"Wow, sure."

"It's going to be *big*," he says.

"Big is good," I say.

"*Huge*," Lisa adds, excitedly.

Biggie exhales a long sigh, "You'll do Oprah, *The Today Show,* Andy Cohen, Anderson Cooper, *The View*." He pauses. "...I've seen your TV clips. You're good on TV, but honey, if you're going to be the face of old age, drop the *wow,* the feathers in the hair, the thrift store chic."

After the call, I don't feel the joy I want to feel. Instead, I feel conflicted and angry for once again not standing up for myself, but I quickly assure myself a *little* rewriting won't hurt, and that the editor might be helpful and not like the editor who destroyed my Jewish Princess novel. At last, the girls will see that my writing life is finally successful.

I call Nanny and Larry to tell them the good news. "I knew it! I knew a major publication was in the cards," I shout. "Plus, get this. A hundred-thousand-dollar advance and..."

"How much does Biggie get?" Larry interrupts on speakerphone.

"The usual twenty percent," I reply, irritated by his response.

"Now you can pay Larry back. He says you owe him a lot of money."

"I didn't say that," he says.

"I'll be paying it back, soon. Not to worry. Also, Nanny, I'll send your manuscript to Biggie, he's huge..."

"Stop the shit! Already you're hocking. Do you think I want to go through what you've gone through? I don't want to be old like you, schlepping with the books."

"Sorry, I'm just saying."

On the verge of tears, I want to tell her that I wish she wouldn't talk that way to me, but I feel too guilty about my past parenting and assure myself that in time our relationship will get better. "Well, anyway, I hope to see you soon. We'll have lunch at the Cheesecake Factory. You love it there," I say, my voice high.

After a contemplative silence she says, "Mom, I'm happy for you."

6

"Avalon is very happy to have you as one of our authors, Bette," says Emily Marino in a low, lifeless voice.

"I am too, Emily. I'm thrilled. Ready to work—"

"Avalon is thrilled about your TV series. Melissa Jones, the *head* of Avalon's publicity department, will go heavy on promotion and coordinate the book publicity with your TV series. We're sending press releases announcing the coming series and the book publications in Europe, US, Shanghai, Turkey, other countries. We removed the self-published version from Amazon."

She pauses. "...I see Anny Applebaum like Anastasia in *Fifty Shades of Grey.* She'll be the first sixty-five-year-old sexy dominatrix!" She chuckles.

"Anny is a writer," I say carefully. I laugh nervously. "She's not into S&M. But, of course I'm open to discussing...*suggestions.*"

"Good," she says, with a relieved sigh. "Your first fifty pages need total rewriting. We need to reveal Anny's sexual side. Up the sex scenes. Sex sells. In other words, she's the first old woman who's into sex. This is a win-win."

As she discusses that, she marks the pages with her notes and where to add more sex scenes and backstory. I'm fighting the impulse to say no and give me my book back and telling myself I don't have to do everything; she's saying to talk to Biggie first. Then Emily says that she will send a detailed memorandum very soon, she promises. After, we gush how happy we are to work together. I hang up and call Biggie.

Right away, he takes my call. Quickly, I relate my conversation with Emily. "...I'm furious, Biggie. I don't mind *some* rewriting but she's hocking about changing Anny Applebaum into that idiot Anastasia in *Fifty Shades of Gray*. Anny Applebaum is sixty-five, has frizzy hair and diverticulitis, and is quirky and real."

Silence.

"Hello? Are you there?" I ask.

"Listen," he says with a long sigh. "Let her send the fucking memorandum, rewrite what you choose to, handle her. I'm not a fucking therapist. Don't fuck this up. Or you and I don't get paid."

"Sure, thank you," I say, somewhat relieved and assuring myself he's right. "I just needed to vent. I don't mind rewriting with intelligent development—of course I don't, but I hate what she says and there are enough sex scenes with the diamond dealer and Anny is not a twenty-year-old submissive idiot and it doesn't make sense and..." But he ends the call.

I pace along my small living room, back and forth, feeling relieved that Biggie said to do what I think best, but at the same time, I'm feeling deeply disappointed that Emily wants me to change my years of character development and she doesn't seem to know who Anny Applebaum really is.

I sit by the window, observing the tree across the street draped by rain and obsessively wondering why I didn't just tell Emily that of course I would not turn my protagonist into a sexual pervert. Once again, I assured myself that once I have a bestseller, I'll do what I want. But I know that like pulling one thread from a tightly sewn tapestry, if I integrate Emily's changes, the protagonist's voice will unravel.

How far back does this people-pleasing disease go? Where did it start? "Always agree," Mother had lectured early on. But it's more than that. It's deep rooted, based on fear that if I don't please authority figures, I will perish. I'm a mess and no matter how painful it is, I must continue to force myself to face my past, learn what happened to make me the way I am, so I can stop it, so I can accept myself and grow.

Is this possible? Just as a thin crack in restored porcelain shows in certain lights, will my submissiveness eventually be seen?

I close my eyes, remembering an incident when I was ten and big and bulgy. At my father's insistence, trying to please him, I gave up my box of cherished paper dolls to my pretty blonde cousin Elena. Hoping for my elegant father's attention, I rushed to hug him, my large thighs rubbing together and making suction sounds, my glasses so thick they had circles in them and I threw my arms around his waist. "Stop drooling, Bette," he said, pushing me away. "Get a handkerchief. All young ladies have a handkerchief."

Remembering this tiny incident hurts. I feel the same rejection I felt at school dances. No one at the table asked me to dance. Mortified, I spent the evening under the table, pretending that I was looking for a lost bracelet.

I call Lisa. She's in her car on her way to see an emergency patient. I tell her about the conversation with Emily, and then with Biggie. "...Anastasia is an idiot," I say, my voice rising. "How dare they demand that I rewrite sixty-five-year-old Anny into a sexpot. And I'd trusted Biggie!"

"So what do you want? *The Pulitzer Prize*? You need the fucking money. Anyway, I'm on my way to treat a fifty-one-year-old producer who was aged out of the industry and is threatening to kill Trump. Oh Mom," she says with a sympathetic sigh. "I'm sorry I'm yelling, but write what's true to you and stop giving these people so much power. You're fabulous. Take charge and your dreams will come true."

"Thank you. I know you're right," I say.

"Then do it."

Not four days later, I receive Emily's ten-page memorandum. She's made notes on every page, suggestions for many scene deletions, and explicit instructions to "sexualize" Anny.

Enraged and disappointed I want to tell Emily I cannot agree to her changes.

But then I think about the WC series, how its airtime coincides with Avalon's September publication, and how fabulous is that? A series and a publication will definitely make my career take off. Again, assuring myself that compromise is necessary, I resume reading Emily's memorandum, marking in red what I will revise, and in blue, what I won't, working until it's dark and I'm exhausted.

A lonely rain slips along the windows and dusk takes over my apartment. I turn on the lamp, enjoying the quick, pink light spraying the sudden dark.

Before I begin the tedious revision the next day, I need to clean up the apartment. Piles of art magazines, books, canvases, and discarded drawings are strewn about the floor. Order, I need order. If I have order, then I can think, write, and look ahead.

I arrange the dozens of charcoal drawings I'd made of women inside boxes into a red plastic folder, re-stack the magazines and books. Finally, I change the water in the blue glass vase filled with yellow roses.

I sit by the window. A sliver of moon slices the sky and streetlights transform the dark wet streets into a luminous dark. I feel disconcerted, like a literary rape victim. There's no way I can change this book, but what do I do?

This has to stop. Why can't I act on what I know to be true? Why do I give so much power to my weak side?

I recall the happy day, when I was thirty-two and still in graduate school. Lisa was at NYU, and Nanny was working as a maid by day, and going to City College at night. In those days, at my age and going to college, I had to wear a tag printed re-entry woman, and while the girls and I were struggling with college and finances, I'd worked on my Jewish Princess novel, and submitted it to my creative writing professor as my graduate thesis. He'd loved it and had sent it to a well-known local literary agent. No one in my family had ever praised my writing, and I was thrilled. Mother had said to marry a rich man, and that women who wrote books were old maids. Shortly afterwards, the agent sold it to a New York publisher. "Big. It's going to be a movie," the agent had gushed. When I'd received a ten-thousand-dollar advance, I'd framed it and Mother had a family party for me. She'd invited the relatives who sat around the coffee table, eating prawns dipped in hot sauce, murmuring they never thought I was smart enough to write a book and was the check real? But I was so happy. I was on my secret journey, and for the first time, I felt I had an ego.

When the publisher invited me to New York, I thought I'd died and gone to heaven. That was until the editor, a hostile blonde woman, crisply informed me over lunch in a fancy restaurant that before they publish the book, I had to change the point of view from first person to third person. Instead of telling her that changing the point of view would change the voice and ruin the book, I smiled and agreed. It never occurred to me to say no. Instead, I spent the next year diligently changing everything, assuring myself that this was my big chance to be a real author, have an identity, and prove to my mother that I could be more than a wife.

But by the time I finished the changes, the voice was gone, and the publisher shelved it. My family suggested I get a real estate license. "You're not author material," Mother said.

Now, the moon is full and I don't want to look at it. It's too beautiful. Too promising. I decide that the next morning I'll call Emily and discuss the memo.

I slip into a half sleep.

Early the next morning, I call Emily. She takes my call right away.

In my strongest voice, my heart beating fast, I tell Emily in detail that most of the changes are useless. "Don't you see? Changing the protagonist's characterization smothers her voice and changes the story? I can do little things—but I can't compromise the characters. I'm sorry, I just can't."

She exhales an irritated, long sigh. "Bette, no can do. *We* at Avalon, feel this revision is *necessary*. Your protagonist needs... to be sexier. The faster you finish, the faster we'll get the book to coincide with your September TV show. Ari Jacobs, our best graphic designer, is sketching ideas for the cover. We see it as sexy. But elegant."

"Uh huh," I say, my heart dropping. "...I hope not too drugstore sexy."

She giggles. "We want the drugstore mentality. Sex sells. We read in the trades that your TV series is going to be even sexier than *Sex and the City*. We are very excited. So, Bette, trust us. Get this done ASAP."

I hesitate. I want to tell her it's not possible, but I fear that if I don't make the revisions, Avalon will pull it. Instead, I agree to get to work. "But I'd like to design the cover," I say. "I'm a painter. I'll send you some images."

"Fine, Bette. Though I have to run this by the publisher. Now get to work."

That upset feeling you get when you know you've done wrong, and pretend you did right, comes over me. But I assure myself that I'm on the brink of fame and fortune and that I won't use all Emily's changes anyway. I tell myself that I'll begin the rewriting in the morning.

The rain transitions to cool, foggy days. Every day at dawn, my green tea beside me, I work on the revision in the early-morning quietness, carefully highlighting lines to add or delete, and pretending I'm happy. Except for my students, I exclude outside life, hardly going outside, not picking up the cleaning or opening invitations or mail. Like trying to catch an elusive, beautiful bubble, all I think about is the coming TV series. Still, knowing in my heart that I am violating my protagonist's characterization, I constantly assure myself that soon this will be a bestseller and a major network TV series, and next time I'll do what I want.

As the weeks pass, the fog lifts, leaving behind layers of sunlight. Often Edwina calls and chirps excitedly about pre-promotion of the series. "This is going to be big, honeybun."

In therapy, like a child searching for a lost toy, I obsess about the revision, painfully trying to identify the sources of my willingness to submit to the will of others. "It's as if my submissive self is winning over my stronger self. When will it ever stop?"

"When you trust yourself," Dr. T. says softly. "Disassociation is a painful disease. It takes time."

"I need this publication and the TV series. My former books are stagnant. When I die, the kids will throw them out with my other things and all my books will end up in garage sales, or in free book bins for out-of-print books."

"Do you think that unless you do what Emily demands, your book is worthless?"

"Look what happened to the Jewish Princess Novel. After it was shelved, I sent the original manuscript to dozens of publishers and agents, but by then, no one wanted it. Years later, I finally sold it to a remote little press in Florida. No one reads it, and there are hardly any sales."

As I work on the revision, time eludes me. From dawn's cold gray light I work until night. The air transitions from dark fog to butterflies and sunlight. Finally I finish working on the revision. No longer is the voice sparkly, but flattened out, dulled. Nevertheless, I assure myself that the book is definitely better structured and that Anny Applebaum is a sexier sixty-five-year-old. "Marketable. Age is in," Edwina gushes on the phone.

Determined to have a great cover, I paint a shadowy woman wearing black, holding a bouquet of white roses, her pale face reflective under a swirling black hat. I send the painting, along with the revision, to Avalon.

A few days later, Melissa Jones, Avalon's head publicist calls. She is working her "buns off," she repeats, on a huge publicity campaign. She's writing press releases and researching everything about me. She likes my brand as an age activist.

"Great."

"You'll be the voice of age. As soon as your TV series hits the air, we're booking you on Wendy Williams, *Ellen*, and other shows. Also, I'm working on getting you on a shampoo ad for older women with frizzy hair like Anny."

"Uh huh. Well, Anny is just Anny. She's not an age."

"Got it," she says glibly. "Anyhoo, we're looking forward to your wonderful book and getting you on the global map. Talk soon."

* * *

On a windy morning just before Thanksgiving, I have the first Skype meeting with the WC team and I'm really excited. I look good on screen. I'm wearing my H&M black turtleneck pulled up to my chin, my hair slicked back and my long, shoulder-length amber and silver earrings with matching rings that I bought from a drugged-out Pakistani who sells jewelry off the truck.

Sitting real straight so that my jowls don't show, I hear the ding of Skype coming on. Everyone is sitting around a mile-long conference table, bottles of Smart Water beside them, while their assistants stand at attention. A humongous buffet table with piles of bagels, platters of ugly scrambled eggs, and shriveled smoked salmon sits along the wall. They're waving and gushing how great it is to be together, finally.

"I got Angie Golden to play Anny!" Joshua Bitterman announces. He stands in front, his shiny hair puffed up and styled, his black silk suit and mauve tie impeccable.

"Wow, she's about sixty too," I smile, pleased.

"Forty-nine," Yesterday corrects with a smile. Dressed in white with ropes of pearls dangling from her swan-like neck, she sits at the head of the table, writing on a long notepad.

"But she's had too much cosmetic work," I say. "Anny Applebaum doesn't believe in fillers and cosmetic work."

"She's a big star and she's hot," they murmur together.

"She'll be great no matter what her age," says Kat Zimmerman, the scriptwriter. She has huge, curly red hair, an arrogant, baby-like face, and she wears a white tank top with a huge Minnie Mouse image on the front. "I love Anny," she says to me with a kiss. "You look like her."

"I am her."

They laugh.

"We love Nancy," Bitterman says, looking at his Apple watch.

"Who's Nancy?" I snap. "My protagonist is *Anny*."

"Anny, Nancy, she's great," he shrugs. "I want to marry her."

"She's fucky fun," says Damian Sterling, one of the producers on the WC team. He looks twenty something, and he's got this slick, Ken doll look about him—thick brown wavy gelled hair, a perfect chiseled profile. He's wearing the industry ubiquitous Tom Ford black.

"We're good to go," Yesterday says. In her smart industry voice, she continues to say how much she *loves* Kat's scripts. "However…we might need a teeny tiny tweak…Angie is unhappy with the Medicare bit. It's not good for her image," Yesterday explains with a smile.

"Good idea," Kat says.

"Not negotiable," I say. "Anny needs Medicare. She's over sixty-five."

Wendy Richardson, a former soap opera producer, chimes in. She's drop-dead gorgeous, with waist-length shiny black hair. She references storylines from *As the World Turns,* while Waters Wilson, a casting director, sees Anny very "Kim K."

"Matt Damon is calling back soon. He's perfect for the diamond dealer," says Bitterman. Frantically, the assistants type notes on their MacBooks.

"Too young," I say. "The diamond dealer is seventy—and hot."

"We're *appealing* to younger, multi-generational audiences." Waters explains with an enervated sigh. "Maybe if Anny were Amish? Big numbers."

I say in my most corporate voice, "I don't want Anny changed... aged out and dumbed down. It's time to end age discrimination and show a real person, a woman who is happy about her age and has goals and..." My voice drifts.

There's a huge silence. Joshua looks up from his phone nervously.

"We're good to go," Yesterday smiles. "...We'll be in touch for our next meeting."

"I love you," they coo, blowing kisses through their fingers.

"Breathe. Hydrate," Kat shouts.

The screen goes gray. I sit staring at the pink rose inside the glass bud vase next to my computer. Once again I compromised myself, aware that Bitterman and his crew are only interested in making money? That they're ageists? Of course they're not going to listen to me so why do I do this again and again? When deep down I know they'll exploit my work?

* * *

"Anyway, the revision is done," I say to Dr. T. "Publication and pilot are set for September."

"I'm happy for you, Bette," Dr. T. says sincerely. "Hold your ground with Avalon. When you get that urge to please, go to the river." Dr. T. sniffles. He's had the flu.

"I just don't want them to change Anny's age. The networks have done it too often. Ageism is a disease. They want fourteen with tits and legs."

He sighs, heavily. "Unfortunately, we live in an ageist culture. They don't reject you, personally. They reject age—"

"By rejecting age, they reject me," I interrupt. "I don't buy this psychobabble that writers are separate from their work. Anny Applebaum is part of me. All my characters are." I hesitate until my anger subsides. "It's so odd—I feel this little person curled in me, hidden and watching. She knows so much, things that I won't face, and just knowing she's there is comforting sometimes."

He nods knowingly.

"I wonder if I was born angry or if situations made me angry, and what the anger really means, how it drives my work. Why I sabotage myself? That I don't think I deserve to have critical success? As far back as I remember I've felt weird, like I wasn't normal like Patty Horowitz, who kicked the ball perfectly in kickball, got perfect grades, and seemed happy."

He stares.

"Anyway, when I kick the bucket, at least I'll leave the girls a legacy."

"I think you already have," he says softly.

The red light clicks on. "Time to stop."

Later at home, at my computer, I'm writing tomorrow's column about breasts. *"Why are men consumed by breasts? Just give them a nipple or a balloon and they're fine and..."* After I finish writing the column, I write notes for the next column, deciding to write "To Viagra Falls And Back," a story about a sixty-eight-year-old surgeon I'd met online and then met for coffee. I want to reveal his obsessive need for a young and "fit" woman as he'd said. I write some notes, not wanting the piece to sound glib or revengeful, but rather to show our culture's obsession with genitalia and ageism. I write: *He bragged about his penis size. Even showed me pictures. The women who turn me on are under thirty. Also I like a tight vagina. He'd gone on to confide that when he was a child his mother made him eat fruit and he hated fruit and it made him gag and to this day if a vagina is wrinkled or hangs it reminds him of fruit.*

After I finish taking notes for the column, I study Emily's latest memo; She is now suggesting a different ending. *Maybe they marry and live happily ever after,* she writes. *Sex and happiness are important issues. Your Anny is too...depressed.*

This time I refuse. *The revision is done*, I email back.

I turn off the computer. I look at the framed photograph of my father at Universal Pictures. He's wearing one of his custom-tailored gray silk suits, his silver hair combed and slick. He stands with several of his colleagues and even in the photograph I can see the dreams in his stern, dark eyes. Next to his photograph is a framed newspaper article about my mother, who at sixteen won the Chopin Contest and a scholarship to Juilliard. A fringe of bangs touches her thin, arched eyebrows; her gorgeous face beams in proud repose.

I turn off the lights and close my eyes and wait to dream. Almost every night I dream about the parts of my life that I pretend don't exist. Consciousness is too painful. Soon, I'm inside a dream. I always know I'm dreaming because I stand behind a tree, watching myself in my life. Lisa is six years old. At a flower stand, I buy a bouquet of marigolds and place them in a ceramic vase in her room. The air is dark and the marigolds glow orange and I'm afraid that up close they'll smell bad or turn brown. I try to rush into her room, scoop Lisa from her bed and bring her into my arms but I can't move.

The holidays are raging. Christmas cards and recycled gifts are coming and going. Avalon sends me a huge box of stale Godiva chocolates and a note saying they're excited about the publication and will send galleys soon. Bitterman and his team send a five-foot-tall ugly cactus that has bugs in it. Anyway, during the holidays the industry turns into a ghost town, but Yesterday texts from Sedona that Kat Zimmerman is almost finished writing the series. "The script is very special," she raves. "You'll see."

So, feeling optimistic on Christmas Eve, I'm at Nanny and Larry's house in the Oakland Hills. It's a cozy house with high, molded ceilings; tall, curved windows; and an open industrial kitchen off the large living room. Puffy leather sofas surround a tall stone fireplace, and the windows face a lovely garden.

I place the Christmas gifts I wrapped in red satin and tied with purple silk roses under the tree. Neighbors and family carry gifts, cats, and dogs, bring platters of food. Nanny's beloved dog Fred wears a red sweater and a Santa Clause hat and the neighbor's dogs are running in and out of the house.

I love this house. It has high ceilings, a patio surrounded by tall bamboo trees; the multitude of glass windows and doors remind me of a small church. My paintings of women inside boxes or lying in gardens hang everywhere.

Nanny, an apron over her red jumpsuit and a headband of red roses holding back her waist-length satin hair, stands in the open kitchen, slicing her homemade pot roast. Larry, who has a head of unruly, thick black hair and soulful, shrewd eyes, makes cranberry martinis.

Couples are drinking and dancing to hot Christmas music playing from overhead speakers. I feel no pain as I'm jiving with this hot African American dude, trying to be cool, grooving, and stumbling in my clunky heels. I'm decked in my H&M red sweater dress, red stockings, sparkling red high heels. I hear my wrist bells clinking, and then Nanny yelling, "Hey. Mom. Don't fall!"

"Hey, you're cool," says the dude, pulling me closer and swinging me around. God, he's something. Go black and never back, Myra always says. But his girlfriend, a blonde white chick with a snake tattoo and mean eyes, glares at me from across the room. Thankfully, Frank, a little person who lives next door cuts in. He spins me like a top, and though he's a dwarf, the man can dance. "You're doing it Bette, just follow me," he says, twirling me around. On my third martini, I'm twisting, turning, stumbling, clunking, but having a ball. Happiness comes in moments. They add up to great memories.

"Don't drink too much, Mom," Nanny shouts.

"Oh, let her! We have a lot to celebrate," Larry says. He tells everyone about my book coming out with Avalon Publishing, and about the TV series in the fall.

There's cheers and applause; everyone clinks my glass.

"So nu? Is the check in the mail?" Aunt Zoe asks. She's about seventy-four, with a huge face and tiny hair. Strands of Christmas beads wrap around her tall, thin neck.

"Actually, it's already deposited," I reply.

"*Exactly* when is the series?" snorts my cousin Crystal, a fifty-year-old divorced social worker, whose husband ran off with her sister and now lives on an Indian reservation.

"They say early next fall. No pilot. Straight to series. It's going to be important."

"That's what you said about your Jewish Princess novel."

"This one's getting to air. Most people never succeed."

"Like your first husband who dumped you on your wedding night."

"Fuck you!"

"Fuck you too!" she says, flipping me the bird.

"So let's have a fucking merry Xmas!" Larry says, waving a tasting spoon. "Let's eat."

Everyone crowds around Nanny's pot roast and kugel and platters of salads and vegetables, all laid out on a long wooden table decorated with small glass vases of red roses and lit, flaming candles. So we're all eating and drinking and then in one swoop, Fred licks all the food off Aunt Zoe's plate. She shouts that Fred needs anger management classes and that her dog Willie is in behavior modification school. Then everyone is stuffing their faces, comparing their dogs, and shouting that our world is shot to hell.

"Trump is doing his best," Aunt Zoe says, pressing her thin lips.

"Best what? Pulling families apart? Trashing Obama, our only real president? He tries his best with hookers. That's it! He dismisses the LGBTQ community. Doesn't let trans people into public bathrooms."

"Do you want to go in a public bathroom with a woman who has a penis?" Aunt Zoe asks.

"How do you know I don't have a penis?" I say wanting to smash in her smug face.

"You're vulgar. Just like your column. The whole family knows it."

"I love her column," says the little person.

Nanny shouts, "Presents!"

We sit on this huge leather sectional couch, Fred next to me. One by one, Nanny calls out our names and we open her beautifully wrapped gifts. Nanny loves Christmas. All year she shops the sales and stocks up for the holidays.

"Oh, an Alexa Dot," Larry says. "Thank you, Bette."

"Mom, I love this bracelet," Nanny says, showing off the silver bracelet I bought at the Museum of Contemporary Art.

"A black cashmere scarf. I love it. Thank you, Nanny and Larry!" I wrap it twice around my neck. "Gorgeous."

"Don't schmootz it up," Nanny says, frowning. "It's for your New York meetings."

Fred loves the huge rubber duck I gave him. Neighbors exchange regifted candles and candies, and soon there are boxes of wrapping piled high and gifts strewn everywhere.

"Nanny is a great hostess," says David, our cousin who fell out of a window when he was ten, leaving part of his head caved in.

I say cheerfully, "Nanny is the writer in the family."

"Don't hock!" she shrieks. "It's Christmas, and right away she's hocking the china with the writing!"

We crowd around Skype, and wave to Lisa on their annual Crystal Cruise to the Caribbean. They're wearing reindeer hats.

I sleep in the guest room with Fred next to me on the bed. All night my arms are around him, his warm breath on my face, his heart beating next to mine. I love him so much. I wonder if I'll ever sleep next to a man I love as much.

The next morning Edwina calls. "Honeybun, Merry Christmas and all that shit. I want to tell you that this Sunday night Anderson Cooper is interviewing Angie Golden about *The Viagra Diaries* and the series. Be sure and tune in."

"Oh, great. How exciting."

"I'm exhausted," she says, sighing. "...I'll be glad when pilot season is over. WC only has one slot for fall and in eight weeks, Bitterman is going to announce our show in the trades."

"Edwina, I so much appreciate all the years you spent on my projects. I just have to tell you this."

"Cut the shit," she snaps. "I'm in pain. Lester left."

"Your husband?"

"I got the fuckhead all his jobs. He's got a dick the size of his arm and the brain the size of a pea. I hate him. He ran off with the twenty-year-old transgender parking attendant. She's gorgeous so it's perfect for him. They can compare dicks."

"I'm...sorry...I don't know what to say..."

She sniffs. "Don't say a word but I'm sixty. If the networks knew, I'd be out of a job. This age shit is a nightmare. I've spent a fortune on new boobs, lips, cheekbones, vagina, you name it. The rat still left me."

Then she rants about how she hates Joshua Bitterman, what an idiot he is, that she had an affair with him once and he has a tiny teeny dick. I feel sorry for Edwina, but I also know not to get too close to her, remembering years ago when my options fell through and I was upset and she was dismissive and emotionally unavailable. The industry is full of broken dreams and people who aren't the way they seem.

8

Sunday evening, I'm sitting close to my TV, watching Anderson Cooper interview Angie Golden. My girls and I are on Skype as we watch the CNN interview. Angie looks gorgeous in sapphire blue, the color of her eyes. Her chestnut hair floats to her shoulders. Unlike Anny Applebaum's facial wrinkles, frizzy hair, and natural look, Angie's face is unlined, and her glossy, pouty lips are full from fillers. In her whispery voice, she talks about Save The Elephants, her foundation in Africa, her 800-number flashing on the bottom of the screen. Anderson asks how it feels to be a sixty-year-old icon.

"Forty-nine," she corrects. "It's painful," she replies, pausing, and then confiding that the paparazzi follow her everywhere, and that recently she'd been on the john, doing her business like everyone on the planet, she explains, when flashing camera lights blinded her and the next day the picture ended up in the *National Enquirer*. She hired Gloria Aldridge, who is suing the photographer for his home and for his children's college fund.

"It's very hard," she says, her fake eyelashes shadowing her face. Finally, Anderson mentions *The Viagra Diaries*.

"I idolize the title," she says flashing a wide perfect smile.

"What is it about, Angie?"

She hesitates and looks confused. "...Well...it's about...a lot of things," she says in an unsure voice. "...Tune in to the show this fall." Quickly, she continues talking about her elephants, and how as a child she "adored" Dumbo, urging everyone to donate. The interview ends.

"She didn't read the script!" I yell on a conference call with Nanny and Lisa. "How is she going to play Anny? Plus, she says she's forty-nine. Like my left foot."

"She's a star, mom. She can say what she wants."

"And you want me to publish my novel?" Nanny snips. "I'll hang upside down from a flagpole before I go through what you go through. The industry makes you sing for your supper and it's cruel."

"It's ageism," I say.

"Stop with the ageism shit," Nanny says angrily. "It's hard shit."

"Well, all in all, as soon as the show and book are out I'm going to make a fortune and name my price. Then they can eat crow. You'll see."

The next day, Melissa Jones calls, raving about the CNN interview. "Avalon *idolizes* Angie Golden. And your *PW*, *Kirkus*, and *New York Times* reviews are fabulous."

"Oh, I'm happy," I say, surprised by the good reviews, assuring myself again that all is going to be fabulous after all, and soon this book will be behind me. "This is all mind boggling."

She reads aloud the review from the *Times*: "*Elder Bette Roseman, age activist, writes about elder horny Applebaum with vigor and fun. She proves that elders can have fun...*"

I interrupt, trying to keep my voice down. "Anny is not an *elder*. I'm an age activist and I've said that I don't like that label. Anny is a woman who represents ALL ages. Ageism affects all ages and races and should not be labeled."

She sighs indulgently. "...Avalon *feels* that your book will be the *first* to show that elders can have fun too. I've reached out to every nursing home in the US, and in Europe."

As I continue to protest that I detest labels, that I don't want Anny branded as an *elder,* but rather as a woman who knows herself, has goals, and defies ageism, Melissa talks over me, emphasizing that Avalon is marketing *The Viagra Diaries* as *ground breaking* for the *elder* community. Publication will be August 21, three weeks before the TV series is on air.

"September third, I've booked you on *Fame, GMA,* and I'm working on *Oprah.* I'll send a schedule. Also, Emily FedExed the galleys and the book jacket for your approval."

Two mornings later, at the crack of dawn, the FedEx guy delivers this huge envelope from Avalon. I tear it open and remove the bound galleys, the audiotape, and a poster-size cover. Is this for real? The cover is hideous, with tiny blue Viagra pills dripping along the front and an ugly, oversized black bra draped over a bed with a walker next to it. My photo on the back is so airbrushed that I look like a cadaver. The audio has the same cover and when I play the audio, the narrator reading my book sounds like a dying cat. I burst into tears. This is the final humiliation, and at last I see that once again I'm the one who murdered and violated not only my book but also my protagonist and myself.

Quickly, I call Emily. I blurt that I *detest* the cover. "...The walker has *nothing* to do with the book and the cover is not creative or interesting and..."

"Jacques is a genius," she interrupts in her overly sympathetic, condescending voice. "*We* at Avalon think it's *brilliant* that Jacques integrated the...*elder* community."

"I told Melissa that I don't want to emphasize any community with any label. Anny is ageless, and my cover is so much better."

"We felt your design, though lovely, is not right for our brand." After a tense moment, she says in her pale, rigid voice, "...Bette, you're having author jitters. As soon as pub date is near, I'll call and we'll arrange to meet with you in New York."

When I hang up, I'm shaking from anger. I want to kick in the walls, call Emily and scream that she's a stupid, untalented fool, that I want my book back, and how dare the stupid publisher turn down my cover in place of the ugly one they're using with the cheap paper. I want to kick the walls in, hating myself for once again creating this fiasco, for not confronting Avalon in the first place and refusing to rewrite.

The night is still, like the stillness after a storm or before an earthquake. Even the old apartment building is quiet. I slip into bed and under the covers and into my dream, where I find myself wandering into a house with beautiful paintings, antiques, and a table set with silver, crystal, and place cards. When I see the names of people I know, I pull the tablecloth. No one is looking and I hide as the crystal breaks and there's shouting and dishes flying in the air and I try to move. I'm frozen and I hear my mother playing Brahms on the piano and will she know that I broke the crystal and will I ever be able to lift my feet and escape this dream and I can't breathe.

* * *

It's the middle of summer and the air is sultry and the roses bloom in front of the apartment building. At night when no one is looking, I pick yellow roses and place them in my pink glass vase by the window. I can't live without flowers, and when I look at the beauty and perfection of a rose—its mutations, colors, swirling petals—I'm sure that there's a higher power.

Though I'm sad about the way my book looks and reads, and disgusted with myself for allowing it to happen, I'm getting excited about the TV series. Bitterman texts that the script is in the "polishing stage," and is fabulous and is *green lit* for air and soon the airdate will be announced.

Melissa begins promotion of the book. She sends me the press release that she wrote, the one she is sending to bookstores and papers, and once again I'm deeply disappointed. Not only is the press release full of phrases like *Anny Applebaum, Elder Queen*, but also the prose is flowery and poorly written and doesn't relate to the book or make sense. What happened to the press release I'd written? Should I call Melissa? Demand that she use my press release?

Wanting Lisa's advice, I call her and complain about how awful Avalon's press release is, how it doesn't represent the story.

"Let it go, Mom. No one reads them anyway," Lisa advises. "Move on. Enjoy the ride. Once the TV series is on air, trust me, you'll call the shots."

Meanwhile, trying not to worry about the book and assuring myself that in spite of the revision it will be a bestseller, I concentrate on teaching my writing workshops, writing my column, and trying to find new material for a novel. But I have block. Looking for inspiration, I read incessantly, rereading Fitzgerald, Hemingway, Plath, Sexton, Woolf, and many past and current authors. Though I don't believe in genderizing art, I'm especially in awe of many women artists and their ability to go so deep into their inner selves and render great works. Art depends on truth. Wanting to go deeper, wondering if I can, I watch films and take copious notes on dialogue, structure, the way the camera is used and how it captures light, and the emotions underneath. I read books on directors, studying how they tell their story by images and light and direction. All those years in graduate school, in the creative writing program, stifled my writing and my confidence. There were too many rules. Just as Jackson Pollock dripped paint into something beautiful and magical, I believe that craft must be driven by the spontaneous creativity that emerges from the subconscious.

But the block persists. As if I've lived a life with amnesia and suddenly start remembering, I feel bewildered and don't know how to be the way I really feel. My moods fluctuate and I find myself calling people I've resented, confronting them about past slights.

"You need to find new ways to monitor your thoughts," Dr. T. advises. But the struggle between my two sides is raging and I find myself craving solitude. I turn to my painting and write poetry. I love writing poetry, how the images caught in my subconscious float to the surface and seep into my poems.

By text, Yesterday informs me that soon I'll be invited to the first table read.

"Can't wait," I text back.

She writes that "boys with the money" have to approve the script. "They adore Kat. They *love, love, love*, what she's writing."

Night falls and night songs begin. These songs are voices from the past. Sometimes these voices are so real I think they're next to me in the room, other times they sound faint, as though trying to get my attention. Sometimes I hear them recite regrets, and I know they're my regrets. When I wake, I write down what I can remember—pieces of images, words—and put them together into messages.

I listen to Sibelius. His music is passionate. It makes me cry.

I close the computer and it's time to sleep.

9

Several days later, on a still, foggy day, I'm at Starbucks working on my next column about why you don't see little people in art galleries or museums or exhibits. It's crowded in the café and I'm sitting at my usual table next to the window. I like to keep a week ahead of the columns and keep lists of themes and ideas.

When I finish the column, I'm shooting the breeze with Father Brian, a hot, gay priest and another Starbucks regular. Father Brian is ranting about his relationship with this twenty-year-old, Tommy, who also works at Starbucks, and he's complaining that Tommy is *incapable* of being monogamous.

"Well, relationships aren't easy. I *know*. At least you have a good relationship with Jesus."

"Jesus, yes, But Tommy's a shit—"

Just then my cell phone rings. A woman with a gnat-like voice informs me that my long-lost, drug addict brother Ricky Roseman has been found on the street and is in a Napa hospital. "He's a sick puppy. He doesn't have insurance and he said you're a big star author and can take care of him. He's on methadone now, but we're not here to support drug addicts. If you don't claim him, we have to send him out to the street and he'll die. I need you here in the next two hours. Or we have to release him."

"I'll be there."

Father Brian offers to drive me. "It's the Christian thing to do. God's will, to help," he says.

In Father Brian's Toyota, on our way to Napa, huge gold crucifixes dangle from the rearview mirror. He's talking about the glories of death, and how he hopes that Tommy drops dead. Meanwhile, I'm remembering Ricky, a redheaded late child—sickly, sucking his thumb until he was twelve, announcing he was gay and Mother yelling at him that he'll get over it—tutored at home because Mother said that like her, he was born with an old heart, and was too sickly to go to school or work. I remember his attempted suicides, constant hospital procedures, the year in prison for dealing heroin. All his life he'd lived at home, until Mother died while watching *Jeopardy*. His grief was huge—I remember his sweater on her pillow, as if he were with her, her television set to her beloved game shows. Because he'd forged her will, he got everything, threatening to kill me if I contested. He ran off with this eighteen-year-old boy who, in a year, took everything he had. After that, I never could find him.

"We're here," says Father Brian, parking in a huge, concrete parking lot. We hurry into the hospital.

I try to get my bearings at the doorway, feeling an enormous wave of sadness. I watch Ricky sitting half-up in this narrow bed, and though he's ten years younger, he has the look of a much older man, resignation visible on his narrow, chalk-white face. His once-red hair is streaked with bands of silver. I'm feeling a mixture of such pain that I can't breathe. To think that I'd resented this poor soul so much that we'd never really known each other. "Hello," I say, at his side. I take his hand.

"Hey, Bette, thanks for coming."

"Of course. I'm sorry you're ill. I'm here to take you home. Not to worry."

Relief turns his ravaged face into boyish joy. "It's not enough that I'm sick—I'm gay and old. They were going to leave me in the fucking street." He blinks, his sunken, unsure eyes on my face. His dentures poke out from his tiny mouth and dark purple circles line his tan eyes, giving him an owlish look.

"Of course I'm here," I repeat cheerfully as I can. "You're my brother."

Tears float from his pale eyes. Father Brian comes in and I introduce them. Father Brian is very kind and places his hand on Ricky's. For a second, Ricky looks confused.

"He drove me here," I assure him.

After Father Brian does some mumbo jumbo stuff, crossing himself and telling Ricky to keep the faith, he leaves.

"Not to worry," I say, overwhelmed now by sadness and not wanting him to see me cry. "You're with me. I won't let anything happen to you."

He nods, as if an affirmation. "I...I read about you, Bette," he says wistfully. "I told all the nurses about you and your books. She's a professor. An author, I told them. My night nurse Dawn said your book was mentioned on CNN and that you're having a TV series. You'll make a fortune. You're a star."

"We'll go to Hollywood," I say, trying to smile, knowing he lived an unlived life without dreams and in isolation.

He shrugs. "Mother always said you were a hippie and a dreamer. But I always knew you'd make it. You're the only one in our family who went to college—who did something..."

A crabby-looking doctor comes into the room. Lanky like Gumby, with a pointed head and tiny glasses, he's clutching a clipboard. In a robotic voice, he explains that Ricky has end stage heart failure, an aneurysm near his heart, and needs immediate hospice care. "He hasn't more than a few weeks to live," he continues, as if Ricky can't hear him. Ricky squeezes my hand, and asks the doctor if he's eligible for a heart transplant.

The doctor frowns. "You'd die on the table. Second, you have no insurance."

"I'll take care of him," I snap.

When the doctor leaves the room, I assure Ricky that he'll come home with me. "You'll see. We'll show them. We'll figure it out. I'm on the brink of getting some money."

His sad, caved-in face lights up. "I appreciate it, Bette. Thank you."

A few moments later, a skinny social worker comes in, a pale brown hairnet covering her thin hair. She has release papers for me to sign, and with them the outstanding seventy-two-thousand-dollar hospital bill.

"I don't have that kind of money."

"Well, you have to make a payment of at least twenty thousand or we can't release him to you. He's on methadone," she says primly, pressing her lips. "If you leave him here he has to go to our restitution department. Where terminal people without MediCal—on drugs live out their last days..."

I take out a checkbook, figuring I'll transfer my book advance savings and, assuring myself that money is coming from the series soon anyway, I write a check. An hour later she calls a van that takes us to my apartment. Ricky is on a gurney, his huge oxygen tank beside him. He's wearing my raincoat over his hospital gown. He has nothing, only a paper bag of some old underwear and medications and prescriptions.

At my apartment, his oxygen tank beside him, he stands in the doorway, his eyes closed as if in rhapsody and he inhales deeply. "Oh, it smells so good in here, Bette. Like Mother's perfume."

"Shalimar," I say.

He opens his eyes and looks dazed for a moment. "Very nice place, Bette," he says with an affirmative nod. "Mother's antique table, desk, her blue vase—your paintings are wonderful. Very nice," he repeats, slightly wobbling.

"Sorry the couch isn't big but I'll give you lots of blankets and make it cozy. Would you like a hot bath? It will be good for you. I'll put bubble bath in it. You can wear my robe and tomorrow I'll buy you underwear and pajamas. Tonight I'll make us spaghetti. You always loved it."

"Sounds glorious," he says, almost shyly.

He unhooks the oxygen and I help him into the bathroom where I fill the tub with lavender bubble bath. "Now hold on to the sides when you get in and out. Call me, when you're ready. Here's my long fleece robe you can wear, and clean towels."

I leave the bathroom and begin preparing dinner. I hear the water sloshing in the bathroom, his humming. I stand in the middle of the room, holding my breath, like holding in the sadness I feel. For so long, since Mother died and he went through the money, he's been living on the street or in homeless shelters. As I open my sofa bed and prepare it with fresh, lilac scented sheets and lots of soft pillows, I remember how indulged he was—overly fed, given cars, clothes, consistent money.

I call Nanny to tell her that Ricky is with me and not to call too late.

"Now you have Ricky there?" Nanny says on the phone. "Next, you'll bring home the homeless nut you always give money to. Ricky makes Norman Bates look normal. Mom, he was in prison for drug dealing and in a million rehabs for heroin. He stole Nana's jewelry and sold it and he'll steal your money too. He'll bring the druggies to your place. Larry agrees."

"I didn't say that," Larry says on the line.

"Ricky is very ill. A sad soul. He doesn't have long. The doctor said so. Compassion is important, Nanny."

She sighs. "...I'll go to Costco and bring some things for him. I'll make my chicken soup."

The following three weeks, I do little outside of taking Ricky to the clinic to get his methadone and shopping for his new clothes, his oxygen tank next to him. While I work at my desk, he spends his days on the sofa bed, happily watching the History Channel on television. Television is all he knows. How he educated himself. From the time he was little he watched cartoons and then, as the years passed and Mother insisted he had an "old heart," he had to be home tutored and needed constant surgeries and procedures and hospitalizations. I remember him lying on his waterbed, medicated, and watching programs on space. As he got older, he took flying lessons and dreamed of becoming a pilot. He got a license to fly cargo planes until he had a heart attack, and then turned to heroin.

To make up for his horrible life, I want to make him happy. But constantly he rants what "rotten breaks" he's had, how everyone has "screwed him," that he's going to "sue" the insurance companies, drug companies, Mother's lawyers. Careful not to mention the past, or to ask why he stayed all his life in Mother's house until she died, I try to change the subject.

Nanny brings Tupperware containers of her homemade chicken soup. Every night, his oxygen tank dragging behind him, he sets my table with Mother's pretty plates, the ones with the orange flowers. He loves to bake, and earlier that day, with the ingredients he'd requested, he baked a pretty chocolate cake from scratch. "It's delicious," I say, eating my second piece.

He looks surprised, as if he's not used to praise. He confides that Mother wouldn't allow him to bake. He recalls a birthday cake he spent hours making her. He'd wanted to surprise her. "It was a white cake. On the top of the cake I designed pink lilies and violets. She threw it out. Homos bake cakes she said."

As if the discussion is closed, he places the rubber oxygen clip on his over his nose and sips his mint tea, a faraway look in his sunken eyes.

As the days pass when Ricky's methadone is due, he gets edgy, but after I take him to the Tenderloin Clinic to get his "dose," as he calls it, he seems subdued and better.

Every day, he straightens my bed cover, sponges the kitchen counter. I remember how he polished Mother's silver, vacuumed, waxed her floors, like Gray Gardens, Ricky and Mother drinking expensive wines and dressed formally in her empty formal dining room.

Tonight, the rain stops. Ricky is lounging on the couch, his oxygen tank beside him. A rubber clip over his hawk-shaped nose, Ricky watches me as I'm writing my daily column. A plate of brownies Nanny baked is next to him.

"You're a star, Bette," he says after a long silence. "I wish I was."

I stop writing. I face him. "You are in your own right. I think you're very bright."

He flushes as if he's embarrassed, or like he can't believe what I said.

"I'm not educated like you," he continues. "I want to be successful too. But my old heart kept me back. I want to do things... travel...." His voice drifts off.

"Maybe you will. You have to believe. Work for things..."

"I'm retired!" he screams so loud I jump. Don't I know that he's had three heart surgeries and didn't have the advantages I had and who do I think I am to lecture him? He screams, "Mother was right!" He says that I'm a selfish bitch and couldn't keep a husband. "You shamed the family when Charley left you the day after your wedding. Mother never got over it. Then you became a hippie and looked like an earth monster. Mother always said your hair was too long and it still is."

I close the computer and go into the kitchen to make tea. Shaking like a leaf, I'm remembering how after Mother died, I found the full bottle of heart pills he was in charge of giving her every day, and I knew then that he had deliberately not given her the pills, and pretended to not notice when she slumped over while they were watching *Jeopardy.* She'd been unconscious for fifteen minutes.

I bring him a cup of tea. Calmed down, like a reprieved child, he plants wet kisses on my face, profusely apologizing. "I'm in pain, Bette. My gut is killing me. I have to go to the doctor at four today for a test. Can you take me?"

I wait in the hospital lobby on the phone with my girls, until a volunteer tells me that after the tests, they had to bring Ricky down to surgery as his aneurysm had burst. “We’ll let you know when he’s in recovery.”

As day transitions into dusk, I worry what has happened to him. Finally, another volunteer informs me that Ricky is out of surgery and he’ll take me to the recovery room to see him. I follow the lovely man along a dank green tiled hall, feeling numb as I always would, all the many times I’d visited Mother during one of her heart surgeries. I feel myself detach and can’t feel my feet. The man presses a code, the doors slide open and I go inside.

In a small basement room with old radiators hissing heat and machines beeping, Ricky is awake in the middle bed and screaming that he’s in pain. I take his hand stuck with tubes and feel faint. “Bette, get the doctor, I’m in pain!” This nurse with a sour attitude is adjusting dials on the heart monitor next to his bed. “He’s in pain,” I say, my voice feeling faraway. “Please call the doctor. Please give him morphine. He’s in pain,” I repeat. “Do you hear me?”

“I’ll give him a Tylenol,” she says, her back to me. “His blood pressure is too low for morphine. I’ll call the doctor and please wait outside.”

“Ricky, I’m right outside,” I say to him, but he doesn’t answer and he looks panicked and is shouting how he’s in terrible pain. Oh, why don’t I stay here and hold him until the doctor arrives? Why do I leave and rush down the hallway?

I wait in the lobby and I don’t inquire about Ricky, telling myself that the doctor will find me if anything is wrong, sinking into that other place and disappearing. But I sit on the orange plastic chair in the back, watching the news listlessly play on the television, until hours later another volunteer comes over and informs me that Ricky is in ICU, on the fifth floor.

Shocked but numb, I take the elevator to the fifth floor, to ICU.

I press the code and a young doctor wearing blue scrubs, with kind, sympathetic blue eyes, introduces himself and sympathetically lets me know that Ricky is intubated and in bad shape. Quickly, he leads me past the noisy, over-lit nurses' station, past huge heart machines and clusters of doctors talking in groups into a tiny room. The doctor leaves. I'm shocked to see Ricky hooked to these huge machines, his tiny mouth grasping the breathing tube, his face white and frowning as if he is trying to tell me something.

"What happened?" I ask the male nurse adjusting dials on a huge heart monitor.

"You'll have to ask the doctor," he says, gently.

"Bette is here," I say to Ricky, holding his warm hand. "I love you, I love you. Blink, if you hear me."

He blinks.

"You're going to be all right. We're going to Hollywood. Hang in there. I love you."

I hold his hand, blue from the tiny, inserted tubes. I'm hunching over the bed, my tears falling on his poor sad face, murmuring, "I love you. Bette loves you. You're my star. Don't you ever think you didn't do great things. Look how you took care of Mother, and you got your pilot's license at eighteen. Remember? Remember how you flew cargo planes? Always, you were easy with technology. I'm a tech moron."

Then a young Indian doctor comes into the room. She whispers for me to follow her into the hallway. She's short and slim, her shiny black hair in a bun, and a red dot between her eyes. In a cold voice, she informs me that she needs me as a witness as she tells Ricky that they are withdrawing his care and can't do any more to help him.

"What? Why? I don't even know what happened! The doctor never contacted me. Can't you let him die in peace?"

"It's a law."

"Fuck the law," I say. "Let him believe he's going to make it."

"Sorry, if you don't calm down, you have to leave. I'll bar you from his room."

Numb, I follow her into the room. She hovers over Ricky's bed, her cold voice informing him that they've done everything possible and that his sister Bette is here and agrees that they have to end his care and to blink if he hears her. A tear comes out of his eye, drops down his cheek like a protest. She dabs it away with a tissue. I'm holding his hand but he pulls it away.

"Ricky, this is not my idea," I whisper, kissing his face. "I won't let anything happen to you. I promise. The doctor doesn't know—you'll make it and we're going to Hollywood." I hold his hand again. But he pulls it away, again.

"You see," I say to the doctor. "He thinks I told you to do this. See what you did! You're cruel and I'm going to report you!" I say, my voice rising.

"You have to wait outside," she says.

A nurse leads me into the hall and I'm crying harder and pressing into the nurse's arms. "They're giving him more morphine now. You can see him in a few minutes."

When I go inside, Ricky's eyes are closed but there's still a frown creasing his forehead and I'm whispering that I'm here. "Bette is here. Bette loves you," I whisper, watching the morphine drip into his arm. The male nurse is working at the machine and my face is on his chest but he still won't hold my hand. He half opens one eye and a tear floats on it. "I love you," I whisper. The beeping slows down and then there's silence. "I'm sorry, he's gone," the nurse says. The nice resident comes in and removes the tubes from Ricky's mouth, arms, and body and pulls a blanket to his chin. "I'll leave you alone with him," the doctor and nurse say, leaving the room.

Ricky is still frowning and his lips are black, his tiny mouth a dark hole, his hands fists. His hair floats back on the pillow and my tears fall on his still-warm face. "Your soul is still here," I whisper to him. "Let it go."

I sit next to him, stroking his face and then, like the quiet that occurs when daylight transitions to dusk or night to dawn, a stillness takes over and I know that his soul left.

The resident doctor covers his face. Gently, he says, "Bette, I'm sorry. He seemed like such a nice man. I'm sorry."

A nurse gives me a brown wrinkled paper bag with the new sweatpants and new beige sweater he'd been wearing when he entered the hospital. She gives me his worn cloth wallet with ten one-dollar bills I'd given him for his taxi ride to the methadone clinic, a driver's license, a faded license to fly cargo planes. How sad, I think. I remember how thrilled he was when at eighteen he passed the flying requirements and dreamed of becoming a pilot. I close the wallet and place it next to my heart. Sometimes when dreams are broken, some people can't go on because that's all they had.

I walk home in the rain. Tears flood my vision as I walk the last hill to my apartment. As soon as I get inside I unpack the tote bag and place Ricky's things on my glass table. Holding his beige sweater in my arms, I sit by the window watching the rain. A brave life, yes, the life inside him was brave.

I fall asleep in the chair, Ricky's sweater in my arms.

I dream that I peek from a hole, watching Ricky on the beach. He is twelve. He is running and he carries a long stick, and a windmill on top of his dark blue cap spins around and around. We stop by a crooked black rock and pick off the sea anemones and then place them in the water. Sea salt stains my very thick glasses. We run into the waves, and as they try to catch us, we run back. Ricky is laughing and the windmill is spinning...spinning...

* * *

Even when we expect a death, when it comes, it has an impact—one you never expect. For the first time in my life I feel grief, a feeling you feel when you're standing on the edge of a ledge, looking down. He's in my dreams. A vase of pale pink roses sits next to the photograph of us at his birthday dinner I recently had at my apartment. Nanny and Larry and our adored cousin Linda stand next to him, holding balloons printed with the number 60. His oxygen tank next to him, wearing the blue shirt and tie I'd given him, he gave a nice speech thanking us and saying he loved us.

Although his death is a blessing and I knew he was going to die, I'm haunted, as if his death has propelled me deeper into my subconscious. In my dreams, I see clearly my mother's beige Tudor house, the beautiful antiques, the orchids carefully arranged inside metal frogs. In my dreams I watch Ricky, a pale, redheaded child alone in his darkened room, vials of medications next to him as he neatly pastes pictures of dogs into a large scrapbook. His room is his world, a room that Mother had decorated in dark brown, with a corporate desk, empty except for a lonely calendar, and dark wood bookcases filled with Mother's choice of golf and football books. I see a framed photograph in Mother's beige room, of Ricky dancing with a girl at Miss Watson's Dancing School. Even at ten, you could see the emptiness in his eyes. She stole his sexuality, his essence, and his ego.

Poor Ricky, he had nothing but his TV, fancy clothes, and fancy leased cars that he constantly crashed. His dreams stuffed into some secret part of him, existing as if he were in some awful play Mother had written.

Next to his photograph, I light candles. At Sinai I plan for his cremation, spending most of my savings on the cremation and nice obituary in the Jewish newspaper. I write, *Ricky Roseman took care of his mother all her life. He flew cargo planes. He's the beloved brother of Bette Roseman...the beloved uncle of Nanny Berman and Dr. Lisa Ann Rafstein.*

I paid extra for a nice velvet bag for his ashes, which I plan on scattering at Baker Beach near Mother's house where Ricky lived all his life.

On a windy, cold day, a man wearing a black suit delivers the bag of ashes. I'm surprised how heavy they are. Myself, my cousin Linda, Nanny, and her beloved Fred all arrive at the beach Ricky so loved, near the house he grew up in. I'm holding the box of ashes close to my heart and we walk along the tide to the end of the beach, to the cave where Ricky loved to go as a child to collect strange rocks and shells. The wind is up and the waves are roaring high and white, slamming along the edge of the tide. A few well-dressed women and men walk their dogs along the private beach, glancing suspiciously at us as we hover by the edge of the water.

I had written Ricky a poem and sealed it inside a narrow glass bottle. I want him to read it. I drop the bottle in the roaring ocean and watch it bob and then lift with the waves. Nanny is next to me and as if Fred understands, he quietly stands next to her on his leash, watching. Crouching low by the edge of the water, I open the top of the velvet bag and streams of white ashes spray the air like smoke. The wind is wild and some of the ashes spray my face, my hair, and my shoes. Frightened that he's getting lost, dis-respected, I rush into the water and hold the bag at an angle and the white ashes spray into the air like streams of kites.

We stand in a circle to say a prayer, and Nanny opens a jar full of rose petals that float into the sky.

We hurry to Linda's car. A lady holding the leash on a large dog, yells, "You threw a dead person's ashes into my private beach! The police are on their way."

As Linda drives past my mother's house, the house exactly the same as it was, even from the street I can feel the pain from the tall, gray and white Tudor like it was yesterday. Mother's bonsai trees are still perfectly shaped along the side of the house and I remember her constantly reshaping the trees as she was always trying to reshape Ricky.

When I'm home I place a shell from the beach on top of Ricky's beige sweater in my drawer, next to his rubber oxygen nose clip. I hang several pictures I took of Ricky during his last days on the walls of my apartment. He's wearing his new blue shirt and tie, smiling, his oxygen tank next to him.

* * *

"I hurt." Dr. T. sits straight. It's the next day and I've been crying for the past fifty minutes. Never have I cried so deeply, as if

Ricky's death penetrated my buried tears and all the sadness is coming out. Between crying, I continue to talk about the past years, saying that I could have helped Ricky, guided him, but instead I had been full of hate and resentment and blame. "He died isolated, his sexuality hidden...his life unlived."

I stop, press the Kleenex to my eyes. "...Strange, I'd always resented that poor soul because Mother showed him love. No matter what he did she loved him. No matter what I did, especially since Charley, she hated."

"That wasn't love," Dr. T. says softly. "Poor Ricky was your mother's need for something else, for her own self-loathing. She's the one who died an unlived life. At least Ricky knew who he was."

Late day shadows spill onto the silence between us.

That night, I dream that Ricky is holding his cat Prince. Ricky is in his tool room, a small dusty room in the basement. He saws wood. Expensive tools hang from corrugated holes on the wall. A variety of nails are inside little labeled drawers. This is where he spends his days. It is his pretend vocation. "He fixes things," Mother said. But he doesn't. He saws wood and listens to classical music. Huge earmuffs are over his ears, as Beethoven's Fifth plays so loud the walls shake.

I'm crying and I want to get out of the dream. It is too sad to watch Ricky's empty eyes as he saws a piece of wood.

I strap myself into a little seat inside a long silver submarine and it slips down into the sea where it's black but the fish glow pink, some have yellow dots on their fins, and flutter like fans...

* * *

It's the end of summer. With publication not far off, Melissa sends press releases to bookstores, newspapers, and to the foreign publishers who are publishing *The Viagra Diaries*. She sends early reviews, which are not too bad. Yesterday texts that everything is moving forward, and very soon I'll read the script.

Meanwhile, when I'm not writing my column, to supplement my income, I concentrate on my writing workshops, and also on my Age March. The march is to celebrate age pride and to end age segregation. I got a few women to help me and Moo Moo who is so well connected, agreed to do the publicity. I call local startup companies and political celebrities. I pitch the age march and ask for endorsements. But it's hard to get through.

Today I call a local celebrity billionaires' office. I pitch his assistant. "We're all dealing with the fucking age! You old ladies and your ageism shit! Get a life!" he screams, banging the phone.

Though the women on my committee start fighting, we somehow manage to get several endorsements and a parking permit for our march.

* * *

The drought continues in San Francisco. I hate the sticky air and the perpetually enervating sun. Without a new story and still having block, I work on my poetry manuscript, which I title "Night Songs." Each song is a regret, or incident from the past, until, at the end, the narrator soars from the bottom of her subconscious to the top. It's a challenging project.

In the afternoons, the light fading into a silver haze, I walk along the hills. I'm trying to figure out a new story; I walk until my legs cramp. In North Beach, I stop at Caffe Trieste for a latte. From speakers Pavarotti sings opera arias, his gorgeous voice mingling with the sounds of cable cars, tourists, and the busy Caffe. In the evenings after cooking a simple dinner, I watch films about painters, dancers, actors, and artists—crying at Margot Fonteyn and Nureyev dancing *Giselle*. Everything about them moves me. Their dancing is a combination of their emotions and craft. A deep connection.

Desperate to find a story, I sleep with a notebook next to me, so when I wake, I can quickly record pieces of my dreams, memories, or thoughts. In therapy I discuss my chronic disassociation, and with Dr. T.'s encouragement, I try to see into my subconscious, where my true self exists—the clue to this condition. In my dreams there's a black door, but every time I try to open it, I wake up.

"I think your trauma is behind the door," Dr. T. suggests.

"Time for romance," Myra says on the phone. "You're a celebrity."

"What does celebrity have to do with romance?"

She snorts. "Everything. Even ugly Moo Moo is having an affair with the twenty-two-year-old sushi chef at Wasabi Ginger. Young is the way to go. Nader is the best sex I've ever had."

"You sound like Donald Trump."

"So honey, I have the right man for you."

"No such thing as right. Who is he?"

"Jake Berman. He's sixty-nine, which means seventy-two. He's a physicist, and a genius. His wife ran off with one of his students and moved to Finland. He plays clarinet in a Chamber Group. He was on my show last week when I interviewed famous scientists. He just retired from teaching at Stanford and he wants to write a screenplay. Shall I give him your number?"

"Well..."

"Well what?" she shouts. "What else do you have to do? Go out with those idiots you write about? Or those earth monster women from your workshops who bend your ear with their boring plots? Go. Do. Meet. Life is short. Look what happened to Maxine Ronstein! She stops at a porta potty to go pee—she has incontinence—a crane pulls it up, her pants are down and everyone is looking, the crane drops the porta potty and the rest is history."

Jake calls. He has this distracted low voice, as if he's thinking about something else while he's talking. I get into a conversation about stars and molecules and Stephen Hawking. "Are we really made of stars?"

Silence.

"I guess I sound..."

"Let's talk in person," he says impatiently. "Tonight? I'll pick you up and we'll go for Thai."

"I'll be ready," I say, thinking Thai food gives me gas.

After the call, I quickly go to Google. Dr. Jake Berman has a tumble of huge, floppy salt-and-pepper hair, soulful eyes under plain glasses, and a ravaged, intelligent face. He's taught at Harvard, and is known for his work on rainbows. He resides in Berkeley and is on the UC faculty.

I dress for my date. He's short, so instead of my four-inch shoes, I wear to-the-knee red suede low-heeled boots I found at this amazing thrift store, with my usual black turtleneck sweater, and a fitted soft leather jacket I found at Thrifty Chic.

Seven on the dot he calls. "I'm in front of your building," he says impatiently. "...I'm in a red Toyota."

Holding the bannister so I don't fall, I hurry down the steps. A beat-up red Toyota is parked a mile from the curb. He waves. I hurry into the car, and without a greeting he drives into the traffic, his car jerking in and out of the lanes, Bach's Brandenburg

Concertos blasting from his car stereo so loud that I can't hear the traffic.

The front seat is covered with scientific manuals, empty Starbucks cups—an array of disarray. Dandruff sprays the shoulder of his dark jacket like confetti, but his angular, Jewish face is interesting...a sensual mouth, a beautiful bumpy nose, and a puff of unruly salt-and-pepper hair that sticks up like a hat. He's definitely one of those nerdy, schlumpy genius types with sex appeal. The kind that women adore for their brilliance.

"I Googled you," he says, driving into another lane so close to the other car that I brace myself for impact.

"I Googled you too," I admit.

"So we're Google-compatible," he snorts.

He drives in two lanes, indifferent to cars pounding their horns, drivers yelling *fuck you!* The music so loud that I can't hear what he's saying but his mouth is moving and he sits low on the beaded seat covers so that all you see is his rather large head.

Finally, we arrive at the restaurant nestled in an alley high in North Beach. It's small with low, red ceilings and Italian chefs who don't speak English. He orders special wine without asking what I'd prefer and sausages for appetizers.

Over the delicious food, I make conversation, chattering on about how much I adore Stephen Hawking and Neil deGrasse Tyson and my insights about the universe. Outside of an occasional comment, he remains indolently silent. But something about his sultry silence, indifference to style and convention, his utter self-confidence, taps into my penchant for emotionally unavailable smart men, and for the first time in many years, I find myself sexually attracted.

Over lattes, I ask about his work with rainbows, but he only shrugs as if I wouldn't understand. "I've always wanted to keep a rainbow in a box."

"You can't own what's not yours. A rainbow is elusive, mysterious and symbolizes diversity and is never permanent." He pauses, intently looking at me.

"I always think if I went through a rainbow maybe I would come out of the other side and I'd be a different person."

"Or maybe you'd be the same interesting woman you are," he says softly. "Maybe you'd view yourself in a new way. That you don't have to please me or anyone." He pauses. "You already please me."

On the way home, the music high, he holds my hand between stops. He stops his car in front of my apartment building and turns off the motor. "I'm staying with you tonight."

I don't protest. I want to.

It's past midnight and we've been having sex for hours. It's been so long since I've had sex, I made sure the lights were out so he wouldn't see the slight fold on my stomach or the sprinkle of age spots on my pale skin. At first, I was really nervous but then all was forgotten; he isn't the type of man who looks at all that. He seeks perfection in his work. He's still on top of me, and my legs are wound around his back. "It's been years since I..."

"I know. I can tell. You're lonely. You crave love," he says, kissing my mouth, my face.

"Well, everyone wants love," I say defensively.

"Love? What is love? There is no such thing."

"You've never been in love?" I ask cautiously.

"Love is for hallmark greeting cards, for twenty-year-olds. But loving is like the rainbow, magical for a while but such beauty cannot be owned or sustained for too long."

"What about Heathcliff? His love for Cathy?"

"Or Romeo and Juliet?"

"Seriously."

"I love sex with you," he whispers into my mouth. "...I love your face..."

"I've never done this—a one night stand, I mean."

"It's about time. It's pretty great," he says.

Near dawn when the light is straggling, we pillow talk about swapping lives. "Who would you swap with?" he asks, softly kissing my mouth.

"Mileva Einstein."

"Why? Einstein was terrible to her, and didn't give her credit for her work."

"Exactly. I'd like to make her do everything right. Because she was a *brilliant* physicist and a woman, only she wasn't granted her PhD. She lived in his shadow and then he dumped her. She died without her dreams coming true."

After a long silence, I ask: "Who would you swap lives with?"

"Newton." He yawns. "...Newton discovered the rainbow, and the telescope. If he had lived, he'd know the secrets of the universe."

"Do you think a time machine is possible?"

"I have to go," he says moodily. "I forgot to leave a key for my tenant."

He's dressing quickly and I'm feeling dismissed. He kisses me on the lips and before I can get up, he rushes out.

I sleep on his side of the bed where it's still warm.

"You slept with him on the first date?" the girls say on a conference call.

"It was a deep connection."

"Has he called?" Nanny shouts.

"It's only been five days."

"Another schmootzy intellectual who can't commit," Nanny says. Lisa lectures that a real guy would have sent flowers the next day.

"Or a text saying he can't wait to see you," Nanny adds. "What you always said men should do after sex."

"He's...unusual."

Lisa sighs. "I have patients binging and purging. I have to go, Mom. Talk to Dr. T. about it."

Two weeks pass and no call from Jake. I'm remembering everything about our date—Jake drawing equations on the napkin, explaining in scientific detail why it's not possible to touch a rainbow. "But I believe you can," I insisted. He laughed and listened patiently to my reasons why I think you can. Then we held hands as I told him about WC, how I needed this series for so many reasons, and that all my emotions and pain found their way into writing and my identity. "Sounds like writing is an addiction more than a profession," he said, critically.

Do I dare call him? Email him? Text? At the library, in scientific journals, I look up his experiments on rainbows and light. Not that I understand a word. I paint on canvas a woman sitting in the middle of a rainbow.

A week later I'm writing my next column, when the phone rings and I see Jake's name. Quickly, I answer. Just hearing Jake's moody voice makes me flustered. He was in Arizona, doing light experiments on the desert. His latest work is on raindrops. He sounds animated.

"Is there a pot of gold on the end of the rainbow?" I laugh nervously.

He pauses. "...I'd like to see you Friday night. I thought we'd go to a Bach concert, then Indian food..."

"Oh I can't eat it. I prefer Japanese."

"You'll like this Indian restaurant.

"Saturday night would be better."

"Not for me," he replies.

I sigh. "Well, okay. Friday night then."

When I see Jake I feel like a girl with a first crush. At the same time, I feel a distance between us, a disconnect, but even still our sexual attraction is palpable. Maybe it's this very distance that arouses me. During dinner we flirted and held hands and after we were finished, we returned to my apartment, undressed quickly, and had even greater sex than the first time. But as soon as it's over, this moodiness comes over him, he wants to leave and I feel faraway and disappointed.

"I thought about this," he says into the dark.

"Are we going to be lovers?" I ask.

"So you can write about it?" he replies. He kisses my mouth.

"Isn't the universe *your* material? Well, my life is mine."

"You plagiarize your experiences before they become something real. You can't separate art from life. You write about the men in your life which is a way of staying distant. If you were close, you wouldn't be able to write about them. You're like a person who commits a crime and then writes about the crime in detail."

"How do you know?" I ask, startled by his insights.

"I know," he replies gently. "I've read some of your books. You think love is like a hallmark greeting card. Love has many faces. Like a rainbow, you can soak in it, love it, want it, but you will never have it."

"So you mean you don't want to be with one woman?"

"I want what I want," he says softly. "You don't know yet what you want."

I fight the impulse to tell him to get out now, I am who I am and I don't welcome his critiques. But then we have sex again.

Almost right after, he dresses and leaves. I slip into a dream where I'm driving around a long mountain cliff on my way to find somewhere I'm supposed to be, but can't remember exactly where it was. But as I drive the cliff becomes more narrow and then there's nothing but ocean and I stop the car. If I drive forward I'll die and if I move backward....

* * *

I start seeing Jake. He calls on Tuesdays and invites me for Friday nights. He never includes me in any social events or asks me out on a Saturday, and even his phone calls are timed always at six. "I can only talk a minute," he says. "I have a paper to write."

But I find him interesting, intellectually challenging, and I want to know everything about him. I download his research papers and write endless notes about his every frown, sigh, moody silence, trying to figure out what he feels and how I should respond. I obsess where he goes on Saturday nights. Then, out of the blue, he invites me to a party at his Berkeley home the following Saturday night and I'm excited, sure that this is my debut to his world. Will his friends like me? Certainly he must want a closer relationship or he wouldn't invite me to his home to meet his friends.

"About time. You're been fucking him for weeks," Myra says on the phone. "This is serious."

"I'm sure he wants to introduce me to his friends as his new girlfriend."

She snorts. "He compartmentalizes."

"Don't we all?"

"Don't make good sex into something it isn't. Besides you don't know anything about him. Moo Moo's latest tycoon invited her to a dinner party at his house. She had tons of extra Botox, spent a fortune on hair extensions, and when she got there he introduced her to his wife. You never know with these oldies. At least Mohammed is mine."

"You and his three wives and six children."

"Well, he's worth it. He has a penis that grows like Pinocchio's nose."

My dream has a terrible silence tonight. I stand inside a yellow circle of light, my black dress flowing to my ankles and a hat made of white roses covering my long hair. My platform shoes are so high I wobble but as I sing a blues song, my body sways and my eyes close in the smoky dark and I can't see the audience through the smoke and my voice begins to wobble and fade and I don't want to wake....

11

Saturday night, an Uber drops me off at Jake's house. Carrying my overnight bag and a bouquet of white narcissus, I hurry up a bumpy cobblestone path past shrubs of drooping rose bushes. It's a blue wooden house with faded white shutters. My high Cuban tap shoes are clicking on the path, and I feel glamorous in my black trousers and new backless, long-sleeve sweater and white feather earrings that dangle to my shoulders. I have arranged my hair into braided rolls and am wearing very red lipstick.

Inside, I push through a crowd of intellectual looking people—the men wear colorful T-shirts printed MIT or Harvard, with huge, unkempt hair, the women with long, curly gray hair and makeup-free faces wear colorful, ethnic shawls and interesting necklaces.

Standing in the center of a huge kitchen overlooking a patio and hot tub, Jake holds court. He's wearing a Harvard sweatshirt, his huge bundle of hair sticking out, and schmootzy glasses. My heart leaps. When he sees me, he kisses me on each cheek, and thanks me for the flowers. "You look sensational," he says, as he puts water into a coffee can and drops the flowers in it. Next, he introduces me to a few people, repeating, "This is Bette, my San Francisco author friend." Then like a shadow he disappears, greeting the people arriving.

I pour myself a vodka shot, disappointed he didn't say Bette, my *girlfriend,* and wondering if I'll meet his tenant.

Suddenly this great slow jazz blasts from the speakers. Couples are slow dancing, including Jake, dancing with this skinny woman no older than forty. She wears spiked heels with an off-the-shoulder blouse, and pale blonde angel curls surround her indolent face. Her long arms are tight around his neck and his arms are around her tiny waist and he holds her in a way that I'm sure they're sexually involved. Just then, this humongous man wearing overalls with huge, dark hair, pulls me onto the dance floor. He holds me so tight that our cheeks make suction sounds. I'm leaning forward too much, stepping on his feet. My eyes on Jake still dancing with the blonde.

"You're hot. Jake likes you. But he's in love with Inga, his ex-wife." He laughs. "She left him years ago for his twenty-one-year-old graduate student and moved to Finland. He always loves what he can't fix."

"Which one is his tenant?" I ask, pulling away from him and trying not to sound upset.

He laughs. "All of them are his tenants. Winter is his latest student and so-called tenant. He's dancing with her."

"Excuse me," I say.

I rush up the stairs to a large hallway, past framed pictures of rainbows, photographs of Einstein, and empty rooms. No signs of a tenant. In the master bedroom, I notice the rumpled double bed. How naive of me to believe that we'd be star-crossed lovers.

In the bathroom, in the medicine cabinet, on one shelf is a row of lipsticks, medication bottles, and female items. In the closet, a woman's clothes hang neatly next to his and I feel not only disappointed, but suddenly aware that I had fantasies that we were going to be a couple.

I close the door and go downstairs.

The music is rising, and everyone is dancing. I pour another vodka and find Jake in the kitchen, an apron around him, making what he calls his "famous chili." With a huge wooden spoon, he stirs the chili in a tall red pot. In precise steps, he tells me how to make the chili and that the recipe was in his mother's family. He loves to cook. Do I?

"Yes, but I'm not good at it."

"I think you're good at everything you want to be good at, Bette." He then calls, "Everyone eat!"

The music stops, and everyone rushes to the buffet table, drinking and stuffing their faces with Jake's chili and gluten free salads. I sit next to a retired mathematician with a long, thin nose and unruly silver hair. As he stuffs his mouth with huge slices of French bread, he raps about Stephen Hawking's death.

"But he died and left so much behind. So many questions," I say.

"But he never got the fucking Nobel Prize," says the mathematician, his mouth full of beans.

Jake is holding court. Most of the women are professors and they stand in clusters, loudly discussing politics. Meanwhile, the men huddle around Jake, who is telling them about his new light experiments. It's his world. A world of questions and brilliance and pondering great things. I feel distant from this world. It's not Jake who is wrong, it's just not my world and I feel disconnected.

Past midnight everyone has left. I help Jake dump the paper plates and cups into plastic garbage bags. We're in the kitchen rehashing the party and Jake is rinsing pots in the large sink. He had a wonderful time and like a wonderful child who thinks whatever he says or does is perfect, Jake is oblivious to the fact that for most of the night he ignored me.

"Did you have a good time?" he asks, scrubbing the pot with a sponge.

"Is it true?" I ask hesitantly, aware that he knows what I mean.

"What's true?" He rinses the pot.

"That you have many tenants?" I laugh.

He shakes the pot of water, and then turns it upside down, letting the water drain out. He faces me, amusement on his intelligent face. "There are many ways to love Bette. It's not one thing. One way."

"This isn't about love. It's about honesty," I say.

"Isn't the great sex enough?"

"Not even that. But without emotional connection, the sex is fleeting and lonely."

"Our sex is plenty emotional." He laughs.

"Only for a moment, then it's forgotten. I thought we'd be exclusive," I reply.

"You need fantasies to enjoy part of a relationship. You're in love with your dreams, your work. Anything more and you'd be bored."

He turns off the kitchen light. "Tomorrow, I'm going to show you something important. Something that you can take with you forever. Now, let's go into the hot tub."

In the hot, steaming water we're looking up at the stars spraying the sky like mashed diamonds. Jake points out various stars, explains each one.

"Do stars grow?"

"They die," he replies, "and new ones are born. Nothing is permanent."

"Something more exists behind these stars."

"I hope you're not going to say God." He sniffs.

"Not the God that religion teaches. I don't believe in religion. But when I see a jellyfish, an ant en route, or a rose blooming, I know there's something behind the entire universe."

The next morning, after Jake makes omelets, we begin our journey. As if Jake knew that I no longer was interested in having sex with him, he'd just slept.

The air is cold, and a mist dampens the garden like silver. He drives his motorcycle. I sit behind him, my arms around his waist. He drives expertly and I feel like I'm flying, mist lying over the bridge like orange lace. Then I see this huge rainbow arc shimmering in the light and it seems so close I can touch it but when I reach out my hand to do so it retreats into its own place. "Hang on, Bette! We're driving through the rainbow," Jake shouts, and inside the rainbow it's so bright that I feel the heat, the colors shimmering on my skin like bits of light. "We went through the rainbow Bette," Jake yells.

At the end of the day he drives me home—we're quiet. We know this is the end. At my apartment he stops his car, turns off the motor and the music, and it's suddenly quiet. When something ends, is over, there's nothing more to say or explain. It's just over. Like a beautiful dream you didn't want to end, it's now in the past.

"I'm glad you liked the rainbow," Jake says, his hand on mine.

"It's forever with me, Jake."

"You see Bette? Sometimes a single moment can last forever. The rainbow is inside you. It's yours forever. Live who you are and don't settle for anything else."

I get out of the car and watch his car rumble up the street.

12

The morning of the table read at WC, I turn on my Skype. I'm excited.

Everyone says "hello," at once, some waving. I'm surprised to see Amen. "What are you doing here?" I ask, laughingly.

"He's cast as Anny's young lover," explains Yesterday with a quick smile. She wears a sleeveless pink dress; her dreadlocks are wound with beads. Kat Zimmerman, wearing slim shorts, red glitter high heel pumps, and a tank top with a huge picture of Superwoman on the front, stands on a box in front of a blackboard. Bitterman stands next to her. As usual, he's dressed in a formal, expensive suit. His puffed-up hair is perfectly styled.

"Okay, everyone, it's time," he announces. "Kat is going to read from episode one to episode fifteen. We're in for a treat. Quiet now."

Kat's fast, husky voice dramatically reads the first episode, a raunchy sex scene with the diamond dealer. She's acting out the scene with wild gestures. Anny's name is now Kitty. She's twenty-nine and a hooker in love with the diamond dealer who is no longer seventy but thirty-one. Marv Rothstein's name is now Sheik; he's thirty-one.

"Excuse me!" I interrupt. "Who is Kitty? Who is Sheik? They are not my characters! What happened to Anny Applebaum and Marv Rothstein?"

A quick silence. Averted eyes.

Kat explains: "Anny is an avatar."

"Avatar?"

"Avatar," Yesterday quickly interjects. "She is Kitty's older self."

"You mean Anny's a cartoon? A Xerox of Kitty only older?" I feel faint.

"The avatar is high concept," Yesterday says with a quick smile.

Bitterman murmurs, "Fucking brilliant."

"The demographic won't support Anny at sixty-five but they'll adore the avatar concept. The networks hate age."

"I hate it. It's stupid," I say.

Everyone is looking at their computers. "I hate it," I repeat. "It has nothing to do with my book. It's silly and I don't want it."

"We're going in a different direction," Yesterday says with a smile. "The avatar motif suits our demographic. It's epic."

"Well, it doesn't *suit* my story."

As if I'm not here, they assure Kat, who is sobbing, not to worry, and promising her that as soon as I realize how great the script is, "how *special* it is," I'll be ecstatic. Kat reads more episodes, each one worse than the other, each with this stupid avatar emerging in Kitty's dreams.

"Stop!" I say. "This is not my project! I won't allow it! It's crap!"

Bitterman looks angry. "Then you want us to pull it?"

"What I want is what we agreed on in the contract. You'll maintain the integrity and authenticity of sixty-five-year-old

Anny Applebaum. Marci Feldstein has a clause in the contract that I'm to have artistic input and approval..."

"Approval of what? I'm using your title. What more do you want?" Bitterman screams. "That you'll have a major show on air? Make major money? Angie Golden, a fucking star, is playing the avatar. It's good enough for her! But not for you?"

"Fuck the avatar!" I shout, shaking from rage.

The screen goes dark. Barely do I have a minute to regain my composure, when my cell phone rings. "Joshua is pissed. What did you do? We're fucked!" Edwina says.

"He's pissed? They used me like a toilet! Dumped their crappy script on me. Betrayed me. Anny is an avatar! A cartoon!"

Edwina signs. "I've got Marci Feldstein on it. She'll talk to Bitterman about the avatar. Then Kat will make script changes, and we'll be good to go. Not to worry honeybun. This can be fixed."

The following days, I try to work. Finally, my lawyer calls, yelling, "Don't you people read? Don't you have a mouth?"

"I read Kat Zimmerman's first draft and there wasn't an avatar. They sneaked it in."

"Fuckers!" she screams. "I told Bitterman if he doesn't kill the fucking avatar, he'd never work in this fucking town again! You people don't read!" she screams. "Learn to read! Speak up! Then this won't happen!"

A few days later, Yesterday calls and assures me that Joshua negotiated a meeting with the studio and Kat is revising the avatar. "We're on the same page, honey."

"What about Anny's age?"

She hesitates. "...Angie Golden refused to be at an age for Medicare. She's out the door. But we're good to go. The network agrees that Kitty is forty-five and that the avatar can go. The issues are the same, and this way we're hitting more demographics. The show is going to be a fucking hit."

"I want Anny to be sixty-five. That's who she is!"

"Everything is negotiable, honeybun. Once we start shooting you can work it out. Let's get the fucker on air. Not to worry."

"That's what you said last time. The answer is no. Jane Fonda's show with Lily Tomlin is hitting seventy plus demographics! I was there first. The networks didn't listen to me. WC treats me like I'm an idiot because they think I'm old. I want sixty-five. Or I'll call Bitterman and say no show."

"I'll tell him." She pauses. "Kat is very upset. She flew to Sedona so she can be near nature while she finishes the rewrite. The trades are announcing the fall shows in a few weeks and it's very important that WC announce *The Viagra Diaries.* And your book is coming out, so don't make any more waves. It will work out...not to worry honeybun. I promise. I miss you.

In my dream I walk on a tightrope but just as I reach the middle of it, I fall off. I remember Matisse said that you must be able to walk firmly on the ground before you start walking a tightrope. I hope I wake soon.

13

Earthquakes rattle the San Francisco Bay Area. I receive an email from Kat Zimmerman who is still in Sedona: *Dear Bette—I'm on the desert with nature—enjoying the insects and blooms—I'm going to make Anny sixty-five, and orgasmic and hot. We'll meet at the Emmys—Kat.*

Relieved that at least she's keeping my protagonist's age and that things are finally going smoothly, I'm feeling more optimistic and I assure myself that this will all work out. But then my long-time San Francisco column editor calls and chews me out about my latest column, "Boomer Orgasms."

She reads aloud from the column: "The oldies think a bowel movement is an orgasm. They whimper like fleas..."

"But Oliver Abbot in Australia says he gets tons of fan mail..."

"He has a communist paper and sends you twenty-five-dollar checks. We have an important paper and pay you plenty. Can't... can't you write about senior pets, goldfish, or something wholesome? Less vulgar?"

"That's not what the column is about."

"You're not Dianne Sawyer. Make your column about wholesome issues and not so vulgar or we'll have to end it."

Disgusted with the editor always telling me to tone down my columns, I continue writing what I want. Almost every day I receive fan mail and Oliver Abbot texts that some of my columns have been picked up by other magazines and that he'll send the checks.

Weeks pass and very soon WC will be announcing the TV series. Edwina has set up a table read so I can hear the script read and Kat regularly texts me. Now everything will be perfect, I think. At last my series will be on air and I fantasize that all my books will then be in demand for films and TV. I assure myself that soon WC is announcing my TV series, and not only will I be relieved, vindicated, but then maybe I'll contact Jake to celebrate.

Even though I've been receiving more fan mail from *The Australia News*, I receive a call from my editor at the *San Francisco Times*. "We're ending *Blast,"* she snips in her hostile voice.

"Why?"

"I warned you. Your last column *fucking* caused a sensation here. We got hate mail. Death threats. The publisher says your work is too vulgar and is letting you go."

"I write what's true. What people are afraid to say about sex and ageism and social issues. What I write is real."

"We're not about real!" she shouts. "We're a fucking newspaper! We need to make money! Next, they'll arrest us for pornographic material! You're not Christiane Amanpour. You're Bette Roseman with a potty mouth and too many liberal ideas. People who are older don't want to read that crap. Sorry. Good luck."

I text Oliver Abbot and tell him that I've been fired from my San Francisco paper. He emails that he's so sorry and that his paper is going under and that he's going to concentrate on making films. He's moving to San Francisco to open a production company and will be in touch.

"So now what?" Nanny asks on the phone.

"I'll find another paper. Or I'll start a blog."

"Larry says he can't lend you any more money."

"He doesn't have to. I'll have a hit show soon. Also my book is about to be published and Avalon said it's a bestseller for sure, with the show and all."

"That's what you said the last three times." She pauses. "Have you paid your life insurance?"

"Yes!" I shout.

"If you're smart you'll marry Professor schmootzy."

"He's not schmootzy and he's not for me. Anyway, marriage is not for me."

"Make it for you."

"I'm happy the way I am. I don't believe in it for me."

"At your age you better believe or you'll end up in assisted living, folk dancing with a gimp on Sundays. My friend Eileen is thirty-one and she has to lie about her age on JDate because even the oldies want young."

Lately, as if I'm putting my broken parts together, I remember more pieces from my past, mostly about my daughters and the time when I was a single mother and aspiring writer in college.

I write: *Anny's plastic turkey is filled with marigolds. Mother sent a white moth orchid. Its petals look like moths. I keep it on the windowsill with Anny's avocado plant and her goldfish Swannie. If you talk to plants, play Bach, and make sure they have sunlight, they bloom. I nurture my plants but I didn't nurture my babies. I feel sad.*

A row of daffodils is so yellow they're almost white. Lisa arranges them in a mayonnaise jar. I like watching their shadows drop along the wall. My flower paintings are stacked along the walls. I sell them at beauty salons, and gift shops.

Don't you think that after art is completed it's no longer art? I think photography captures moments alive but only painting reflects your soul. Nancy Epstein stacks thick expensive art books on a glass coffee table. They are shrink-wrapped.

"*The Viagra Diaries* is officially published. I just saw it on Amazon!" Nanny says excitedly on the phone.

"It's a month early...are you sure? Avalon didn't tell me it's out there."

"Well, it's there. Congratulations. Gotta go."

I go on Amazon and sure enough there is the book and the bio and Melissa's awful press release that says the book is about "elder love."

Beside myself, I call Biggie Delano, ranting that the book came out early on Amazon, but there aren't books in the stores. No one has received press releases. "Only a couple tiny, local lesbian stores have Melissa's press release and only one or two copies of *The Viagra Diaries*. This is terrible. This happened to my Jewish Princess novel and it was disastrous."

"What am I, your therapist? I'm your agent. I sell books. I don't distribute them. Who do you think you are? Jane fucking Austen?"

"Well, sorry."

"Let Avalon worry."

"Okay, sure," I say, calming down. "Anyway, I'll see you in a few weeks in New York. I can't wait. Be sure and watch me on *Fame,* NBC."

"Why not Oprah?"

"Melissa set me up on *Fame.*"

"No one watches *Fame."*

"...I..."

He already hung up.

I call Emily who assures me that Avalon wanted to "beat the punch," ahead of the TV series and not to worry. Then I call Melissa, reporting the names of the bookstores that don't have the book, or her press release. "And where's the *People Magazine* review you'd promised?"

"It was an *email,"* she replies.

"Didn't you follow up? Make a call? *People Magazine* is important."

"I have fifty authors to follow up with, Bette. You're lowest on the list."

"*Fame* also needs books. Also, Andy Cohen needs books. I'm going to be on their shows and they don't have press releases or books and my name is spelled wrong on Amazon and on your press release. Melissa, this is terrible. Here it's going to be a TV series and..."

"Bette, as soon as your TV series is announced, I'll call all the stores. Meanwhile we're comping you and your daughter at the Pierre Hotel in New York. We're also planning a luncheon for you in your honor. Not to worry, and see you soon."

I tell myself to let it all go. "It's in the fates," I tell Nanny. Also, I feel sorry for Melissa. I can tell she works really hard and she's under a lot of pressure and I realize that I've been demanding and I don't want to be one of those bitchy authors. I realize I've been lucky and though I haven't had a bestseller, I've published a lot of books and even had made some money. Not to mention that I have Lisa and Edwina always helping me. Still, I tell myself that from now on I just have to take a stand. Also have more compassion for those I work with. So I send Melissa a note thanking her for her work and telling her I can't wait to meet her in New York. At Nordstrom's, I buy a pale pink silk scarf for Melissa, and for Emily a yellow silk scarf dotted with tiny pink flowers. I send Edwina a black silk scarf with tiny white roses.

Two days later, Yesterday calls and reports that in five days WC is announcing that their network is producing *The Viagra Diaries* and revealing the September airdate. "It's going to be great, Bette. This is it."

"But I haven't seen the final script. I was going to go to a final table read," I say, trying to sound cheerful.

"Kat is in Mexico polishing it. She needs to be with nature."

"Uh huh."

"Not to worry, Bette. WC is already setting up locations. It's all good."

So feeling optimistic again, figuring that as soon as the WC series is announced I'll have enough money to hire a real publicist to call bookstores, Lisa and I concentrate on preparing for New York. It's an exciting time. I want to feel positive.

Until, two days before Lisa and I are leaving for New York, I'm home at the computer and by impulse, I check *Variety* just to see if there's any news. I read: *WC green lights VIRGIN ALIENS for their September slot. The Viagra Diaries is pulled.*

Shock. I feel the hot disappointment in my body, like when the Jewish Princess novel was pulled, and I feel my body slowly detach into numbness. My hands are shaking and my head feels hot. I call Edwina and demand to see the script as soon as possible. In an hour I have the script in front of me. All I had to do is read the first page to know that they'd lied to me. It's worse than it was the first time. The avatar is still there, only now a main character. No wonder no one wanted it. I call Edwina and tell her that I'm going to sue WC for going against the contract, and that they ruined my script. "Fuck Bitterman's stupid avatar!"

Edwina calls, trying to humor me, assuring me that Bitterman will pursue another network."

"I don't want him or Kat. They raped my work, Edwina. Lied to me. Then threw it out like an old sweater."

"Honeybun, Bitterman complained that you made too many conditions about age. Also he wasn't complimentary about your book. It's the title he wants and he's wedded to his script. When Angie Golden pulled out, he'd had it. You criticized the avatar and Kat had a nervous breakdown. He's worried about her and says she's a great talent." She sighs heavily. "Not to worry. I'll submit the script to other networks."

"No one will buy the fucking avatar," I say angrily. "I don't want my title or name on it. Let him exploit someone else. Either they use my story or nothing. They're ageist pricks! He used me. I'm going to sue WC when I get back."

She sighs. "...Honeybun, we're all disappointed. They went in a different direction, but know honey that I believe in you. We're on the same page so hang in there, Bette. I'll get the project on air the way you want. I'll get back to you. Miss you."

But no matter how much I tell myself that I don't need a TV series, I know that it's over, and I know it's my fault. If I'd stood my ground, even gone to another publisher and refused to rewrite, things might have turned out differently, and I would have known that I didn't sell out.

The following days I concentrate on meeting Lisa in New York.

15

New York is beautiful. God, I love it. Just being here makes me feel renewed. I'm in a taxi on the way to the hotel. An hour ago, Lisa called from her cell phone and said she's at the hotel waiting. "Hurry, Mom. Can't wait to see you," she says on the phone.

As the taxi driver passes in and out of lanes, yelling and flipping the bird at other drivers, I'm admiring the skyscrapers, people rushing, the noise, lights, energy, remembering the years Lisa was at NYU, my occasional visits, the time I was here visiting my publisher about my Jewish Princess novel. No matter how disappointed I am about the TV series, I'm relieved that I am taking responsibility and that I have a new journey ahead. Mostly, I'm excited to see Lisa.

The taxi screeches to a stop on Fifth Avenue in front of the Pierre Hotel. As I enter the mirrored lobby, I remember that my father used to stay here on business trips all the time. He must have been so lonely, so unhappy, I think.

Inside the lobby, perfumed groups of men wearing Armani suits and turbans huddle about the open cocktail lounge and the carpets are so thick my heels sink in.

Rafi, a gorgeous young boy who walks like he's floating, his cologne drifting behind him, carries my duffle bag and leads me to our room on the eleventh floor.

When Lisa opens the door, we're hugging and jumping up and down, glad to see each other. She looks beautiful, wearing a dark green woolen dress the color of her eyes and gold jewelry. Her auburn hair flows past her shoulders in Rita Hayworth-style waves. Our suite is huge, with tall windows overlooking Central Park, plush green carpets and two double beds, and a bar and a sitting area in the living room area. "This is a gorgeous suite. So nice of them," I say, dropping my things on the chair.

"You look great, Mom. Love the hair and the black turtleneck. See, everything is coming up roses."

"Let's order a late dinner and then get some sleep. We have a busy couple of days. Jammed. Tomorrow, a car is picking us up at five a.m. to bring us to *Fame* for makeup." Lisa opens a huge menu and I remove my tall leather high heel boots. A rain has begun and slams the windows, city lights flickering like gold sequins.

We order two New York steaks, baked potatoes, ice crème parfaits. We chat about WC, how really stupid Yesterday is, gossiping about industry people, even laughing.

She takes my hand. "Don't be sad, Mom. Avalon is treating us like royalty. Tomorrow, you're on *Fame*. You'll knock them dead. Sales will go off the chart...you'll see, Mom. WC will eat crow." She pauses. "...Sometimes, I miss developing shows."

"Maybe you can combine your work someday—advise the psychological interiors of characterizations in movies..."

"I've thought about that." She smiles.

She talks about the work she's doing in her practice, her intense voice full of wisdom and compassion. She especially likes working with kids with sexual identity issues. "It's horrible not to know who you really are. To live a fake life."

"Like poor Ricky."

She looks reflective. "Mom, don't be sad. I know you feel guilty about Ricky. You did everything you could."

"For years I didn't contact him. I resented him. He was a poor soul, suffered so much. Had no sense of self."

"Remember, you grew up in the same household. You've suffered too, and still suffer. You inspire me—how you constantly work and develop your own emotional growth." She sighs. "...I didn't get the job. At the interview there were a dozen twenty-five-year-old blonde psychologists..."

"...I'm sorry, Lisa. It's ageism. Even at your age. But you'll get something better. You have the experience, the wisdom. You'll see."

She sighs. "There's a job opening for a psychologist on *The Bachelor*. I'm going to apply for that. Anyway, I'm not even forty and I'm pissed about the ageism. You're my hero, Mom."

Our dinner comes. We dine on salmon and salad and fresh rolls with butter by the window, New York's bright lights blinking at us through the storm. We talk about our work, our dreams, and in this moment I feel that if I should die later, I know what pure joy is: pure admiration and love for this beautiful, lovely, wise woman, my daughter and nothing else is as important. Not even the fame and fortune I've always dreamed of. I can't die not until I know who I am, not until I let the girls know and how much I love them. I have a way to go.

Sleeping soundly, I'm in the middle of a dream where I see my mother, wearing a white dress and crying. I'd never seen her cry before and her eyes are full of pain and she's apologizing to me but I'm turning away from her. As she comes towards me, I dissolve. Bells are ringing and I'm trying to find them.

"Mom. Wake up. The car will be here in twenty minutes."

At five a.m. we arrive at NBC. I'm wearing a black suit, ankle strap platforms made of fuchsia leather, and a huge yellow silk flower pinned to my lapel.

In the green room, a long buffet table laden with platters of shriveled, dry scrambled eggs, burnt bacon, muffins, and pots of stale coffee sit against a wall.

In a smaller room, celebrities I recognize are having their hair and makeup done.

Igor, a very tall, thin man with huge tattoos on his long neck and arms, applies my makeup. While he works, dozens of charm bracelets make clinking sounds.

"Your skin is thin—so pale," he says, peevishly.

When I'm done I look like an old tart, and I hate the makeup. "...I think red lipstick is better...less eye shadow?"

"Dear, this is NBC, not Starbucks."

He turns his back and begins working on a very young news reporter I recognize. He finishes the makeup and it's time to go on air.

Quickly, this tiny intern with a huge head ushers us upstairs into a small, airless room so brightly lit that I can hardly see the host through the dusty white haze of light. Armando, famous for his interviews of national authors, advises me to only look at him. "Do not look anywhere else."

"Sure."

He can't be more than thirty-five. He's handsome, with a huge puff of shiny brown hair, perfect features, and smooth olive skin. A very young assistant puffs his hair with a metal comb while he rolls a lint brush along his fitted black jacket.

"I can hardly see you through the light," I say, trying to sound cheerful.

"Just follow my voice," he instructs. He smiles. "I *love* your book. Very sexy."

He starts the countdown, and then introduces me as *Bette Roseman, the author of* The Vagina Diaries *and the new face of elder life!* "What do you have to say about age and sex, Bette?"

"Well, first, I'm the author of *The Viagra Diaries*, not *The Vagina Diaries*. I don't believe in labels like *elder.* I believe that all age matters. Numbers don't."

I continue to talk about Anny Applebaum and her quest for age equality and undying love, until he interrupts and starts ranting that sex is *rampant* in the nursing homes, citing that his grandmother was raped. As he continues making quips and stupid jokes about nursing home sex, hogging the interview, he slowly raises his voice to say, "Okay folks. *The Vagina Diaries* is at every major bookstore! Terrific read."

On the huge screen behind him is a picture of *Green Pastures* by Jenna North, published by Avalon. An 800-number and Amazon's website flash in huge letters under it.

"*Green Pastures* is not my book," I interrupt, trying to smile.

"Whoops. Sorry folks. *Green Pastures* is next. But run out and buy *The Vagina Diaries,* published by Avalon Publishers."

Devastated, Lisa and I walk all the way to Avalon Publishers for the luncheon. Holding hands and getting soaked, we decide that even though things went wrong, everything is good. "All good, Mom." We hurry into the narrow building and take a wood-paneled elevator to the fifth floor, where Avalon Publishers is.

The so-called luncheon in my honor turns out to be Emily, Melissa, and Gloria Katz, the publisher. We're in this dusty room with long tables of pathetic paper cups and flimsy, stained paper plates and a cheap bottle of champagne next to a huge, blown up poster of my book cover.

"Everyone had the flu," Gloria explains with an insincere smile and darting, dark eyes. She's so tiny I can hardly see her, like she's standing in a hole. Her huge yellow hair is knotted on the top of her head into a point. An African necklace covers most of her thick neck.

"Everyone saw you on the show today. It was wonderful," says Melissa, a Neanderthal-huge woman with a flat, pale face, and nervous eyes. Her hands shake slightly and her bulging gray eyes look anxious.

"Wonderful?" I say, incredulously. "Only thing is that not one copy of my book was at NBC. I'm sure you sent them copies but they put the wrong book up on the screen. No business like show business," I say with a thin laugh, aware that they're shooting each other knowing looks.

"I was a talent agent for a top agency," says Lisa. "It's not acceptable that the wrong book was on the screen or that they didn't have books. Sales are very important now."

"My new intern made a boo boo," Melissa says nervously and I feel sorry for her. Her thick, nervous fingers touch the tops of several cookies arranged in a circle on a paper platter before picking up one heaped with yellow crème.

"Bette has been calling bookstores and asking them to order," Lisa continues. "This is not okay. Your publicity department dropped the ball. No one knows about the book."

"Let's celebrate Bette's wonderful book," Emily says quickly. She has short, tan hair and pale gray eyes that match the color of her suit. She opens the bottle of champagne, pouring the warm liquid into paper cups.

In our tense self-conscious silence, Gloria explains in an efficient, corporate voice that Ingram, the main distributor, is printing *The Viagra Diaries* one at a time."

"Print on demand?" I say incredulously. "Like self-published books? That's not what I signed up for."

She sighs heavily. "...Because the WC option was...canceled we feel that we can't put a fortune into inventory. Stuck with returns, God forbid. So we decided to do a wait-and-see."

"See what?" Lisa challenges.

"If there are book sales," Gloria Katz snaps. "If the book can stand on its own without a national series behind it."

"Sales are everything," Emily lisps.

"So you bought the book because of the series?" I say.

"We love the story. We're committed to the book," Emily interjects.

"...Let's all toast this wonderful book," Melissa says in a high voice. "Who knows, it might be the next *Pulitzer*. We all worked so hard on it."

As they make fake conversation, trying to sound happy, I feel like I've arrived at a party on the wrong day. Everyone talks at once, pretending cheer instead of doom, Melissa promising to bring books the next day to the Andy Cohen Show, the publisher raving that I'm so "talented" and she can't wait to see my next book. Emily, glancing at her watch, announces with a forced smile that she has an "editorial meeting."

In the rain, Lisa and I walk back to the hotel, trying to pretend we're not gloomy and upset, but knowing now that the book is probably dead and that Avalon only bought the book because of the impending TV series. "Next time," I say, "I'll stand up for myself. I'll never rewrite unless I know it's necessary or have a connection with the editor. I blame myself."

It's evening. Lisa is upstairs on the phone with a suicidal patient, and I'm downstairs in the hotel's cocktail lounge with Biggie Delano. A pianist nearby is playing Cole Porter songs and couples talk quietly at tables arranged around a huge mirrored bar. Biggie is a tall, large man with a beautiful almost cherub-like face. A mass of unruly blonde curls like a Roman gladiator sit flat on his perfectly-shaped head. He has a sensual mouth and his sentences are sparse, economical, as if he's used to editing his words. Over vodka shots, I'm ranting about the TV show being pulled and Avalon not bothering with the book as a result. "On *Fame* they didn't even have the book on the screen."

"A disaster," he says, peevishly. "Unless it's Oprah it doesn't matter much anyway." He waves his hand as if waving away my protests.

Between popping cashew nuts into his mouth, he says little, as I continue ranting that Avalon is printing on demand, that there's no distribution, and no books in the bookstores, and how much I hate the rewrite and how it spoiled the book's original voice. Between shots I'm repeating that I should never have agreed to the rewrite.

As if he's heard this a thousand times and is bored with anything but bestsellers, he orders another drink. "Well, your sales stink. You have no sales on any of your books. No matter what, the public decides what they want to read."

"Stink? *The Viagra Diaries* has only been released for four weeks. It came out early, with no promotion, no books in the stores, and it's not even on Avalon's website."

"Stinks," he repeats, indolently. "The series is pulled. The book doesn't resonate. It's done. You know the score."

"Anyway, what about the sales in Turkey? China? Russia? Italy? Their books look great."

"What about them? A few fucking royalties where the money is at most a hundred bucks? Your audio didn't sell more than three copies and no one wants to read 'old,'" he continues, gesturing impatiently to the nearby waiter and ordering another round of drinks with their most expensive caviar.

"So are we celebrating?" I say, sarcastically.

"Honey," he says sympathetically. "Write another book. I'll sell it. Write your truths. In two years, call me."

"I *hate* the Avalon editor and I should never have rewritten, and she was so stupid..."

"Do I look happy?" he snaps. He spreads caviar on a tiny round toast.

"I want the original *Viagra Diaries* to be out there, the Avalon version has no sparkle. It reads like an essay. Can't we get them to run the original?"

"It's dead," Biggie sighs. "Let it go."

Just then Lisa appears, and Biggie orders more caviar. Over more drinks, they talk shop, Biggie bragging about his bestselling authors and gossiping about which producer is screwing who, while I'm devastated and shitfaced to the winds. Depressed and dizzy, I say goodnight to Biggie and Lisa and finally stumble upstairs to my room.

When Lisa comes up, I'm in bed, watching CNN. Lisa says that Biggie didn't pick up the five-hundred-dollar tab. "Avalon will pick it up. Serves them right," she says.

She undresses quickly and clicks off the TV. Lying in the silent dark I pretend that I'm slipping into sleep and not devastated.

"This is a glitch, Mom," she says, her voice thin in the silence.

"I'm sorry this has all turned to nothing. You worked so hard on helping me for years," I say.

Silence.

"It's all my fault. The rewrite. I should have insisted to see the script before this happened."

"Mom, you're my hero. Don't you know this? You never give up. You stay with it, and because of you, I keep going too. Now go to sleep. We have a big day tomorrow and I'm tired. I love you. Good night."

"Sorry," I say, again. "Sorry you've worked so hard to help me."

In the dark we toss and turn, and then we sleep.

The next day it's still pouring rain. The New York streets are slippery and crowded, but I love New York, its diversity and glamour. Pretending there isn't gloom between us, Lisa and I to go the MOMA, lingering by our favorite Manets, Pollocks, and Joan Mitchell's murals of abstract gardens. "I love the way Manet uses black...his figures of women."

"They remind me of your paintings of women, Mom." Her green, woolen beret is the color of her eyes.

After the museum, dark now, we take a taxi back to the hotel and in the lounge, we eat grilled cheese sandwiches. After packing for home, before going to the Andy Cohen show at eleven p.m., we bring our bags to the lobby and check out. Amir, the head desk clerk, gives us the bill. "Credit card, or cash?" He smiles, revealing perfect too-white veneers.

"Avalon is paying the bill. They comped us. They made the reservation, and I'm their author," I say with a smile. "Here's a copy of the book." I place a copy on the desk. He glances at it.

"I'm sorry, Madam. Avalon called this morning and said they are not responsible for this bill."

After the WC announcement they stopped everything. I open the bill and am shocked to see that including the room service and cocktail lounge charges the total is $1,755.42.

"I'll pay, Mom." Lisa reaches for her wallet and gives Amir her credit card.

An hour later a long, black limousine picks up to bring us to the Andy Cohen show. In the Green Room we sit on comfortable leather chairs and a young assistant wearing green suspenders and a jumpsuit offers us drinks. Lisa and I decide to have a vodka shot. Shortly after, Melissa arrives with a few books. Dressed in a plain gray suit, she looks exhausted and anxious. In a frustrated tone, Lisa tells her that Avalon did nothing to help this book and that she had to send her own books to bookstores and TV stations.

Melissa yawns. "Without the TV pilot Avalon feels that they can't put any more money into this book."

"Not to worry Melissa. Everything will be fine. You did a great job," I say, feeling sorry for her.

Andy comes in and he's so lovely, personable, and nice. His producer leads me to the set, which is so bright I can't stop blinking. He guides me to the bar where I'll be the bartender, and instructs me that when Andy mentions *The Viagra Diaries* and holds up the book, to hold up the blue martini set in front of me. "Just smile and hold it up."

At Kennedy Airport, before we go to our different gates, Lisa and I say goodbye. As we always would when she was a child going to camp, or coming home from NYU, we cry. In her arms, I'm sobbing, and together we're crying out our disappointment and our love for each other.

"Mom, I love you. You're my hero," she says, kissing my cheek gently. "Call when you get home. We'll see each other really soon. I'll come up. Or you'll come see me."

As I hurry to my gate and I turn around, she's still standing there, waving.

* * *

The following weeks, to get things in perspective, I try to process my disappointment. But the next night is my first big book signing. For the past weeks I'd been calling the event manager, this post-hippie girl with attitude, informing her that I've received RSVPs from at least seventy-five students and colleagues and to please be sure to order enough books. With an irritated yawn, she had assured me not to worry.

But I remember my book signings on my past books when there wasn't Amazon or the internet, when authors depended on bookstores to order their books, riding trains on cold nights to out-of-the-way bookstores in little towns, fantasizing there'd be crowds. I remember when only two people showed up and the manager had only ordered one copy. Then the friends who'd buy one copy would pass it on to twenty of their friends. But writing and becoming an author is what I'd chosen, and though I don't fancy myself to be this great writer, no matter the reasons, my work has always been a calling and the most important thing in my life.

So the next night I arrive at Book Owls, a huge bookstore at Opera Plaza, decked in my Joan Crawford platform glitter heels and my usual black turtle neck, and wearing a burgundy bowler hat with a huge, green silk flower pinned to the side. When I arrive, I'm stunned to see that at least two hundred people are lined up. I'm thrilled, recognizing former students from twenty years ago holding several of my other published books for me to sign. All the chairs are filled, and soon people are standing in the back. What really touches me is that many of my former students, in honor of *The Viagra Diaries'* protagonist Anny Applebaum, are wearing Joan Crawford-style shoes, bowler hats, and Anny's trademark: oversized silk flowers pinned to the side of the hat or a shirt lapel.

"Honey, you made it," says Karina, a former student. She's eighty-five and small, with a young face and vivid, intelligent blue eyes. She clutches my first self-published version of *The Viagra Diaries.* "Sign this. I'll buy the new one too."

Several former students ask if I'll help them get an agent, or read their grandkids' manuscripts, or tell me long stories about their near misses and close calls, really touching. Then Nanny arrives, decked in an orange Lululemon jacket, slim pants, and very high heels. Tiny orange flowers are woven in braids along her flowing, black satin hair.

"You look great, Bette," Larry says, with a tentative smile. "Quite a crowd."

They sit in the very front row, next to Myra, who's wearing a short skirt and gray snakeskin boots to her thighs. Her hair is in a high bun on her head, and her dozens of silver bracelets clink as she moves.

As I always do before a reading or speaking event, I'm feeling exhilarated, high, with a sense of my body floating above the waiting, seated crowd. I remember the year of taking voice lessons, too nervous to even read. Now I love it.

Finally, the manager stands at the podium, her disapproving eyes and wrinkled mouth pressed, waiting for complete quiet. She makes a little speech about the bookstore and reads from Melissa's press release. In a shrill voice, she announces: "Bette Roseman, the voice of *elders*, will read from *The Viagra Diaries.*"

Trying not to fall into my habit of hunching forward and leaning on the podium, after I emphasize that I don't believe in labels like elder or senior, after the applause settles to quiet, I begin reading the first chapter, acting out Anny's inflections. When it's over, to applause and whistles, I throw my hat into the first row. Nanny catches it, laughing. Then the manager announces that there will be a brief moment for questions, and after, the book signing.

"When is the TV series going to be on air?" asks a tall, thin man standing in the back.

I explain that the TV series is on hold, but that possibly another network will take over.

"That sucks," says a shy woman in the front. "I was looking forward to seeing a series about a woman over sixty."

"Typical of Hollywood," says another.

"Is the diamond dealer real?"

"Everything is in the book is real. I sell out everyone and myself."

More laughter.

I answer questions about writing—do I write in the morning or at night? Do I write at a certain time every day? Do I have a personal life?

The questions continue for hours until the manager, looking irritated, takes the mic and announces that I will now sign books. A huge line forms and, feeling excited and high on the night, I begin signing books.

"I went to the junior prom with you," says this nervous man who shakes. He confides that he has a rare disease. "I read your books on tape."

"Oh yes. Seymour. Yes, of course I remember." Remembering how handsome he was in high school, how I adored him, I sign his book *Love always, Bette.*

The line is moving fast. People I never expected to be interested are here—the pharmacist from Walgreens, typists from twenty-five years ago, strangers from the neighborhood. Amazing. For the first time, I don't feel invisible or alone.

But in a few minutes, twelve books later, the manager announces. "Sorry! We're out of books. Stand in line at the front desk to order." People leave by the droves, not bothering to stand in line at the desk and order books.

As I watch the store empty out, my heart sinks, and I feel both sad and angry. After I say goodnight to Nanny and Larry, assuring them not to worry, that I'm fine with everything, I approach the bookstore manager, who sits behind the front desk at the computer. I tell her that I'm devastated that at least seventy-five people left without ordering, and that I had told her ahead of time that I'd received at least a hundred RSVPs. While I'm talking, she looks at me like a stern teacher would at an unruly, impossible child.

"I'm sorry you're *devastated,"* she says, in a mocking tone. "Now if you'll excuse me, I have other authors, and work to do."

I stand there a second, wanting to say, *Hey. I work hard too! I'm not some privileged white woman. Why are you so hostile?* But she's turned her back to me and slowly, I leave the store and hail a taxi home.

16

Fall arrives and crisp, yellow leaves float along the hills like paper stars. *The Viagra Diaries* is not selling, and I blame myself for not standing up to the editor and for butchering my own work until it had no sparkle or character. Once again, fearing my own judgment, I'd placed myself in the victim position. When you're not true to your own convictions, everything falls apart. Now the bookstores are returning what they originally ordered. I'm frustrated that I'd let my weaker self take over; I feel cheated and angry, like I knew the answers but pretended that I didn't.

To make things worse, the hostile manager who'd only ordered twelve books reported me to the chain's corporate office, claiming that I'd been nasty to her. An executive from the head office calls, and in a scolding tone she informs me that their stores will not carry *The Viagra Diaries* or any of my books. "We do not tolerate rudeness to our employees," she snaps. "You're not worth it."

I protest that the manager had only ordered twelve books after I informed her that there would be at least a hundred people there. "Your store lost sales."

"End of conversation," she snaps, and ends the call.

Upset, I sit by the window and concentrate on the tree across the street. After the morning rain, the branches glisten like crystals. I think about the night of the book signing, playing back my every word. Had I been rude? Was I so detached from the reality around me, that I couldn't feel what the manager was feeling, that her integrity had felt challenged? Or was I so angry about the twelve books that I had a nasty tone? Yes, looking back, there were times that I'd smile at someone's rebuttal or mistake but still felt entitled to have their unconditional positive responses to my orders, challenges, and opinions. Even worse, had I been so furious at Avalon and WC that I took out my frustration on her?

I watch the tree, thinking how true nature's essence is.

For hours I lie awake, going over past altercations, defensively insisting I had nothing to do with anything. A wind is blowing, and the rattling sounds mingle with Mr. Wilson's music thumping upstairs.

I slip into a heavy dream, the kind where the air is thick and you know you're dreaming and can't get out until it lets you out. I'm hiding behind a tree at Happy Valley and the fading sun turns the acres a myriad of pinks and greens. I'm watching Ronald play his horn—when he's drunk and sad he plays his horn. Tall oak trees rustle in the breeze. Lisa and Nanny are asleep in their pretty rooms. He holds the horn tight. We are strangers and I caught him on rebound from Charley, so I can torture him until he leaves.

* * *

"I feel empty."

"Empty because you're not writing a new book?" Dr. T. asks.

"Yes."

"It's not enough that you've published eleven books? That you're in a small percentage of artists and writers who have any success at all?"

"I created my disasters. I let my weak side take over. I botched my book, made bad decisions, and have no money. Here I am pushing seventy and still dealing with disassociation. Not feeling is...painful. Not feeling whole. I feel as though there's a hole poked in my psyche where my truths leak out, and then the fake me takes over."

"Your mother made you feel defective and was unable to separate you from her own feelings about herself. Early on, to feel safe, you disassociated.

We sit in a long silence. My dark glasses are on so that he won't see the sorrow in my eyes. Then he says softly, "Ironically, disassociation has taught you to find and process your own memories and emotions."

"I always say I can only love sometimes because I'm afraid if I love all the time it will go away."

He smiles. "Love is the effect of loving yourself. Then you'll know how to love on your terms, the way you want it."

I pull another Kleenex from the box next to me. Dr. T. waits. He knows that when I smile, I'm detaching. Or when I cry, I'm ascending to consciousness. "I wish I could wake up and feel whole. Will this disassociation disease ever stop?"

"It's not a disease, but rather a defense mechanism," Dr. T. says sympathetically. "But it can be treated, and you work hard at looking deep into your psyche, extricating buried feelings from the past, and processing your findings. You lick your own wounds. You don't need anyone to do it for you, and that is why your capacity for loving is great. You will be found, Bette. Don't give up hope."

A wind rattles the window. He sits slightly forward, which means the session is ending.

"The other night I had the most incredible dream," I say after a long moment. "I was walking along a flat road looking for my self and carrying a bucket of stones. Each stone was a memory. Surrounding the road was the most beautiful field of roses—roses as big as clouds. At the end of the road was a woman wearing a flowing white dress. She had my face and silver hair, and she appeared so calm, so interesting and happy. She was wearing violet stone bracelets. I gave her the bucket of stones. She emptied the bucket and arranged them one by one each along the edge of the road, and she said we'd find the original trauma. Some of the stones were hot and some had little ridges on the edges with lines etched between tiny words. There was one black stone with white writing, but as I touched it I awoke."

* * *

I struggle to face my reality. Like opening a gift and finding it empty inside, I panic that unless I write another project, my career is over. Then it dawns me: I'll turn my column into a blog based on my experiences with the industry. Yes, I'll write a tell-all about the ageist Hollywood industry. I'll write the truth about how the networks change a writer's work for ratings, power, and money. Yes, I'll transition from writing my column to writing a manifesto about writers and what they do through in the industry. I create a blog and name it *Blast,* like my former column. I write an introduction and ask readers to write me and post their stories on my blog. I add a button that says "Respond."

As the days pass, I write not only about my personal experiences as a writer, but also about the ageism in the industry. I feel alive. I can't wait to get up in the morning and write. When Edwina calls, I tell her about *Blast* and she warns me to be *careful.* "Trust me. If you write and complain about the industry no one will want your work."

But I don't care. Daily, I work on the blog. I write: *...the industry, meaning the networks, agents, studios, are made up of twelve-year-old male executives who seek power. They hate age. Unless you're twenty something, they change your original scripts and books, rewrite, and dumb down your work. Many of the story developers are twenty-something girls who think because they have MFAs in creative writing, they know everything. Their faces glowing from age crèmes and Botox, they talk like valley girls ending each statement with questions and they turn your material into monsters or aliens or lovesick girls.*

I write about Bitterman and Yesterday and Kat who changed my sixty-five-year-old protagonist Anny Applebaum into a thirty-two-year-old avatar. *Ageism in our youth-oriented industry reveals that the networks don't understand that life itself is a learning process, an unfolding, not just TV ratings. They have no vision.*

What do you think?

Almost immediately, the blog goes viral. Writers, authors, actors, filmmakers of all ages write on my blog that they're also tired of their works being sold, optioned, and then hacked, trashed, and changed. Writers over forty relate their horror stories about how, after their TV and movie options were ended, network writers stole their themes, stories, characters, only changing the names. "Literary rape," many claim.

I'm on fire. This manifesto is not to trash people in the industry, or for revenge, but to reveal ageism, shed light on where there is often disrespect for female writers over fifty.

I write about the overflow of young, hot literary agents who rave about your book, then never contact you again. Or the agents who send generic letters saying: '*Unfortunately your work is not for us,"* when you'd never sent them the work in the first place. There are the writing conferences full of very young, smug agents who sit on panels, lecturing rules about how to write, submit, and what the "market wants," discouraging older people who want to write. As if they are an exclusive club, and unless you're twenty-something, have rehabilitated from prison or sexual abuse, or have won literary awards, you're not allowed in. I write about how so many female agents and successful authors are competitive, and mean to other women who are trying to make it as writers, too.

Why should art be age-exclusive? Especially, why should age matter?" I write.

Every day, up at four a.m. with my green tea beside me, I write the blog until late at night, recording my inner feelings about the process of writing and the continued saga of *The Viagra Diaries*. In the evenings I try to read the thousands of responses from writers flooding my blog about readers' personal stories and complaints about bookstores, publishers, and agents who express interest and then never contact them again, or about writing workshops that overcharge and exploit young, ambitious writers. Many write about ageism and how some agents didn't want to read their work if they were over sixty. "I love your blog, Mom. It's true, funny, and outrageous. Keep going."

* * *

Winter transitions into early March and swooping rains flood the hills. The blog is growing so fast I can't keep up. Except to teach my writing workshops, work on my age march, or take quick walks around the hills, I hardly go outside and rarely answer the phone. Winter is beautiful. Fog covers the city like a halo, and the air is cold and dark. The rosebushes are empty but the trees glisten, sway, and are so alive. Winter is my time to stay submerged in my subconscious, and peer out. I love the solitude, the routine and rituals that I use to write. I feel joy.

Today it's a cold day and my small space heater is on. A strong wind is blowing the tree across the street, and branches lie on the street like sad dolls.

Edwina calls. "Good news, honeybun. Satan Bernstein, executive producer at HBO, is *salivating* over *The Viagra Diaries*. He thinks it's yummy and wants to option it. Angie Golden wants back in, but when I called Bitterman he complained that because of your blog he's receiving death threats and he won't release the rights. So I have to keep Satan on ice."

"I'm sick of it all," I say.

After a hesitant silence, she says: "Bette, please make nice with Bitterman and Yesterday, and do a lunch. This fucking business is all about relationships."

"It's not. Bitterman is about betrayal and money, and I don't want to do a lunch with them."

She exhales an exasperated sigh. "The avatar is a celebrity. *The Hollywood Reporter* article makes fun of WC and the avatar. *People Magazine* is running a story titled "Diary of An Avatar."

Bitterman is out for blood. If you don't make nice he'll wipe the floor with you and you'll never work again in this town."

"It's his problem. I don't care."

"Honeybun, I spoke with Marci Feldstein. She's going to advise you. She'll give you a call tomorrow."

The rest of the day I work on the blog. Not feeling well, I go to bed early, watch a Netflix film, and slip into a dreamless sleep.

Around three a.m., I awake with cramps like you wouldn't believe. I'm pacing the floor, assuring myself that I probably ate too much pasta and that the cramps will go away, but they get worse and my back hurts so much I can't bend. Worried my cancer came back and spread, I quickly put on my coat, grab my purse, and text Nanny that I'm going to the ER. In agony, I call a taxi.

"What is your pain one to ten?" asks a tired-looking nurse in admission.

"Twelve."

The nurse takes me right into ER. Wearing a cotton gown, I'm in a bed behind a curtain, next to a man who's screaming for a fix as a nurse inserts an IV into my arm. A doctor with a Mohawk thumps my back, and in a shrill voice, shouts to the tired-looking orderlies, "Contrast abdominal CT scan! Hurry."

An hour later, in ER again, the same doctor says I have diverticulitis and double pneumonia, and that my heart rate is off the chart. "Ten more minutes and you'd be dead!"

I'm moved upstairs to a room that I share with this Mexican woman who shouts on the phone in Spanish. A young nurse with long blonde hair and cranky eyes injects morphine, and I float into oblivion.

I wake to Nanny and Larry looking grave and standing by the bed, holding a bouquet of pink roses. "Mom, we love you. We're here."

The days pass in a blur. I'm living in a world of blaring lights and noisy hallways, hooked to machines, IVs in my arms. And I wonder if I'm dying, if this is the way my life will end. I can't die without feeling my feelings, embracing my daughters and telling them my story so they can break the angry cycle between my mother and her mother. Will my daughters empty my computer and dump files of unpublished books, half drafts, poems in process? I didn't write a decent will, and so far I have little to leave them. I don't want to die without seeing my beloved tree one more time, lying on the grass by the ocean on a warm day when sunlight scrapes the sky, without arranging pale pink roses and peonies in my blue crystal vase, inhaling their perfume, or listening to Bach as I slip into sleep.

Every day, Nanny walks me along the hallways, on her cell phone, whispering to Lisa about my progress. Being so ill transforms my view of life, and I begin to think that before I die I must rearrange not only my values but so many of my thoughts, my wasted anger at people and situations long past. I'm so fortunate that I have my wonderful daughters and the means to live in the little world I'd carved out for myself. I want to work harder at staying connected and not detaching.

Five days later, I'm released and I can't wait to get home and back to my writing. But I feel weak and tire easily and still have breathing problems. Nanny worries about me; every morning she arrives pushing a huge cart filled with Tupperware containers of her homemade chicken soups, Jell-O, puddings, and delicious, organic casseroles. In the afternoons, to build my strength,

Nanny and I walk outside to admire the roses in bloom and the light dropping on the hills. She holds my arm tight and sunlight flickers gold dots along her flowing, dark hair, and as she lectures that I have to eat better, that Lisa says I'm too negative, I assure her that I'm fine and take good care of myself.

"But I worry, Mom," she says officiously. "You have to stop living like a homeless person."

"I take care of myself."

"You do not!" she shouts, her face turning red. "You're seventy. You think you're eighteen. You're going to break a hip wearing those platform fuck-me shoes. You eat shit, fries, chips, produce from the dollar store. I paid Jose extra to clean your place and he said there's mold in your fridge and Larry says that every time he's at your place, he gets bites."

"I've never seen a bug."

"Jose said he saw bugs."

"Not one bug," I insist.

"Lisa says you have high anxiety and that you are bipolar. Eileen Blumenthal's mom is your age and she's in assisted living. She wears flats and knits, not five-inch platform shoes and H&M clothes."

In the next few weeks, still taking antibiotics and going to doctor appointments, the health trauma passes and I resume writing the blog. As I answer the growing questions, I write about ageism, cosmetic surgery, why women mutilate themselves, their lineless faces shiny like porcelain dolls. Is it just to look young? To please men? The irony is they look older as they look less and less real.

I write about the dumbed down TV shows like *The Bachelor: Which gives a false and bad image for all women. To think that after a quick meeting, receiving a wilted rose, the women are in love. Though entertaining, the highly rated show, The Housewives, also gives a false image: the women's daily glam squads guarding their faces like soldiers, stylists choosing their clothes, hairstylists designing perpetual hairstyles. Their quest for eternal youth, wealth, will produce unhappy daughters. They are only concerned with their appearances, wealth, and eternal youth.*

As the blog heats up, Edwina is furious. "I'm working my balls off to get you a deal. Stop critiquing highly rated shows! How dare you?" Edwina says on FaceTime.

"It's a sociological issue," I reply.

"Fuck sociological! It's about money, honey."

Mendelssohn's violin concerto plays loud, the music reaching my soul. Night is here and the music evokes memories of past loves.

I close my eyes, remembering Bob. Tall, Norwegian, with olive skin and the bluest eyes you've ever seen, after my divorce with the girls' father, a single mother and penniless, going to college at night and working at a bank. He'd been so kind to me and to the girls, and for a long time, we'd lived together. But except when I was writing and painting or haunting art galleries, I was so disconnected to myself that I couldn't connect to him on any level. Until I met Noel David, a well-known dealer of contemporary art. Hanging out in Noel's gallery, I followed his every move, went to his every opening, his lectures on minimal art. I'd leave poems or drawings on his desk and he'd say, wistfully, "You're talented Kid. I love your style." Totally in love, one night I'd asked Bob to leave. "As soon as possible," I said. "I'm in love with Noel. As soon as my next novel sells, I'll pay you back. I promise. We'll be friends..."

Just like that, without feeling what he was feeling, I kept on typing, until, carrying a box of his things, Bob left. I continued typing, his hurt footsteps retreating on the stairs.

* * *

Marci Feldstein calls and she's furious that I'm writing about Bitterman. "He's suing you for defamation of character!" she screams. "You think I have time for this nonsense? I have Streep and Pacino to deal with, and now I have to deal with the WC morons! Stop writing shit about the fucking avatar! And it's your fault that you didn't protest it in the first place. Now I have to clean up another dumb author's mess."

"It serves Bitterman right," I say. "He betrayed me. Ruined my project. Now he won't release the rights."

"You people are idiots! You don't read! You dream. You exploit." She shrieks a litany of complaints about authors, what a total idiot cocksucker Bitterman is. "These ball heads are putting me in the grave! Meanwhile don't write anything more about the asshole."

"He deserves it. He changed my protagonist into an avatar. I never want to see them again."

"Do you not hear?" she screams. "What do you think I'm doing? Playing with myself? I'm breaking my ass to get you what you want!"

"Yes. But..."

"Stop hocking and let me get to work! You people are morons!"

WC announces the lawsuit in the trades. Bitterman badmouths me as an old hack. "The book is a dog, poorly written," he reports. Sales tank. But I know that I'm doing the right thing and I feel relief. I concentrate on turning my blog into a book.

But the publicity doesn't stop. As if *The Viagra Diaries* is no longer a book, but a campaign, *Variety* writes an article titled *The Avatar Problem,* citing industry crimes—like hijacking authors' ideas and concepts and turning them into theirs. Authors on talk radio rant about Hollywood hacks distorting their good works to suit ratings. They hope that Congress legislates laws that prevent networks from changing writers' original works or the ages of their characters.

Tonight, I'm at the computer writing my next blog, when I recall driving through the rainbow; Jake said that when you're true to yourself, your dreams will come true. I wonder how he is and would love to tell him that his rainbow helped me realize that there's not one way to be or to love, and that some moments are worth a lifetime. I want to tell him that I admire his work and that I now believe work to be the key to our growth.

Usually at this time he's home, cooking—several times he brought me Tupperware containers of his homemade fish soup—or playing his clarinet. I call Jake's home number. It rings several times and his answering message is not on. Next, I text—he always responded to texts—but no response. I email, but it comes back. Thinking he might be out of the country, I click on his private university email, sure that he'll answer that, but an obituary comes up. Stunned, I read: *Professor Jake Feldstein Professor Emeritus died from lung cancer, his wife and friends with him at his home...He...*

I read two more pages about his achievements, his generous foundation to help young students, the memorial at Chapel of the Chimes in Berkeley, remembering his constant coughing. I recall Jake saying he'd been married, very much in love, and how broken he was when his wife had left him for a rock star and moved to Finland. He never said they'd divorced. You never know what's in a person's past and I respect that sometimes it needs to remain private.

I lie in the dark on my bed thinking about death. In the past when I'd think about it I was terrified and would put it out of my mind, but now as I'm getting older, I'm looking at it as a journey, as maybe another path of dreams. If we came from a seed, like a rose blooms again I'm sure that our soul blooms into something else. But then, I wonder who the beings are who come to me in the night. Usually, this happens near dawn when I wake with a feeling that someone is pulling me, as if trying to pull me from the bed, and sometimes I feel their thin, bony hand, like a grasp or a message. During these times I keep my eyes closed, to make sure that I'm not dreaming or imagining this, listening to the traffic outside my window, my heart beating hard until the pulling stops. Once, I opened my eyes and saw a spray of light so blinding I closed them again.

* * *

The next few weeks I'm ignoring what's going on with the lawsuit. In the time between teaching my writing workshops, I'm spending a great deal of time working on my blog. Most of my advance money is gone and I don't make much money teaching the workshops. Though I've learned to budget and live without money, at times I feel panicked and think about taking a job in a hat designing place. Then out of the blue, I receive a text from this huge LA literary agent, Evan Allen. He read my blog and thinks it's great and funny; he sets up a meeting for a Skype call the next day. Since the New York trip, I haven't heard from Biggie Delano and I think, what's the harm in just talking with him. "See what he has to say," Lisa advises.

"You got the bastards," he says, the next morning on Skype. He's about fifty, tall and slender and golden, as if he's dipped in golden air. His wavy hair is the color of corn and an air of glamour hovers over him, like he's a real-life Oscar. Yet, under his genteel manner and confident, deep voice, his tone is impatient, and I sense if you're on his bad side, he has a tongue that can slice you in half. He wants to represent the blog and suggests that it needs a more powerful storyline.

"It's a manifesto about ageism in the networks," I emphasize. "It isn't fiction."

"You need an arc," he snaps.

"Arc?"

"Yes, arc. Haven't you heard of an arc?"

"Yes, but this is a manifesto on ageism in the networks. It's about..."

"No one gives a crap about ageism. They hear the word *age* and it's over." He laughs. "They're interested in the lawsuit, the hilarious *Hollywood Reporter* article 'Diary of an Avatar,' the gossip. I'll sell this fucker over the phone."

Amid his various phones ringing in the background and a nervous-looking young assistant dropping pages on his desk, he discusses which "dick producers" he'll pitch the blog to. He frowns, exhaling an exasperated sigh. "I'll pitch it as *The Diary of An Avatar.*"

"It's titled *Blast*," I correct.

He frowns. "Hey! Either you want me to sell it or not."

"Biggie Delano is my agent. I have to talk with him first."

"Biggie Delano is a fart! His nose is so long from his lies that he can't get through a doorway. Everyone in town knows he sold *The Viagra Diaries* based on WC's so-called TV series. Now Bitterman won't release the rights and the other networks can't re-develop it. So let's get *the* blog into a pilot before the whores fuck with it. I know these whores. All they care about is the money. Trust me."

As he continues to trash Bitterman, I'm thinking keep your options open, for once be smart and let him try to sell the blog. And if he doesn't, give it to Biggie Delano. "Okay, I'll give you four weeks," I say after a pause. "...If you don't sell it, it goes to Biggie Delano."

After the call, I decide, so as not to burn any bridges, to call and tell Biggie about my deal with Evan Allen. So I call, and his assistant puts me right through.

"Long time no see," he quips.

I tell Biggie that I'm in the process of putting my blog into a book. "Evan Allen loves it, so I gave him three weeks to pitch."

"Did you sign anything?" he asks with an exasperated sigh.

"No."

"Don't sign anything," he repeats. "When you have the book, send it to me. I'll review it. Let me know what happens."

I resume work on the blog. I feel good about the way I handled this, and I'm enjoying working on the book. But Edwina hates the blog and she warns me that the "word on the street" is that I'm a "sour old lady," and that the blog trashes the networks. "No one wants your work now honeybun. Let me concentrate on *The Viagra Diaries* and there's still a chance. I can't handle you getting arrested. You know Bitterman is a rat and loves publicity, even bad publicity and he's foaming at the mouth."

18

"I warned you to stop writing shit about WC. Now we have a lawsuit going!" Marci Feldstein screams on the phone. "You people don't listen! You authors have your head up your ass!"

"I only wrote the truth," I say nervously.

"What do you want, a fucking medal? You people think you're so fucking smart. Now not only do I have to save your ass, but I've also got to make pussy suck Bitterman pay huge legal fees."

"What if he wins the rights? What if I lose?"

"I don't *lose*." she screams. "I have clients waiting. Clients with money! Clients who read! Until court, keep the trap shut."

Everything goes wrong. The lawsuits and bad publicity surrounding *The Viagra Diaries* hurt my career and my book sales—though they were small before, now fall to nothing. Not even Edwina takes my calls, and every time I call Evan Allen his assistant says he's in a meeting. I'm receiving hate mail from people who say that I'm a lousy writer and a sour grape whore. *Hollywood Dateline*, *Star Movie Magazine*, and *The National Enquirer* publish pictures of Bitterman next to an image of an avatar. The headline reads: *Elder author, Bette Roseman is suing Joshua Bitterman for breach of contract, for aborting* The Viagra Diaries.

Sometimes, you think that nothing changes in your life, but if you persist on exploring your subconscious, suddenly things change. No longer is my singular dream of fame, fortune, and visibility so prominent. I yearn to write something literary, which means simply to go under the surface and integrate the deepest of my emotions with craft.

"You need to get out of yourself," Lisa advises. "Do something important that has nothing to do with your writing."

I resume my volunteer work at Shanti and do weekend training to help those dying from HIV and terminal cancer. I start a support group called Letters to Cancer, where women with stage four cancer write letters about their deepest feelings and how cancer changed their lives. I hope to publish their letters in an anthology and donate the money to Shanti. Their spirits and courage humble me.

Past October, when the sun retreats into the trees, my former editor of the Australian News, Oliver Abbot, calls. He moved to San Francisco and he's living on Alabama Street; he's recently opened *Castle Production Company*. He invites me to meet him for dinner the next night in Japan Town, and I agree. For five years he published my columns in Australia, and though we never met I feel a natural bond with him. I'd also admired his critiques on film, painting, music, and ballet, was always impressed by his insights.

"Is he single?" Myra asks on FaceTime.

"He's fifty-eight years old. Anyway, my column used to run in his newspaper for years."

"Go for it. As soon as they're sixty they leave the toilet seat up and wear Depends."

"Why do you think everything is about sex and genitalia?" I'm irritated.

"Because it is. Mohammed misses me so much that on FaceTime he strips naked, masturbates, and his penis blows up."

"He's a pervert," I say. "He's raping you. And you let him."

"I don't see it that way. He asks first. Lots of men do this."

"Are you crazy? It's like saying 'I'm going to rape you, is that okay?' Report him. Don't fuck him."

"He's lonely for me and I don't want to end up in the me too movement with those bitter old ladies."

"You're the one who is acting like a lonely old lady craving attention or you wouldn't let the creep expose himself."

"Men are pathological," she continues. "Look at poor Moo Moo. She meets this fabulous lawyer at her fundraiser to save the mice, and turns out he has a vagina."

"He can't help that," I say. "He might be a great guy."

She yells. "Are you crazy? Anyway, he should have told her first."

She continues to rave about her fabulous dermatologist Seth, and her recent laser treatments, lecturing that a woman has to keep looking young. Constantly she has cosmetic procedures and brain MRIs to make sure she isn't dying from cancer, worrying about age and death. But I love her loyal friendship, along with so many other things about her.

"Honey, the younger the better. All you have to do is blow on it and it's up up and away."

Tonight the sky is full of stars. I sip my ginger tea, letting my thoughts sift through my mind, dredging them up as they come. Disappointment is part of making art, I think. From disappointment there is first pain, then self-confrontation, then new choices. It is not only about technique. Craft comes from daily practice, like choreographing steps and then rehearsing them into a semblance of expression.

Risk is the key to good writing. Except for my Jewish Princess novel, and a couple of others, I'd not risked anything. Without the risk of diving deeper into yourself, knowing your truths, exploring them, you only have commercial projects.

I am tired. The stars shrink and some diminish. It is time to dream.

19

"Hello, I'm Oliver." He extends a hand and we shake.

Sometimes a moment you least expect changes your life. He has the most beautiful, artistic, intense face I've ever seen: high cheekbones, very full lips, dark olive skin, and piercingly dark, emotional eyes. Just the way he stands, as if he owns the ground, makes you just want to stare at him. He's about my height, with a hip-length fitted black jacket accentuating his small waist that fits as if it's painted on his graceful, slender body. A wide silver bracelet covers his narrow wrist like a statement. I feel as though I've been dropped inside a dream and I'm not going to get out.

At a discreet table in the back of the darkened restaurant, we drink hot sake and I talk nonstop, repeating nervously about how great it was writing for his paper, while Japanese music plays softly in the background. In his gorgeous British accent he talks about how he'd admired my column and that he loves the blog. "It's fresh, progressive, and off the radar," he says sincerely.

We sip our drinks and eat shrimp wrapped in seaweed.

"I read that you were a dancer in the Australia Ballet Company before you started the paper. Why did you stop, and when did you start making films?"

His intense eyes fill with light. He relates that he was raised in an orphanage in London, and that his father was African American and lived in Kenya, and his British, Caucasian mother died when he was an infant. From a young age he'd studied ballet and dreamed of becoming a dancer like Nureyev. A wealthy uncle raised him while he studied film and journalism at Cambridge, but his conservative uncle disapproved and he dropped out of school to pursue his love of ballet. He spent years dancing with The Australian Ballet, until he was in a terrible car accident and broke his foot in several places and had to stop. After his uncle died and he inherited money, he bought the failing but progressive *Australian News* and became its art critic. After the paper folded, he decided to move to San Francisco and make films.

He orders another bottle of sake and we eat more appetizers. I'm mesmerized by his confidence and exotic allure. He smiles. "You look different from your headshot, from what I'd thought. You're quite ravishing."

Flushing at the compliment, I quickly talk about the years of writing the column, and especially how I was always thrilled that he never edited out what I'd written.

"Why did the *San Francisco Times* let your column go?"

"The editor of the *San Francisco Times* said that the paper's uptight donors complained that my columns were too controversial and vulgar."

He frowns. "I think that WC turning your protagonist into an avatar is vulgar. I think changing a writer's work is vulgar. I think playing to the monkeys who only want to see youth at its worst, with blown up faces and sex, is vulgar. It's vulgar that your former San Francisco editor fired you because you wrote the truth about ageism."

I nod, moved by his passion, the fire in his voice.

"And some would say the feathers on the side of your ridiculous, wonderful hat and your platform heels are vulgar, but they're you. They're real. They're ageless."

I sip more sake, feeling lightheaded and staring at his androgynous face, his tumble of shiny dark waves. After a long silence, I ask: "...Were you ever..."

"...No, I've never married," he interjects with an amused grin. "I'm married to my work. When I'm writing a script, dancing, making a film, I'm in love. I can't get close enough. When the dance is over, there's an emptiness. Then, like a scavenger, I collect observations, people for my next project."

"I get it," I say eagerly. "I think that the concept of love is an outdated, ancient ritual and it destroys true romantic love."

A melancholy comes into his eyes. "Love is vulgar. It needs so much. If it gets too close it fades away. It must be independent, exist from your soul, be whole on its own and not depend on outside sources. Or it can't last."

After a long silence he says: "I read *The Rise and Fall of a Jewish American Princess*. It's a wonderful, honest, and sensitive novel, and beautifully written."

"How did you come across the novel?" I ask, pleased by his compliment.

He smiles. "I was in a used bookstore and found it in a bin of free out-of-print books. The title intrigued me and then of course I recognized your name from your column. From the opening page I was hooked. It's so above your commercial fiction." He pauses, a curious expression on his face. "In the book Dianne figures out Charley married her to avoid his married secretary's claims that she was pregnant with his child. Is this true?"

"Yes. Years after the annulment, I called the married secretary. She admitted that when she told Charley that she was six months pregnant with his child, Charley had promised that as soon as she got a divorce, he'd marry her and he'd take care of them. But three weeks later, to get out of a jam, he'd married me, knowing as he took our wedding vows that as soon as she gave birth, he'd dump me. After one day in Hawaii, he said he'd made a mistake and took me home." I pause. "My father dropped dead from a heart attack a month after Charley won an annulment."

Oliver presses his hand on mine. He knows I'm feeling emotional. "My father was a screenwriter at Universal. He dreamed of one of his original films becoming a movie but not one of his scripts was ever made. The only way I could have a voice and express my rage at Charley's betrayal was to write *The Rise and Fall of a Jewish American Princess*. It's dedicated to my father."

"It's a compelling and sad story," Oliver says after a contemplative silence. "But your protagonist Dianne rises against all odds. Even though the story opens in 1960, women of all generations and cultures can identify with Dianne's emotional abuse, that she had no voice, how she was blamed." As he continues to discuss the novel, he holds his gaze, as if he feels with his eyes. He pauses. "Why was the novel not marketed?"

"It was my first novel. When the novel sold, the editor insisted I cut most of the scenes, including the Happy Valley section when my protagonist Dianne was married to her rebound husband, a wealthy drunk, and they had two daughters and she fantasized about leaving and becoming a writer. I revised until the voice was gone, and then the publisher shelved it. Years later I published it in its original form."

"I'm sorry," he says gently.

"But it was my fault. Obviously, I have a problem."

He smiles. "At least you're aware of it."

He pauses, looking at me intently. "Bette, one of the reasons I wanted to meet you is to tell you that I want to make a film based on your Jewish Princess novel. It would make a wonderful film. I want us to collaborate and make a film not just about a brutal rejection, but also about Dianne's inner struggles and her exploration of the subconscious. I can't pay you up front and the distribution will be small...mostly art house. I can only pay you a percentage of the profits. We'd both be taking a chance."

I'm taken aback. "...I need to think about this."

"Of course," he says quickly. "Take your time. It's a big decision."

I nod, suddenly uncomfortable by his penetrating, watchful eyes, as if he sees into me. He resumes discussing my work, confiding confidently that he wants to make a film that holds up for generations. "Just as Dora Maar inspired Picasso, you inspire me, Bette. In your imagery I see the layers of Dianne's mind. Like Dianne, you're complicated. I like complicated. I want to get to know you."

"...It's...late," I say quickly, and pull my hand away. I look at my watch.

"The subconscious is our wellspring of inspiration. The composer Virgil Thomson said that." He stands. "Call me when you're ready with your decision, and we'll get together."

I hurry outside and grab a taxi. All the way home, I keep my eyes on the moon. It is so bright I can touch it, and I'm remembering Oliver's androgynous, beautiful face, how underneath his long, silent pauses is passion, fury, and artistic genius. Oliver is a chance to tell my real story, to make sure it's told the way I want it.

At home I sit by the window and play back the night. Definitely a surprise. Everything about him is compelling...his deep, beautiful voice, contemplative silences, intelligent insights, and knowledge. Expressing his love of film, he made quick references to directors, obscure films he'd loved and details why. Well-read, he discussed books from dance history, from Julie Kavanagh's biography on Nureyev, which we'd both read, to Olivier and Burton's different acting styles and their rendering of Shakespeare. His energy, curiosity, artistry, and strangeness are intoxicating. As Jung said, he has the creative fire in him, and I think, I must work with him.

The traffic outside fades and the night is quiet. Fate always directs your path and Oliver's dream of turning my novel into art is here and though I'm broke, I know I must take the risk and follow my fate. Yes, change is necessary to exhume the past and the darkness that resides in unlived houses.

I go to bed. I close my eyes, my mind scraping my past, searching for incidents and feelings that I'd buried. Slipping into sleep, I dream that I'm floating on the bottom of the ocean, memories emerging from my open mouth like bubbles.

I'm lying in a lovely glass box. One leg is caught inside a hole. I crawl out and play Brahms on a violin. Mother plays the piano. Light falls on Mother's hair like a halo. My parents' wedding picture is on the piano. They sit on the edge of a chair, their hands locked like graves. They don't look at each other and Mother sits primly, her legs close together. She is a virgin. Daddy's eyes shine like a young boy on a great adventure.

Mother's sad, ivory fingers wander like listless dancers along the keys. Why does she not smile? Why does she not love me? Is it because of my failure with Charley? I am not a daughter but a failed dream...her dream? I can't breathe.

I shrink up.

We're at the dinner table. I'm thirteen, gawky, and sad. Nannie, my grandmother, sits across from me. A thin, brown hairnet covers her pale tan hair. Daddy eats his dinner neatly, his head down.

* * *

The next morning Lisa calls.

"Well?"

"Well what?" I reply.

"Did you have a great time?"

"He's very interesting."

"And?"

"He wants to make a film based on my Jewish Princess novel."

She sighs heavily. "Hank Googled him. Not only did his newspaper go bankrupt, but he's made five films and they didn't make a cent. He's living on borrowed money."

"He interested in making art," I say, feeling defensive.

"Art, fart, Mom. You need money."

"Money isn't everything."

"Since when?"

"You and Nanny help a lot. I appreciate it. But I need to collaborate on something true and my story needs to be told. It's an opportunity and I sense he's the real thing...really wonderful."

"Now you'll be all obsessed with work again. You haven't been here since your meeting with Bitterman. Almost a year ago." In her therapist tone, she explains that the reason I haven't is because I'm afraid to be close and this is because I never had maternal bonding. "You had bad breast, Mom. That's why you only connect to your work." After a heavy silence she says, "... Spock is missing."

"How could he be missing? Doesn't he have a chip?"

I quickly say, "You must be in grief. I'm so sorry. I hear you. I do. Cats come home. I know he'll come back home, know because you love him and he knows it. He loves you."

"Is she right?" I think, after the call. It's true I only visit when it's work related. I force myself to remember Lisa as a child—brave, studious, sad. She had so many losses so young—first Ronald's parents who she'd adored, and then she lost me, as I was never there. At barely seventeen, on a scholarship, she'd left for NYU and never returned.

Deep down, she must feel the same cold, lonely pain I feel when I remember my parents, this feeling of abandonment. It's time to face those years when Lisa was a child and to understand why I was so detached.

All night I think about what Lisa said. My dream is full of Lisa as a child, while I stand in the shadows, detached, watching, wishing I could feel the pain I know I feel. It's time to transition to a new place—a new self.

The next morning, I call Edwina and excitedly tell her about Oliver Abbot's film proposal. Years ago, Edwina had read the novel and submitted it to studios, but everyone passed.

"There's no money in Jewish virgins," she says. "Oliver Abbot is no one and Jewish virgins don't sell."

"It's not about virginity. It's about emotionally abused women. It's about Dianne's rise above adversity. A *Rocky* story."

"I know, honey. I read it. Remember? No one wanted it. I'm dealing with *The Viagra Diaries*. Everyone wants it. This fucking WC lawsuit is a publicity godsend. After the court hearing, trust me, there'll be bidding wars."

"Evan Allen loves my blog," I confide. "Are you interested in working with him?"

"Evan Allen is a whore. A rat. And there's no money in blogs. Honeybun, I have to jump. I'm late for agent camp. We'll talk soon. Ciao."

Next, I call Oliver and inform him that I read the contract and mailed it to my lawyer. "I'm excited about working on it with you," I say.

We make a date to meet the next day at his loft.

Past noon the next day, filled with eager anticipation, I ride a freight elevator to Oliver's loft, which is on Market Street, near the streetcars. A very young, gorgeous, artistic-looking girl, wearing a black leotard with waist-length black hair and deep-set hazel eyes, greets me. "I'm Rain. You're Bette. We're excited about your project."

"Thank you," I say, wondering if she's Oliver's girlfriend. She introduces me to Joe, Oliver's production assistant, a tall, slender man in his twenties with curly gold hair and happy blue eyes.

"So you've all met," Oliver says, emerging from a side office. A black turtleneck sweater pulled to his chin accentuates his artistic, sensual face. Once again, I'm taken aback by his strong artistic presence.

After Rain and Joe leave to scout San Francisco locations, Oliver leads me into the loft. It's huge, at least four thousand square feet, with pale tan wood floors, industrial floor-to-ceiling curved windows, and a mirrored wall with a ballet barre.

"Do you still practice at the barre?" I ask.

"Every day," he replies.

Framed photographs of Margot Fonteyn and Rudolf Nureyev hang from the walls, alongside Oliver dancing *Giselle* and posters of films he's made. Bouquets of white narcissus fill modern glass vases. Wonderful African masks and artifacts sit on tables or hang from the walls. I admire a photograph of Oliver posed in Swan Lake, his beautiful muscular legs extended.

"You look like a perfect Prince Siegfried," I say, slightly flushing.

He smiles. "I was seventeen," he says with a wistful sigh. "Now. We work. But it's cold in here. I'll build a fire."

He drops logs into the fireplace. Even his smallest movements are graceful and dance-like and exude artistic elegance. Just the way he touches the wood, as if everything he wants has a strong meaning. As if only beauty and art matter.

Soon the flames rise, crackling and dropping orange shadows, and the room warms.

We sit on a low black leather couch. A copy of my Jewish Princess novel is on a square wood table, the pages divided by yellow slips of papers. Oliver gives me a blue folder. "Bette, inside is the contract. Read it carefully. It's a simple contract, money on the back end if the film takes off."

I place the contract into my bag. Brazilian music softly plays from overhead speakers. Oliver discusses his plans for the film. He has a low budget, from grant money and his own money from refinancing his home in Australia, and he hopes to finish the film as soon as possible. Except for the Hawaii scene, the film will be shot in San Francisco. To budget, he's hiring unknown local actors.

"I admire your willingness to take a chance on an unknown project," I say.

"Without risk you have nothing." He lights a thin brown cigarette and exhales a contemplative stream of smoke.

With intensity, he discusses the look of the film, the trajectory. He plans to weave Dianne's past and dreams into the story. "To be fully present, you have to relive the past, and it's important to reveal Dianne's interior life as the story moves forward."

"Sounds like you have studied Dianne." I say.

He replies, "Her inner life is vivid, smoldering, exciting, and different from her actions. I want to capture her conflict."

The flames rise high in the fireplace. For what seems like hours we talk about the novel and how he sees the film. He knows every detail of Dianne's gestures, homemade clothes and unique style, her colloquial stammering words, and her perpetual pain. Never have I felt so artistically connected to anyone. Easily, feeling confident that I can express ideas without being dismissed, I confide that more than anything I want the film to be Dianne's story, her narrative, and her voice. "For the first time, I want her to be authentic, with my point of view and not yours."

Oliver nods as if he totally understands. Wordlessly, he gets up and switches on the track lights, which make a popping sound. "How about I order takeout Chinese?" he says cheerfully. "I'm starving. You must be too."

I nod.

Over shrimp and asparagus, we talk about film. He has an enormous knowledge of directors and how the camera and lighting can reveal emotions. "I want to reach into Dianne's psyche and to reveal what isn't said in the book."

"Do you think I didn't reveal all of her?"

He pauses. "She holds back," he says softly.

Wind rattles the windows and the flames in the fireplace warm the room. As if I'm sharing my inner secrets with him, I feel comfortable with him in a way I never have, not with anyone else. Enthusiastically, between eating, we discuss specific scenes from the novel. As I listen to him vividly express his ideas, I want to touch him. Touch his dark, smooth skin, kiss his sulky lips, and caress his cheekbones that shape his sculptured face. Everything about him is beautiful, magnetic, romantic, but strong. He's like a beautiful leopard about to pounce.

"...I'm not sure about the gun shop scene," he continues. "... Dianne not only buys a gun, but she has hardcore sex with the sleazy gun salesman. She becomes a sexual vampire...her sexual violence is out of character."

"That she wanted sex?" I reply incredulously. "She needs to prove to herself that she isn't frigid as Charley had publicly claimed. Dianne *needs* to end her virginity. He stole her innocence, he..." I stop, aware that my hands are trembling.

"Bette, I want to know everything about you," he says after a long silence.

"You do. You've read my novel."

"Oh, I think there's much more than Dianne," he says with a quick grin. "I think you're enormously talented. I also think you underestimate yourself."

"...It's late," I say. "...I have to go."

He'll drive me home, he insists.

"No, it's fine."

"Please, let me."

On the way home in his open Jeep, the wind blowing through my hair, admiring the cold black starless sky, I know that my life has changed. In a strange way, I feel as though we've inhabited each other. From my novel, he knows so much about my inner life, as though we we're sharing our deepest secrets.

He stops the car in front of my apartment. The motor runs noisily in the night's silence. "Bette. We're going to work closely together."

"We already have."

"I'm going underground to write to work on the script. When I have a good draft, I'll call you."

I open the door and rush into my apartment.

Something extraordinary happened tonight. I feel as though I've been riding a rubber raft in a turbulent ocean, the raft going every which way, and finally I'm riding on a direct course.

* * *

The next morning, I read the contract and then, eager to make sure that everything is intact, I rush to the post office and mail it overnight to Marci Feldstein.

The following days, before I start working with Oliver, I'm eager to finish the blog and begin turning it into a book.

Today, a storm prevails over the city again, heavy rains soaking the fog-covered hills. But as the day passes and I tire of the tedious job of turning blog posts into chapters, my thoughts turn to Oliver.

I write: *He walks with his feet slightly extended, his head high, his beautiful dancer body close to himself. There's an animal magnetism about him, as if he's always inside the moment and in perpetual thought and search for meaning and beauty and he doesn't hold back. An aura surrounds him like a beautiful rainbow.*

My cell phone rings. It's Marci Feldstein, the lawyer. "Who is this loser guy you're bothering me about?"

"Oliver Abbot is a filmmaker. As you can see in the contract I get money if the film does well, and I just wanted you to look at it and before I sign to confirm that it's intact..."

"Look, you people don't listen. If you want to sign it, go ahead. But I don't have time for small shit."

"If the film is successful, there'll be money and..."

"Idiot!" she screams. "I don't do back ends. I do money up front. Enough!" She ends the call.

Two days later, I receive the contract back by snail mail. Quickly, I sign it and send it to Oliver. He texts that he's working day and night on the script, and when he has a draft he'll be in touch. Thrilled that the film is in process, for the first time I feel new hope for a new journey.

20

"Four networks turned down your blog. They said it's too 'insider,'" Evan Allen says on the phone.

"Did they read it?" I ask, annoyed by his snippy tone.

"They read my log line," he snaps.

"Did you tell them I'm turning the blog into a book?"

"They're not interested. They want you to change your age. They said the public won't take anyone who is seventy, seriously."

"I won't do that. It's laughable."

"I warned you that they don't like that you're seventy."

"So do they want me to die?"

"Just to change it."

"Well, I won't. The blog is a manifesto exposing industry ageism."

"Hey! Next you'll think you should be on *Sixty Minutes*!" he shouts.

"Well, it's best we don't work together," I say. "Anyway, I'm busy. I'm collaborating with Oliver Abbot, who is making a film based on my Jewish Princess novel."

"Hey! No one gives a flying fuck about a Jewish Princess. You have a bad reputation, and no one wants your projects."

I happily text Biggie Delano and tell him that Evan Allen is out of my life and that as soon as I finish turning the blog into a book, I will send it to him. He replies that he will read it as soon as I send it.

Diligently, I get to work. Compared to writing a novel, with the dozens of drafts and layering, this process of turning the blog into a book is just a matter of sorting out posts and making sure the ageism theme is passionate and powerful, and about how ageism stains our entire culture, how it affects more than just writers. It exploits and dismisses and victimizes. Instead of honoring age and experience, it shames age. I'm working fast, isolating myself, but I know that I have this obsessive tendency to work all the time, become totally hermetic, and ignore my daughters, so I vow to see Nanny more often. Oh, what a mess I am. Do I do this because I'm afraid if I don't write what I think, what I feel, believe, no one will remember me? Hear me? Know me? Or worse—if I don't keep writing my opinions, ideas, dig into my subconscious, then I'll disappear and never rise to consciousness? I wish I could stick a pin in my heart and let out all the feelings. It's really weird to love your kids so much, and not feel what they're feeling, as if you're locked in a closet and peeking at their life through a hole.

I start seeing Nanny more, taking BART to Oakland. Together, we sit and talk in her pretty garden, butterflies floating in the air and Fred chasing his ball. When I'm with Fred and hold him close, his heart beating against mine, I know this is the way love feels. I remember when I'd had uterine cancer, how after my surgery

Nanny brought Fred over to visit me and he'd sleep next to me. Dogs have emotional intelligence, and a capacity for loving way beyond humans.

But then poor Fred is diagnosed with stomach cancer, and the vet says he's suffering and hasn't long to live. Nanny, in deep grief, plans a goodbye party for Fred and invites her neighbors and their dogs. I'm devastated.

When I arrive at Nanny's home on Saturday, neighbors and their dogs mingle on the patio. Fred, wearing his royal blue sweater, lies listlessly on his favorite polka dot bed in his favorite spot by the window that looks out at Nanny's garden, where he plays every day. His favorite toy, a stuffed yellow bee with black stripes, is next to him. Barney, a rescue dog Nanny adopted two years ago, sits next to Fred, licking him. Since I'd seen him two weeks ago, I'm shocked by his changed appearance. His now-thin pale tongue dangles from his half-open mouth, and his breathing becomes so heavy as he tries to sit up; pain lies deep in his eyes.

One by one, dogs Fred has played with for years lie beside him. Neighbors bring flowers and gifts for Fred. As I watch Fred and his friends circling around him, I feel this overwhelming compassion, thinking that Fred not only knows he's dying, but he's at peace. I can feel it. He's had such love in his life and I believe that if you're loved and have felt love, you transcend.

This beautiful black lab, who has given me unconditional love, whose golden eyes I have looked so deeply into I could see his soul, is leaving us, and as I tell myself this and kiss his face, I feel as though the ground is breaking under me. I can feel his suffering and I hold him close, whispering how much I love him, singing *Mr. Blue, Grandma loves you*, his warm nose next to my cheek. I feel his soul, and my tears spill onto his fur. I hold him all day, with his heart beating against mine and as if he knows he's dying. He looks straight ahead, fixed on some distant point, perhaps the rainbow ridge. Nanny made cookies with Fred's face on them and serves a special lunch for the neighbors who, one by one, say goodbye to Fred.

After everyone leaves, Nanny, Larry, and I sit with Fred, who is panting hard now. Near dusk he has a seizure, fighting for each breath, his tongue hanging out. I whisper how much I love him, but I'm struggling to stay present, to not slip into blank numbness, fearful that if I can't stay in this moment, Fred will feel like I abandoned him.

"It's time," Nanny says tearfully.

"Yes, call the vet."

In tears, Nanny calls her vet and he sends over a lovely young woman with waist-length golden hair and soft blue eyes. Gently, she whispers to Fred. Nanny dims the lights and turns on Fred's favorite music. Nanny covers Fred with his favorite blanket—the one with boats on it—and rocks him in her arms, whispering to him, loving him, Larry on the other side murmuring, "Good boy. Good boy. Daddy loves you."

"Fred, I love you," I say. "I'll see you in my dreams, always." I kiss his heart.

Barney sits nearby, somewhat removed as if respecting Fred's privacy, his large, worried eyes full of grief. After the vet gently injects Fred's leg, he quickly slumps in Nanny's arms, his stuffed bee next to him, a smile on his face.

Barney sniffs all over Fred's body, and then, as if acknowledging Fred is dead, he goes to his bed in the back room, his head down.

While we sob in each other's arms, the vet removes Fred's body from the house. Nanny and I sleep in each other's arms, while Larry sleeps next to Fred's bed.

I stroke Nanny's hair, inhaling her still-baby-like smell. She whimpers like a baby, her small sounds of grief coming from somewhere within her that is so deep, so full of pain. Clutching Fred's stuffed bee, she curls in a fetal position. "So sorry, Nanny. So sorry," I whisper, feeling helpless.

"Fred was my child, Mom."

"I know. He was my grandchild. I know," I repeat.

She sleeps then. I slip into sleep, and dream that Fred and I are in the most beautiful garden of roses blooming like blown up stars. Sunlight warms Fred's satin fur, and my arms are full of roses. Nanny holds Fred's special container of bottled water with one ice cube, and his special treat cookies. He's romping in the sunlight, Barney following. I place a yellow rose inside Fred's collar. We run with Nanny and Barney towards the ocean....

The next morning, before I leave, Nanny sits in the garden where Fred played, pale and in deep grief. Larry is upstairs in his office, too sad to talk.

Fred's toys are scattered about the garden, and his favorite blanket is still spread on the lawn where he always sat in the sunspots to watch butterflies float in the air. "You must be in grief like I can't imagine," I say tentatively. "...I feel pain...I want you to know how much I loved Fred. And love you. I'm sorry that I seem so...remote. Feelings are hard for me. I'm so sorry."

A piece of sunlight lights her pale face.

"Mom, I know you love me and loved Fred. Fred loved you too. I want to give you something to show our love."

I unwrap the blue tissue from Fred's favorite stuffed animal, the bee. I hold it close to my heart. "...This will always remind me what true love feels like. Thank you, Nanny."

In the subsequent days, though I feel deep grief, I feel Fred's presence, like you do when you feel loved by a being you can't see. I resume my work, but stop often to hold his bee, remembering what his love felt like. My dreams are full of Fred.

Tonight, his bee on my pillow, I dream I'm walking along the flat brown road and hurrying to the rainbow bridge, holding Fred's stuffed bumblebee. I hear Fred's bark; it has a special sound, a light happy sound, so I walk faster, through the rainbow. My skin is pink and blue and yellow and red and there on a lovely wooden bridge is Fred and he's wearing his red collar with the golden heart engraved with his name. As I hold him close, I feel his heart beating through mine and he's wagging his tail. Other dogs romp around him, and in the distance there's the most beautiful field of grass and he leaves me and happily romps on towards it.

21

The rains stop and the air smells of damp sunlight and the nights are cold. Change is subtle, and sneaks up on you. I can tell there's change not just by new events and interests but inside I'm feeling less disconnected. When you work hard at facing your past, there are reprieves, sudden feelings of lightness, of something new.

While waiting for Oliver to finish the draft, I concentrate on the blog, working from early in the morning into the late afternoon when I go for my walk.

I walk to the Marina Greens, along the edge of the ocean. A mist of pink fog hovers over the Golden Gate Bridge and a lovely, cool breeze floats over the water blowing the top of the waves like bands of white lace. For a while in amazement I observe the seagulls clustered like bouquets along the edge, eating bits of bread people drop for the birds, thinking how utterly elegant nature is, and fragile life is. At any moment change occurs. Lost in my thoughts I sit on the bench and remember shortly before Ricky died, we'd sat on this very bench, and how much he enjoyed feeding the seagulls. On the way home, I admire the flowers in bloom. I carry a small scissors in my pocket and when no one is looking, I cut three ice pink roses. At home I arrange the roses into the small glass vase I bought at the flea market and hand-painted with flowers.

Then, Oliver emails the finished script. Eagerly, I print it out, and sit by the window, the script on my lap. At first I'm scared to read, scared that it will be awful, or that he changed my characters and voice. But once I start reading, I'm in awe of his beautifully clear prose, compressed lines, imagery, and how he reveals Dianne's inner struggle to really feel her feelings and find her whole and true identity. Dianne is authentic. Down to her unconventional style, the gardenia she always wears in her wavy hair, her platform ankle-strap shoes, he captured Dianne's funkiness and vulnerability. It's as if he studied me, how he integrates Dianne's clunky walk, her self-conscious gestures and habits, her dramatic way of talking, and strange elusiveness.

But he changed my ending. In my novel, twenty years later, when Dianne discovers why Charley had married her and that he had set her up to fulfill his own needs, she uses the gun and she kills him. In Oliver's ending, Dianne finds her identity as a painter and writer and walks blissfully into her future.

I drop the script on the floor and watch the stars fade in the dark and then I call Oliver. He doesn't answer the phone so I text him and write that I love the script, but that I'm not happy with the ending. Immediately, he texts back to come to his loft the next day at four p.m. "*We'll talk about it,*" he writes.

After a while, I get up and close the window, the impatient roar of traffic fading. No stars or moon tonight, only wet, blank darkness. I watch the moon until it fades and I go to bed.

The next afternoon, the loft full of late afternoon shadows, Oliver and I discuss the script and I'm telling him why I think that Dianne needs to kill Charley. Oliver disagrees vehemently, and as he expresses passionately why his ending is better, his voice rises. At the other end of the loft, Rain and Joe and two new interns—young handsome boys who answer phones—scout locations, perform various tasks, and talk quietly.

Between our debates about the ending, Oliver smokes a thin brown cigarette, exhaling agitated puffs of smoke while I continue to explain why my ending works and why Dianne must kill Charley in the end. Oliver listens moodily. And am I imagining that he and Rain are exchanging intimate looks? Or that last night when I'd called him, was Rain the reason he didn't answer the phone?

Oliver continues. "...The audience *understands* Dianne's rage, and wants her to rise above it, to transcend. So that the audience will root for her. I do not like the ending you insist on."

"Dianne needs redemption, Oliver. Don't you see that?"

"Not killing Charley *is* Dianne's redemption," he says softly.

Oliver sits very still, his emotional eyes burning into mine. "Dianne defies all odds, Bette. She rises in a generation where it was hard for women to have a voice, to be anything but a wife. But Dianne pursues her art and is successful." He pauses, looking at me incredulously. "Why would Dianne throw all that away?"

"For justice," I reply.

He smiles, knowingly. "There is no justice. If she kills Charley, she's lost all stakes. Also, it isn't in her character to kill."

"You never know what's inside a person," I say.

"I know what's inside you," he says.

"That makes me nervous."

"I know." He stares intently at my face. I turn away.

He changes the subject to the list of locations he's shooting with Joe. He wants to finish the film before his money runs out. He plans on shooting the Hawaii scene at the Royal Hawaiian Hotel. "You'll have your own room. All expenses will be paid."

"I'll be there. Is everyone going?" I ask, trying to sound casual.

He nods impatiently, and then he continues to explain his plans for the film. He's auditioning actors and has hired the actor who will play Dianne. "She has the emotional range to play Dianne young, and older. She's never made a film, but she's been on the New York stage."

"It's late," I say, standing. I call a taxi.

"I'll walk you outside," he says, taking my hand.

The air is cold and a few stars blink in the sky. We stand huddled on the dark street, waiting for my taxi. I say, "I love the script, Oliver. I smell rain. Do you? I love the rain, it makes me feel...inside."

He kisses me on the lips and it's one full of tenderness. I tighten my arms around his neck and press my body close to his and we stay like this until the taxi appears.

I pull away and hurry into the car.

Inside my dream I kiss Oliver again and again and when he moves away I feel anxious and I try to cry out not to leave but I can't move my mouth and I'm crying because I can't reach him and he's fading away like a funnel of dark smoke.

* * *

"But I wonder if he was kissing me, or Dianne. When he talks about Dianne he sounds...dreamy. In love. As if he's falling in love with her. Almost faraway."

Dr. T. waits.

"He knows Dianne. I almost feel jealous of her. Does he know me as well? Yet I feel...an intimacy with him I've never felt."

"Sounds like he knows your work, and that he wants to make a great film."

"He hates the gun. He wants the film to end with Dianne on her way to the light. I like that she blows Charley's head off. She made him accountable."

"Did you ever think about killing Charley?" Dr. T. asks after another long silence.

I hesitate. I shrug. "In my dreams I kill him. It feels good."

He looks reflective, and then gestures to the empty chair next me. "Imagine Charley is sitting in that chair next to you. What will you say to him?"

"I'd say I want your apology."

Silence. It's the end of my session. I can always feel it. He blinks twice, sighs, and sits forward. He says with a sympathetic smile, "Bette, rage is an authentic emotion. It's what you do with it."

It's late and night falls into my living room. My pink light is on and the television is on mute. My therapy session upset me. Did Dr. T. really think I'd kill Charley? Doesn't he know that women like me, ex-Jewish Princesses, don't kill people? Besides, my rage is safe in my fiction, and in my dreams. Doesn't Dr. T. know this?

But rage is unpredictable.

I've been thinking about my therapy session, about Oliver's insistence on a different ending.

In my closet, on a stepladder, I remove a square wooden box from the top shelf. My arms tingling, I open the box. It's so strange to look at something you've done, something so forbidden in your daily life. As I stare at the small black gun, I remember the day in court. Charley had won the annulment based on his claims of fraud, and he'd done it publicly with reporters recording his testimony; he claimed that he couldn't consummate our marriage because I was mentally ill and sexually frigid. I'd gone straight to the gun shop and bought this gun.

I hold the gun, my hand trembling, feeling removed from my surroundings, like seeing someone you know and pretending not to, assuring myself that I'd never use it, just wanted to know what it felt like to hold it. And then I place the gun into the box.

I have trouble sleeping. Finally, I slip into a dream. I'm twelve. I play Chopin's Minute Waltz. I hunch nervously over the piano, playing the notes carefully, or my teacher Mr. Rodetsky will slap my fingers with a thick yellow ruler. I play Chopin's Minute Waltz again, nodding with each beat. Mother shouts nearby, "You made a mistake! Play it again!"

I turn the knob on the tall black door. I wish the door would open and let me see my secrets.

A huge bird with wings like trees and a thin, yellow beak like a knife slams toward me and I'm trying to run but my legs won't move and I know the bird is going to....

* * *

Almost daily, Oliver and I study the rushes and, in detail, we discuss specific scenes that work or don't work, debating lighting, dialogue, and characterizations. A perfectionist, Oliver works tirelessly. As if choreographing a dance, he strives for a seamless surface and a complicated interior. Gently, he teaches me craft issues and this awakens and inspires my own creativity and spontaneity. "I love the chaos in your work," he says. "A scramble of imagery lurking in your subconscious. It is what interests me about you, and about Dianne. Untold secrets."

"But don't you think we're different?" I ask, increasingly jealous of his love for Dianne.

"No. I think you're the same. But she's willing to reveal more." He smiles indulgently, as a patient parent smiles at a too questioning child.

I continue to ponder this, wonder what he's really seeing, thinking, if he knows that I'm attracted to him. All along, I'm in awe of his talent, how he compresses dialogue—asks, what does it say? Is it necessary? Why? When he lashes out at Joe, or an intern, because of a mistake, he reveals a volatile temper, but after he cools down, he's apologetic and tender. For Oliver it's all about the work. Nothing else. He is his work, and I admire this about him and understand it and feel that somehow we connect to our secret selves and that we communicate through our collaboration.

Is it fantasy? Am I imagining that he's attracted to me too? Since the kiss, I'm flirtatious, but he's been...distant. Or it is that he's so much younger? But in his world he doesn't think about age or gender or differentiation. He's a creature of beauty and men, women, and all who are different are drawn to him. At his loft, there are always beautiful young girls who are dancers or actors, and young beautiful men who want to be filmmakers and who want to work for him. His very aura is intoxicating, and when you meet him you know that he's a star. His beauty is a sexual magnet to men and women, and he exudes sexuality and joy and passion.

Does he prefer men? Or both women and men? Truly gifted people are always bisexual or gay. With Oliver it doesn't matter to me what his sexual preferences are—all I know is that he's the most intriguing, gorgeous, gifted man I've ever met, and I'm falling in love with him.

Sometimes he's moody, and retreats. "Bette, I need time alone, to think about my work." He disappears for days. Other times he's genteel, courtly, and brings sensitive, thoughtful gifts—a shell we'd found on the beach during one of our walks, a first edition of Plath poems that he found at City Lights Bookstore, or a marvelous silk scarf that he found in a special shop. He loves to dress, loves fashion, and introduces me to new colors and fabrics. "You have your own style, Bette. I love that nothing ever matches, is always a little askew." Often, we roam about Chinatown's narrow streets, lunch on pork buns at a tiny restaurant above a laundry, or sit outside at North Beach Café where we eat raviolis and French bread. He makes me feel, know more about myself, my own desires, flaws, and needs. "Your soul contains reference, life is your canvas. Use it," he always says. Everything about him is art—the way he cooks and arranges food, and flowers. Even his sudden outbursts if something isn't the way he wants it isn't about temperament, but about his reach for artistic perfection. He's real. He's perfectly imperfect. But then as we spend more time together I find myself jealous of his attentions to his friends, to other things. I try very hard not to fantasize, like I would with other men, that we're a couple, and to construct seduction plots. This time it's different. I'm different.

As if my dream for fame and fortune and a network deal had dissipated, when Edwina calls, relating that every network is "salivating" for *The Viagra Diaries,* I feel as though that saga is in another time zone. "Honeybun, this time the project will make it big. Big," she repeats.

"Edwina, I'm immersed in the film. Unless someone offers something creative I don't care."

"Well care! Your Jewish Princess novel is outdated. *The Viagra Diaries* is going to be big. Big!" she repeats.

It's a dark day with silence in the trees. Oliver and I are at Tosca Café in North Beach, drinking coffee. Once again, we begin debating Dianne's redemption.

"I'm not sure I believe in redemption," I say. "Art doesn't always depend on redemption and sometimes redemption isn't possible."

Oliver pauses. "Through writing, Dianne begins to rise to consciousness. She's so brave, so artistically gifted...lovely..." His voice drifts.

"Brave? Why do you think she's brave?" I ask.

"Because she's willing to be vulnerable. To take risk."

"I feel you love Dianne and not me," I say, watching his face for a reaction.

He blinks as if thinking, the most tender expression on his gorgeous face. "...When we're working together, I make love to you. Our love is pure, without scars. Without expectations, and recriminations." He pauses. "In Swan Lake, Siegfried's fatal flaw is that he expects sexual and romantic love in one person, and it's disastrous."

"So you can only love me when you're working?" I persist.

"Remember Bette. Dianne is you, and you're Dianne. The love I feel for you is something else. It's our own. Now let's work."

We resume working, both taking notes as we exchange insights about the script. Gently we lock fingers or exchange a hug or sudden insight. When sunlight fades, arm in arm, my mind still on what he'd said about love, we walk about North Beach, exploring the shops. A haze of fog lays over the park, and church bells mingle with the sounds of cable cars ringing and the bustle of tourists and crowds along the narrow cobblestone streets. Wearing his snakeskin boots and a black turtleneck, just by the way he walks, you know he's a star of something and people stare.

In a shop displaying Indian jewelry and fabrics, Oliver purchases a beautiful amber necklace. "I want you to have this," he says, placing it around my neck. "It's the color of your eyes." He kisses me tenderly on the lips.

"Thank you," I say, moved by this beautiful necklace. "...I'll treasure this necklace, forever."

Later at my apartment, night spreads, and lying on the sofa, I turn on the pink light, thinking about Oliver. He's so removed from the conventional ideas about love, yet he voraciously reads Byron, the romantics, poetry. Though he protests love, he's very romantic, leaving me little notes, giving me a special flower wrapped in tissue.

But what does he mean about love? If he loves Dianne, doesn't he love me? Or is he unable, like me, unable to love outside of his work? Then again, what does it matter?

"You love Oliver because he can't love you fully," Lisa suggests on FaceTime.

"But he does love me. But he can. I feel it."

"So it's sometimes?" she says.

"It's perfect. What I feel for him is perfect. I feel intimacy. Does it always have to be holding hands, a valentine's card, seeing each other every minute?"

"No, of course not. It sounds like for the first time you feel intimacy with yourself. Oliver is a creator and his main relationship is with himself. It sounds like for the first time you're not falling victim to some idea of romance and true love. This sounds promising. I'm happy for you Mom, but don't obsess, spoil it, create a disaster."

I dream one of my anxious dreams.

Hi ho, hi ho

Some enchanted evening.

I stuff Charley into a metal box and peek at him through a hole. I watch myself compose music. I see the notes clearly on a long sheet of coffee-stained paper and I hum the melody. I see clearly without my glasses. In my kitchen I'm at the typewriter, writing. Nanny, wearing long pigtails tied with colored glass balls, is swirling a pink florescent hula-hoop around her thick waist. Lisa is fifteen and ironing, her long hands smoothing the edge of her blouse, pressing the iron, steam making a halo around her delicate face. She is five-ten and bends over the ironing board, her plastic aqua eyeglasses sliding along her nose. Her hands are red from washing dishes.

I want to hug the girls but my legs won't move and no sound comes from my mouth as I try to tell them that I'm sorry. Sorry. Sorry. Sorry.

I awake to a thunderous sawing sound. It's six a.m. Groggily, I get up and open the window. Across the street several men wearing orange vests are cutting down my beloved tree. Branches lie on the sidewalk like broken limbs. As the men talk loudly, I feel the tree's pain. How dare we invade nature as if it can't feel? As if a live lobster can't feel boiling water? "Please stop! Stop!" I shout to the men.

The men look up, grin, and resume sawing. Oh, poor tree, poor lovely tree, cut because a wealthy neighbor had been complaining that the tree cut his view of the Bay.

22

"These fucking paparazzi will photograph their mother humping a rat," Marci Feldstein complains.

It's the day of the WC hearing, and I'm in LA at the courthouse. Lisa is inside the hearing room with Edwina Miller, and Marci Feldstein and I stand in the hallway. It's muggy, at least ninety-one degrees—typical LA weather—and it's hard to breathe. My hair is frizzing up, and my new H&M gray linen pantsuit is wrinkled. A huge white silk flower is pinned to my lapel, and it scratches my chin.

Indifferent to fashion, Marci wears a purple jogging jacket, matching baggy pants, and flip-flop rubber sandals. She carries a flat, worn, brown leather briefcase. She's huge in figure, with thin hair that sticks out in every direction, her glasses so thick they have circles in them, and yet she has a glamorous presence and confident aura. One that comes with achievements, devotion to work, and power. Known as the most celebrated lawyer of the stars, paparazzi cluster in front of the courthouse and in the hallway, photographing her, and two reporters are asking if Bitterman is going to be charged on fraud. Like waving aside bothersome flies, she waves her thick, ringed hands at them, shouting, "Go! Go boys! Get a life! No one famous here. Bette Roseman is a poor author victimized by the network fuckheads."

"Now Bette," she says, her face close to mine. "When you're on the stand, WC's piece-of-shit lawyer Aristotle Sussman will try to scare you. Just answer yes or no, no fancy explanations. I'm proving that Bitterman ignored the contract and lied to you about the avatar. So don't open the trap!"

"Sure."

"Get it?"

"Yes. I promise."

"Judge Judith Gross is for women. Thank God we've got her today."

She stares at me like a parent stares at a lying child. "You people have to learn. You don't listen. Time is money. Let's go."

Inside, the room is small and airless. Edwina, Amen, and Lisa sit in the front row. I sit between Lisa and Marci. Yesterday, her assistant, Joshua Bitterman, and his lawyer sit on the other side. Huge ceiling fans spin hot air around the room.

After we pledge allegiance to the American flag, this six-foot tall fifty-something judge with a stern, tiny face and huge hair piled on top of her head, wearing humongous blue robes, sits at a desk perched on a high platform. Like a priestess overlooking her disciples, she looks out at the courtroom. Then she starts this lecture about fairness in her courtroom—that she's tired of male network executives fucking over women. She minces no words.

After each lawyer presents his or her case, I'm called to the stand. Lisa squeezes my hand. "Break a leg, Mom, but not literally."

Carefully, I walk up the narrow wooden steps, my high heel tap shoes making clicking sounds. Sweating bullets, I take a seat next to the judge's desk. I cross my legs, glad I'm wearing a pant-suit. The fan blows my flyaway hair into my eyes. I brush it away, my silver bangles clanking up my arm.

Aristotle Sussman, this unctuous, worm-like man with puffy hair and a spray-tanned face, starts the questions. I'm sitting really straight so I don't hunch. At first, the lawyer speaks so softly I lean forward, but then as his voice rises, I keep my mouth near the small microphone, but my breathing makes squeaking sounds.

"Did you not know about the avatar in question?" He presses his full, red lips.

"I *never* authorized the avatar."

"Yes or no!" he shouts so loud I jump.

"Well, yes, I knew about it..."

"So they told you about the avatar?" He smiles.

"Yes. But after they changed my character..."

"Yes or no!" he screams.

"Yes." My voice echoes.

"Yes what? That you knew about the avatar? Didn't they read the script to you at a Skype table read?"

"But that was after they'd promised not to change my protagonist..."

"Yes, or no."

"Yes."

He continues to shout, "Not only did you know about the avatar, but you authorized it?"

"No. That's a lie."

"I object!" shouts Marci in her big voice. "He is abusing the witness."

"Objection granted." The judge smiles at me.

"That will be all," says Aristotle Sussman, a smirk on his face. Yesterday is whispering to her assistant Ava who wears a pink knit pussy cap.

Marci gives the judge a copy of our contract. In her smart, strong voice, Marci summarizes that WC never discussed the script with me, or invited me to see the changes. What WC had agreed to in the contract, she explains, is that my protagonist, an age activist, would remain sixty-five. "They changed Anny into a thirty-two-year-old avatar." Then Marci cross-examines me.

"Is it true, Bette, that WC agreed to keep your protagonist's age?"

"Yes."

"In fact, outside of one Skype table read, they never invited you to see the final script?"

"Yes."

"They never told you about the avatar before you saw it at the table read?"

"No. They never did."

"Did you express in your first Skype meeting that you wanted Anny Applebaum, the sixty-five-year-old protagonist you worked years to create, to keep her age? And they agreed?"

"Yes, definitely."

"When you discovered that Anny became a thirty-two-year-old avatar, did you protest?"

"Yes. They promised to revise."

"Did they?"

"No."

"WC promised and announced a September air date?"

"Yes."

"Tell the court what happened."

"Two days before I was to leave for New York to do a national promotion about the series and the book, WC pulled the show. I had to find out by reading about it. I lost book sales, TV bookings, and book signings. The book became a joke."

"So they held up your project for a year, promised you a show and a lot of money, but ruined your book and then pulled the show. Left you holding the bag."

"Yes. They chose *Virgin Aliens*, a teen show."

Laughter.

"You may step down."

Marci cross-examines Joshua Bitterman, dressed like he's getting an Academy Award, in this black suit, pink shirt, and pink tie. He's so spray-tanned, he's orange. As Marci throws questions at him, he becomes defensive and nasty. He blames me. "Bette Roseman knew all of this. She even said the avatar was a wonderful idea. I have an email to prove it."

Yesterday is mouthing kisses to Bitterman. I recall sending an email to Bitterman shortly after meeting, consumed by my please disease, telling him how excited I was to be working with him. Finally, after extensive questioning, Marci asks in an impatient, ruthless voice, "Did you or did you not change Bette Roseman's protagonist from a sixty-five-year-old writer into a thirty-two-year-old avatar?"

"Bette writes trash about us."

"Why did you pull the show if you loved it so much?"

"We haven't pulled it. It's put aside for our next season."

"Bette is not only left with an avatar, but no paychecks. I rest my case, your honor. I would like expectation damages for the author. A seventy-year-old woman, she may not have long in this world."

The judge orders that WC has to give up the rights and pay the hefty legal fees, a fine of twenty thousand dollars to Bette Roseman.

Edwina and Lisa cheer, along with other writers in the courtroom. The judge reads a lengthy speech citing copyright cases and examples of networks stealing and breaching contracts.

Outside, Marci and I hug. Everyone is crowded around her, cameras clicking. I'm trying to smile, gushing how great I feel, but wanting to go home and get back to my routine of writing all day.

"So next time, don't call me," Marci quips. "You people have to learn to read, listen, speak up."

"Sure. Get it." I laugh.

She grimaces. "So don't call me. I'll call you when I want you to pay up. Good luck." I watch her walk away, and Edwina appears. She fans herself with a folded newspaper. She rants that now I'll be free and that the court publicity will only do good, and that her phone is ringing wild.

"I have a call in to Satan Bernstein, honeybun," Edwina says. She wears a wide- brimmed straw hat with a black ribbon dangling down her slim back.

"Well, I'll...see."

"See? See what? That we're going to make a fortune? We're good to go! He's salivating for *The Viagra Diaries*. Josie Greenblatt, she's the most powerful packager in town, is also salivating for *The Viagra Diaries.* As is Richard Greenberg at Netflix." She air kisses my face twice on each cheek, and hurries to her car.

"It's time to get to the airport, Mom." I follow Lisa to her car.

On the way, her Smart car bouncing, between talking on conference call with her patients, Lisa lectures that I need to speak up, to take charge from now on to make sure this doesn't happen again. She tells me that because of my over-dominating mother, I'm terrified of authority figures. She has sick patients, she rants, a lost cat, a busy life, and she doesn't have time to call my agents, sell my books, and advise me about the industry anymore.

"Sure. I get it."

"Get what?" she shrieks. "You get into these messes. I had to close my office today. I have a domestic violence workshop to lead today and I can't go through this anymore."

"Well, I appreciate..."

"Stop appreciating. Do what you really want. Maybe it's the film and forgetting about your other projects. Decide, or the party will be over and you won't have the success you deserve. Shit! The traffic is a nightmare!" she shouts, crossing into another lane.

"I'm leaving for Hawaii in a few weeks," I say. "Oliver is shooting the honeymoon scene there."

"Wow, that's great. Sounds like you like him a lot?"

"I admire him. Besides, he's much younger."

"Don't make that an issue. Sounds like he hasn't. You need to enjoy it. You also need empathy for yourself. Do you understand?"

She stops her car at LAX in the no parking zone. She gets out, and on the curb we hug tight. "I love you," I say.

"I love you too, Mom," she says tearfully. "Remember, the case is over now and you have a new beginning and a new journey. Believe in yourself. I love you, Mom."

I hurry into the airport, my backpack bumping against my back, thinking about what Lisa said, and I assure myself that it's time to exhume the past, to face the future and a new path of dreams.

* * *

When I'm not working on the film, I finally finish turning the blog into a book. I send it to Biggie, hoping for a sale so I can have some money. But my mind is on Oliver and the film, and my past projects seem as though they were only necessary steps to be where I am.

Day and night, Oliver is in the editing room. As if choreographing a dance, seamlessly, he makes cuts, splices, and moves time. Besides his execution of story, it's his artistry that makes this more than a film. It makes an experience...he takes the viewer into the characters—as if he inhabits them. He is his art. There's a nobility about him that comes through his art.

Often after these editing sessions, Oliver and I have quiet dinners out, discussing the film, going over a scene or the imagery. The more I'm with him, the deeper in love I fall.

"You love him because he can't love you fully," Lisa says on the phone.

"But he does love me. I feel it."

"Joe? Other men? Does he love them too?"

"I'm not sure he has other men."

"You are and your instincts are always right."

"Does love always have to be sixty years together? Marriage? There are different ways to love."

"I agree, Mom. I just don't want you hurt."

As Hawaii draws near, I brace myself for the honeymoon scene when Charley tells Dianne that he's made a mistake and must take her home. This scene arouses my rage at Charley and once again, I think about confronting him.

"It's time to make him accountable."

"You already have," Dr. T. says.

"How?" I reply.

"Your book."

"It's not enough. He never apologized to my parents. For my father, I want to confront him and ask for an apology."

He warns, "It's dangerous. Right now you have so much going for you. Don't spoil it."

"I want an apology," I insist. "Then I'll feel closure."

"Send him the book then. Don't waste your time."

Late at night, I lie on the couch, facing the moonlight.

I wonder if Dr. T. is right. Is confronting Charley really dangerous? As the night draws near, I'm lost in my subconscious, remembering, watching images appear. A siren passes outside and its anxious sound invades the dusty quiet of my apartment. Tired now, I get into bed, carefully place my eyeglasses on the nightstand, and settle under the covers.

I listen to the wind tap the windowpanes, a sad wind, like my father's sighs.

I slip into sleep and into a dream where the sunlight is so bright, the bay shines like mirrors. I am twelve years old. Mother and I have lunch at Fisherman's wharf. She is happy because I'm on the honor roll. I like seeing her happy. I rarely see her happy. Mostly, she sleeps, or cleans, or yells at Rick. I eat the fresh crab salad quickly, because I want to swallow the happiness. I don't want it to go away.

After lunch, she holds my hand and we walk along the pier, looking at the tied-up fishing boats. I read the names on the boats and imagine the families who own them. We watch a fisherman hold live crabs like an obstetrician holds a newborn baby upside down, and then we watch as he drops the crabs in a tall vat of boiling water. Do the crabs hurt? I hear hissing. I think the crabs cry. I think they feel pain. I cry. Mother impatiently says, "Bette, don't be so emotional."

We pass a store and in the window are beautiful seashells. I stare at a lovely pink shell in the window. Mother goes into the store and emerges with a gift wrapped in tissue paper. "For you," she says with a rare smile. I unwrap the tissue paper and hold the pink shell to my heart, and then to my ear. "You can hear the ocean in it," I say, feeling joyful. "I love you," I say, flushing from embarrassment. She flushes too.

23

Today, Oliver is filming the wedding scene.

I arrive at the Fairmont Hotel, where Charley and I were married in 1960. As I walk through the lobby, I'm remembering the hours before the lavish wedding Mother had planned in three weeks. Mother rented a room upstairs where I'd dressed. Her hairdresser Ning Ning backcombed my hair into a wide bouffant, and then carefully attached my grandmother's lace wedding veil over my face, the long train curling behind me.

I enter the Gold Room, where Charley and I were married. Joe, Rain, and several cameramen, stylists, and makeup artists huddle about the large, mirrored room. Outside, cable cars chug up Powell Street and the same crystal chandeliers hang like jewelry.

Oliver introduces me to the young actor who is playing Dianne. Jane Rose is my height, with thick, wavy dark hair arranged in a 1960-style bouffant, her eyes shadowed in blue. An Audrey Hepburn-style ivory taffeta wedding dress accentuates her slim figure.

"Bette, I have inhabited Dianne."

"Oh, I'm sorry," I quip.

She takes her place next to the actor playing Dianne's father.

The actor playing Charley is tall and slim like Charley was, with a shiny puff of pompadour-style black hair. Known for his work at Broadway Theater, the actor's demeanor and overly styled chic captures Charley's shallow arrogance.

Feeling slightly shaky, I sit on a red canvas chair next to several men and women clutching clipboards, some talking in low voices on their cell phones. This is truly a spec film—one made with little money—and yet the set perfectly reveals the sixties. Every image, the clothes, makeup, every detail exactly as described in the novel.

About a hundred extras wearing sixties-style clothes portraying wedding guests sit on small, gold-gilded chairs. Charley takes his place underneath a Chuppa made of white gardenias and roses. I hold my breath.

"Action!" the director calls. The room diminishes to a quick silence.

The "Wedding March" begins. Dianne, a lace veil over her translucent, innocent face, and her father, Lou Roseman, slowly walk arm-in-arm along a white runner.

The music stops, and after the father lifts Dianne's veil and kisses her on the cheek, Dianne stands under the Chuppa next to Charley. The Rabbi in black robes begins the ceremony. As Charley and Dianne repeat their vows to love till death do us part, the camera moves close-up on Charley's averted eyes, and Dianne's eager, young face.

"I now declare you man and wife!" the Rabbi shouts with glee.

After Charley and Dianne step on the wine glass and the Rabbi declares them man and wife, they kiss lightly on the lips.

The tall, ornate doors open to reveal the other half of the room, full of round tables set with ice carvings of swans, and seated guests. A twelve-piece orchestra plays the "Hawaiian Wedding Song" and couples slow dance. The camera is close-up on the bride and groom dancing stiffly, Dianne's train wrapped around her arm, and her eyes half-closed.

I close my eyes, remembering dancing with Charley to the "Hawaiian Wedding Song," dreaming of that night when I'd end my virginity.

I can't breathe.

I can't breathe. Oliver gave birth to my story and turned it into art. I feel like I'm feeling it for the first time.

I put my head down, taking deep breaths, until I'm aware that I'm in the present and not in 1960.

"Cut!" the director shouts.

After the shoot, Oliver and the team and I have dinner at Tony's Pizza in North Beach. Everyone is high on the film, laughing, talking, drinking, and eating. I'm trying not to notice that Rain and Oliver are talking to only each other, debating the difference between Balanchine's dance purity and Paul Taylor. She looks very beautiful, wearing an off-the-shoulder jade sweater and a tight black leotard. Jealous, and feeling emotional about the wedding night scene, I leave abruptly.

It is late. At home, I go right to bed. I close my eyes, listening to the dark, and wait for sleep. The wedding night scene upset me and my mind is alive with memories.

I slip into my dream.

I stuff Charley in a metal box and peek at him through a hole.

Three blind mice, I sing.

Three blind mice.

A piece of light shines on my father's thinning silver hair as he writes on a yellow legal pad with a long, gold pen.

Ricky bounces a huge orange rubber ball against the wall, and then throws it at the window and glass shatters. My bird Moonlight dies in her cage and Mother flushes her down the toilet and oh wake up please don't let her find me behind the tin-thin door....

* * *

It's summer, when the fog is pink and the roses open like umbrellas. The film is almost completed. Only a few scenes are left to shoot. I don't want the film to end. I don't want him to end. At times it's painful working on the film, like I'm in my past and sometimes it's hard to transition into my present. There are many steps that lead to change and though painful, Charley led me to Oliver. Facing each episode of my past is helping me go deeper into myself. I believe in fate but one's fate is not usually seen, but felt. You have to follow it. So far, I haven't heard from Biggie Delano, or even Edwina, but I'm too consumed by the film and Oliver to care. It all feels so glib, so long ago.

Today, I'm going with Oliver to film the happy valley scene. Oliver got permission to film the same suburban house from the book, the house that I'd lived in when I was married to the girls' father.

When we arrive, Oliver and his team set up the cameras on the patio and lawns overlooking the rectangular pool with turquoise-color water. I sit in the back, remembering living in this beautiful home on the hill, unhappily married.

It's a warm day, and a low, hot sun drops sunlight along the long green lawn.

"Action!" Oliver calls.

I watch the actor playing Dianne and the actor playing her husband, a hulking, handsome man wearing a cowboy hat, lunch at a glass table in the garden. The husband pours wine into a large glass, while Dianne, wearing dark glasses and a yellow sundress, picks at her salad. Their two very young daughters play nearby. Sprinklers twisting and dropping sudden thuds of water on the grass powerfully capture the unhappy silence. The husband tells sick jokes, slurring his words and laughing before he finishes them, while the camera is close on Dianne's unhappy, taut face.

Time plays tricks. You think it's something long-gone but every moment, feeling, observation, and experience is stored in our memory bank. I watch Dianne's stoicism, how she ignores her little daughter who is clutching a rag doll, crying, "*Mommy, I fell," and I'm trembling from self-loathing and compassion for my child. I see how angry and detached I was.* I want to rewrite the past and start over. *But I can't get the time back only self-awareness.*

After the shoot, Oliver drops off the team and we decide to relax and enjoy the day and go to the aquarium in Golden Gate Park.

Inside the muggy aquarium, we wander through the corridors, gazing at the myriad of creatures that live in the sea. It's so magical and makes me wonder if maybe we're the creatures and they're looking at us the same way. For a long time in wonderment, holding hands, we gaze at the jellyfish, transparent creatures floating like glass mushrooms. "You can see their souls," I say.

"Let's have some tea," Oliver pulls me into the daylight.

At the Japanese Tea Garden, we sit at a table, next to a waterfall dropping into a small pond of large goldfish. The garden is set amongst azalea bushes, dwarfed trees, wisteria, and other magical blooms. Next to us is a small wooden bridge. A beautiful girl in Geisha clothing ceremoniously pours jasmine tea from a black iron pot into our hand-painted ceramic cups. We sip our tea and relax totally, observing a little gray squirrel holding and eating a large nut.

We discuss the film, how it's going to look, Oliver worrying if he's running out of money, about the distribution. I confide that I worry that women of today will not sympathize with a nineteen-year-old virgin. "No woman today is a virgin unless she's a religious fanatic."

"It's not about virginity or if Charley is gay," Oliver states firmly. "It's about Charley's brutal emotional violence and Dianne's subsequent struggle and rise against all adversity." Oliver pours more tea into my cup. He discusses the power of emotion, and how Dianne finds herself through art. "Emotion builds suspense and conflict and truth and she doesn't release it with a gun."

"Shouldn't the perpetrator of cruel exploitation be punished? Should he not get the death sentence?" I ask.

"His soul is in jeopardy," he replies softly. "He is empty. She writes about her pain and redeems herself through art. She doesn't need to punish."

He continues to talk about the value of probing deeper into one self, that making art is simply going deep into something you feel is important, and then extricating your emotions so that you can make it alive and felt. Everything about him is honest and real. He has total belief in himself—yet I feel something brooding, and he talks little about his past.

As the day turns to shadows, and the sound of foghorns blow through the trees, we sit quietly, each comfortable in our reflections. At this moment I know what feeling in love is. It's not a description or an idea or a fantasy, it's this deep connection, each secure in our own self, but our souls together. Even when I'm not with him, he's with me. As if I've internalized him. The little squirrel finishes eating his nut and scurries away, and holding hands, we leave and walk through the park.

* * *

"So is he gay?" Moo Moo demands.

"I don't know. Nor do I care."

"I heard he was gay."

"Why? Because he's an artist?"

"India Feldman said she heard he was—he goes both ways. She knows that he was with a guy for years."

"As I said, I don't care. I adore him."

She starts confiding then about the men she dates, rich men, men who donate to her causes, men who take her on Crystal Cruises. Her latest is a much younger ex-count who gives her jewelry. "But he likes kinky sex. He wanted me to pee on his face like he's a toilet. Another freak. These men either want to see your list of medications or your bank accounts or are perverts."

"I'm sorry, Moo Moo."

She sighs heavily. "You arty types never end up good with the men. Look at Myra. She has that Mohammed. He exposed himself at Peets. India saw him. She complained to the manager."

* * *

Oliver directs the wedding night scene at the San Francisco Airport Motel. A wedding bouquet of white roses lies on top of a plain wood dresser and a white chiffon nightgown is on the floor by the bed like a dropped handkerchief. You can hear the jets taking off from the airport and spasms of blue lights flash along the ceiling. "Blue Moon" plays from a radio on the small wooden nightstand. I sit in the back, next to Rain and several people working on the film.

The actors playing Charley and Dianne lie naked on the king-size bed, their bodies pale silhouettes in the dark. Cameramen hover above them.

"Action!" Oliver calls.

Dianne and Charley kiss, the camera close on Dianne's eager face. Her long arms are tight around Charley's neck, and slowly, as if holding back, Charley moves on top of Dianne, his long, slender body slightly suspended. Dianne whispers, "Do it now, Charley. Please Charley."

He stops. "Not tonight. I'm tired."

"I'll make it hard. I can, Charley."

He moves away. He lights a cigarette. His zippo lighter makes a snapping sound. Dianne's legs slowly slide down. Her arms are flat by her side. Smoke rings slowly rise to the ceiling and then dissolve. The music stops.

"Cut!"

The room is dead quiet. Then the team applauds. I feel dizzy and place my face in my hands, my body detached—whirling, whirling, whirling, disintegrating.

"Bette, are you all right?" Rain asks, concern on her beautiful face.

"I…feel dizzy, I…"

"Let me get you some orange juice. Don't move."

After I drink the juice, my shaking stops. *The power of emotion*, Oliver had said. Yes, he's right. He skillfully integrated Dianne's emotional shock into the scene. At last I feel what I had written in my Jewish Princess novel.

At home, near evening, I find the diary that years ago I'd asked Mother to write. I'd kept it hidden. I blow the dust off the cover and I open the black notebook with white dots on the cover. I read her flowery prose in her neat handwriting.

I lived in a grand house on Liberty Street, with tall gold bannisters and high molded ceilings. Every Sunday we had music salons and I played Shubert Songs and Mother sang. Afterwards Mother made pancakes with real whipped crème.

On Saturday afternoons I played the organ for silent films at the Castro Theater, I was paid two dollars and I would go to Nathan's Delicatessen and Nathan would open the big wooden vats full of dill pickles and I'd pick out the best one. He'd wrap it in waxed paper and give it to me.

Tears coming to my eyes, I continue to read pages of detailed and beautiful descriptions about her music salons, her beloved piano teacher, and how happy she'd been when she won a scholarship the Chopin Contest and a scholarship to Juilliard. *But Mother sewed costumes for the opera and we didn't have money for me to travel or buy clothes. So I went to Miss MacAteers Secretarial School and then I met Lou. He was very grand and a screenwriter for Universal.*

When she writes about my engagement to Charley, her writing has energy, an excitement. *Bette married a wealthy prominent man. The Socialite Gazette photographed Bette and published a story about Bette. Everyone in town was envious. It was a beautiful wedding. Lou mortgaged our house to pay for it. But on their three-week honeymoon in Hawaii, Bette became mentally ill for some unknown reason and Charley had to take her home and the marriage was annulled. Bette adjusted nicely.*

I close the notebook. Her word *adjusted* makes me sad. Her denial, defenses, deeply etched into her soul. That small incident with Charley in 1960 had destroyed Mother. Until she died, she suffered the humiliation and shame that I'd felt. Poor Mother. Not to know why and who you are is a true tragedy and always ends in broken dreams. It's time to forgive her and myself.

I call my cousin Linda, who finds my mother's address, where she'd grown up on Castro Street. The next day I plan to see where she lived, to finally face her truths.

The next day I'm on Castro Street. I love Castro Street—the rainbow flags and bookstores stuck between fetish, leather, and candle shops. Same-sex couples and gender free couples stroll hand-in-hand along the paved, glittery streets.

I stop in front of the majestic Castro Theater, admiring the gorgeous Art Deco structure where Mother played the organ on Saturday afternoons. I stare at the ornate golden doors and the huge marquee, imagining my mother on the enormous stage, playing the organ to accompany the silent films. I'd seen photographs of her when she was a teenager and she was beautiful, with waved gold-colored hair, and wearing pretty, flouncy dresses that my Grandmother made.

I cross the street, passing fading houses and following the directions I'd written on a slip of paper, looking for her house. A festivity exists in the air, and you can hear music pouring from the myriad of cafés and restaurants.

I stop in front of a narrow, peeling, wooden-planked house set between a laundry and a fetish store. The address coincides with the address I'd written on the paper.

I stare at the house, remembering Mother's lavish descriptions of *fine marble, music salons and gilded staircases.* My poor darling Mother. She was like the mother in a Jane Austen novel, wanting her daughter to marry a rich man and Charley was her Mr. Darcy. She always had a dream of wealth and social position, and no matter how she decorated her house into a palace or gave expensive dinner parties, she never achieved her dreams. But she made sure that I would have what she thought she didn't have. So when Charley, who she thought was a "catch," brought me home a day after my lavish wedding, her dream was destroyed and she never spoke to me about him again and died angry. For the first time in my life, I feel overwhelming sorrow and compassion for her. As I stand here gazing at her peeling house, I see clearly, and with deep regret and sorrow, the times I was mean to her, ignored her when she was ill, when she had birthdays, always hating her, blaming her. "I'm sorry, Mother," I whisper. But I'll never understand why she kept Ricky away from his sexuality and from the world.

I touch the front of the house as if touching her, thinking that no matter what, mothers and daughters, like trees, are rooted forever into the past and the future.

I walk up the flight of stairs and peek through the glass pane on the narrow front door. I look into a dark hallway, not like she'd described as *curved and regal.* When I hear a dog bark and the sound of footsteps, I hurry down the stairs, into the street.

I walk home, the sunlight spraying the streets and warm on my face. A new beginning, I think, hoping that my mother also has a new beginning. Maybe our lives are lessons and like school, and depending on what we learn, we go to the next journey.

* * *

It's my birthday, and Oliver takes me to see the San Francisco Ballet perform *Giselle.* He brought me two dozen white roses, and I wear one on the lapel of my grey silk cape.

We sit in orchestra seats, holding hands. Enthralled by Adolphe Adam's music and the beauty of the dancing, I hold my breath. When Giselle dies from a broken heart, I feel tears running down my face. Of all the art forms, ballet unites technique with music, and ignites the deepest emotions. Oliver is very still, and I know that he too is feeling what I'm feeling.

After the ballet, we dine at Oliver's favorite Russian Café. On the walls are photographs of Nureyev, Fonteyn, and local dancers. It is a small, dark room. A violinist plays Russian love songs. High on the evening, between discussing the ballet, we drink vodka shots, dining on potato puffs filled with caviar. Wearing a black velvet hip-length jacket tight at his waist and a blue silk turtleneck, Oliver looks like a romantic prince.

I say, "Often I watch videos of Fonteyn and Nureyev dancing *Giselle*. They seemed very much in love."

"Nureyev was in love with Eric Bruhn," Oliver says.

"But couldn't he be in love with Margo too?"

"They were in love when they danced."

"So they could only be in love when they danced?" I ask.

He nods. "Creative communication is the height of love. Nothing can compare."

"You mean you don't believe in romantic love?"

He smiles indulgently, and kisses my hand. "Bette, don't spoil the beauty between us. You always want something else."

"You mean love?"

"I mean we both want a lot from each other."

The evening is over. We are quiet on the way home in Oliver's car. I hold the bouquet of roses in my lap and think about what he'd said about love. When we're collaborating I feel heightened emotions, close, but loving. I don't want anything else in the world to intrude.

At my apartment, he stops the car. The motor is running.

"A nightcap? Brandy?" I ask.

"I'm exhausted," he says after a long pause.

"Is it..."

"It's not you, Bette," he says quickly. "We'll talk another time."

I get out of the car and I hurry into the building, running up the stairs.

* * *

"You need to get out more. You're a local celebrity," Moo Moo says on the phone.

"Hardly."

"Arnie Gutman is sixty-ish, a widower, a billionaire, and a writer. He just published a memoir. I gave him your number. Go out with him."

"I don't like blind dates."

"Well, like them. Or you'll end up folk dancing on visitor's date night at a senior home."

"I'm fine without a man."

"That's what they all say. Do me a favor and meet him."

An hour later, he calls. He has a German accent and a heavy voice. He sounds charming. I agree to meet him the next evening at Bubbles Club on Nob Hill, where there's ballroom dancing.

"But I don't ballroom dance," I protest.

"Just hold on to me, close your eyes, and spin."

I laugh. I agree to meet him the next night at the club.

"Bette? I'm Arnie Gutman."

He kisses my hand. He's so tall my neck hurts to look up. He has a huge puff of perfectly-styled silver hair flecked with dark spots. He's amazingly handsome and way older than Moo Moo said. Dressed in an obviously tailored jacket, he stands straight. At a table overlooking the dance floor, I drink a vodka shot and he drinks a sherry.

"Moo Moo said you're fifty something, and a famous author."

"Liar on both counts," I laugh. "I'm seventy, and not famous."

He smiles. "Anyway, you're beautiful."

"Moo Moo said you're sixty-ish."

"I'm eighty-one."

"You're a very handsome man."

He's really interesting, asks lots of questions and seems interested in everything. He's written a novel. He wants to tell me about it. As he talks story, I'm sure that Moo Moo told him I have Hollywood contacts and will help him. Plus, he's hard of hearing and I find myself shouting. Over the sounds of the orchestra, he continues to talk plot. The novel is about Nazi Germany during the holocaust and how he and his family escaped to Shanghai and then to the United States, where he fell in love with a nun. He pauses. "It would make a wonderful movie."

"Wow. Sounds...interesting. The nun bit. Of course she gave up the veil?"

"Well, you have to read to find out."

"Interesting," I repeat.

"I brought the book. It's in the car."

Just then the orchestra plays "Moon River" and Arnie leads me to the dance floor. We're slow waltzing. My glitter platform high heels are making clunking sounds on the wood floors and the black net flowers on the side of my hair are slipping. I'm leaning too far forward and my legs are cramping, but it's really fun.

Over dinner, he continues to talk about his writing process, how Oprah is reading his book and I'm wondering where Oliver is. We dance a few more dances, including a tango, and he's dipping me and holding me and he's really an excellent dancer.

While we sip our coffee, he continues to talk story but I don't mind because I love his dreams and the book actually sounds interesting. A buzzer rings out from Arnie's watch. "Whoops. Bedtime!" He stands.

Outside, we get into his Tesla. Hans, his driver, navigates the driverless car. Arnie insists that staying on top of technology is the fountain of youth.

Finally, after a scary drive up and down the hills, the car stops in front of my apartment building. Arnie gives me a paper bag. "My book," he says reverently. "Take your time reading, Bette. I'm sure the producers you know will fight over it. We'll talk about a cut for you."

I don't have the heart to warn him that it takes years. That most of them don't read unsolicited material, or if they do, they rarely read. But why spoil his dream?

Carrying the book, I hurry into my apartment.

The next afternoon, Moo Moo calls. I'm thanking her for introducing Arnie, and that I liked him and am going to read his book.

"He's dead."

"Dead? Who's dead?"

"Arnie. He's dead."

I'm stunned.

"His housekeeper found him sitting in his wing chair, still dressed in his evening clothes, his stereo blasting Viennese waltzes."

"Oh my God!" I say. "I can't believe it."

"Honey, after sixty, they drop like flies. My last guy took me to the movies and when the lights went on I thought he was sleeping, but he was dead. Dead as a doornail."

After the call, I sit by the window, staring at the clouds changing shapes. I recall Arnie's dream of having a movie made of his book, his wistful hope. His vulnerability. I'm glad he died with his dream intact. With each person we meet, you learn something. I'm glad I met Arnie. He taught me to never give up my dreams.

* * *

Nanny asks if I'll help her with the new book she's been writing about Fred and rescue dogs. Thrilled that she's reaching out, I agree, and promise to have lunch waiting. "What about your novel? I could send it to Biggie Delano."

"I told you, don't hock. Nothing is ever enough."

"Oh, I'm sorry," I say meekly.

"I'll be there tomorrow at noon.

At noon the next day, Nanny arrives, carrying her backpack and homemade banana breads carefully arranged inside Ziploc bags. "They're so delicious, Nanny. Thank you."

"Don't eat them all at once. You'll get sick."

"I promise."

She wears shorts, red high-tops, and a tank top, her jet-black hair flowing like satin. "I made tuna sandwiches. The way you like, the crust cut off."

She blinks. "You set the table, Mom. It looks nice. The yellow roses are so pretty. Thank you for going to so much trouble."

"I'm sorry it's a rarity. This is a great day for me having you here."

At my mother's antique drop leaf table, we eat tuna sandwiches and drink iced ginger tea. Nanny chats with a light in her eyes about her new puppy, Susie, rescued from the slaughter trucks in China. In detail she relates stories about Susie's new dog friends, her classes, her special foods and how much she loves her. She shows me pictures of Susie on her phone.

"She's adorable. I love her. Love her story," I say. "She's your child. My Grandchild."

"Mom, I have something…to tell you."

"Oh my God. Is…"

"Larry and I…are adopting a child."

"Oh my God. Oh, Nanny. I'm so happy, really happy for you."

She continues to tell me that they hope to adopt a Syrian refugee child from an orphanage in Amman, Jordan, and that these children are victims of horrors and consistent war and available for adoption. "It's a long pull, Mom. They have to have proof that the child is an orphan. We're waiting to hear from the adoption agent we're working with."

"Your child is waiting for you. I know it." I laugh. "Does Lisa know?"

"Of course. I tell Lisa everything. She wants to be Auntie."

"I always worried that you never wanted a child because I was such a horrible mother. I wish I could go back."

"Mom, you weren't horrible. Self-centered, yes, and you put our lunch sandwiches into the freezer and they'd thaw out in my lunch pail, but you were loving and fun and creative—I was always in awe of you. You taught me how to dream." She opens her laptop. "Let's get to work."

She designed the layout and it's beautiful. The stories of dog rescue are told from Fred's point of view. Each page is more beautiful than the next—the photographs and the stories Fred tells about his dog friends, about Nanny and Larry, and his view of the world. "You see, Mom," she says, turning the page. "It ends with Fred on the Rainbow Bridge."

"It's a wonderful book. So alive. As if Fred is talking."

She smiles. "...I liked your suggestion that Fred's point of view should be in first person. It's more immediate. It came alive."

"Yes, I think so. Nanny, I'm glad you're writing. I loved your novel, but you said you never want to publish it. So I was worried you didn't want to write another book..."

"Mom...I have something else to tell you." She bites her lip. Pauses. "I wasn't going to tell you but an agent in New York loves my novel."

"I'm...blown away. Not surprised, not surprised at all. Oh Nanny, I'm so proud. Proud of you. So proud," I repeat.

"All right. Enough already." She bites her lower lip, looking pleased. "When you get back from Hawaii, let's meet every week and work on this. I enjoyed it so much. I want you to help me get this book finished too." She looks at her watch. She has to get home. I hold her tight, sucking her cheek like I would when she was a child. "I love you. Love you so much. I'm thrilled for you."

"I love you more, Mom. You're my heart."

I watch her rush down the hallway, until she disappears into the street.

Near evening, I open the cardboard box labeled *Lou Roseman*. Several of my father's screenplays are in this box. After Mother died, I found this box in her basement. I touch the yellowed scripts, each bound with a faded blue paper cover and imprinted Universal Studios. I open a script he hoped would make the big screen. I read a beautifully written episodic story about a boy who quit school at fourteen to support his mother and sister and worked in a projection room of a movie theater in Los Angeles until at eighteen he was hired to work in the mail room at Universal—his tragedy and rise. I read until I finish.

I close my eyes, remembering when I showed him a short story I'd written and he'd carefully written tiny notes in the margins, explaining that I needed to develop the plot. I saved and framed the story with his notes and often look at it. It hangs above my desk.

24

In one week, I'm leaving for Hawaii. Oliver has been busy polishing the film and I haven't seen him very much. Wanting to say goodbye to Myra before I leave for Hawaii the following week, we're at Miller's Deli, having lunch. Excitedly, I talk about my future grandchild. Our talk then goes to the Age March I'm planning. "We have to fight ageism and celebrate age pride. Ageism is a disease," I say, biting into my chopped liver sandwich.

"Helen Epstein was blowing a forty-nine-year-old rock star and her hair extensions got caught in his zipper and came off. Poor thing is bald. He ran like hell." She pauses. "Don't look now."

I look up, squinting my eyes, and see the diamond dealer. He blinks like a child in a fearful moment, not knowing whether to leave or stay, but then the waiter leads him to the only empty table next to us.

"He saw you," Myra hisses.

"Don't look, Myra," I whisper. "But wouldn't you think he'd say hello?"

"Of course he's not going to say hello! You wrote about the tiny bumps on his penis, that he's cheap, farted in his sleep, and that he's a serial JDater. Bette, everyone in town knows that Marv Rothstein in *The Viagra Diaries* is Mel Braverman, the real diamond dealer."

So during lunch, Myra talking incessantly, I can feel Mel listening to our conversation, his back turned so he doesn't have to face us, while I'm remembering the last time we'd spoken to each other. I'd just finished writing *The Viagra Diaries* and when he lied again about being out of town and was instead on the singles sites, when he invited me over to his home I'd said I no longer cared to see him.

"He's leaving," Myra whispers, her hand covering her mouth.

I watch him exit quickly, leaving most of his BLT on the plate.

Several hours later, I sit in the evening dusk. I can't stop thinking about Mel. Something about his slight slump, over-styled hair, expensive, neatly ironed jeans make me sad. Early on in our relationship I discovered that after nights of wild sex, he'd take me home in the early hours of the morning, always feigning that he had work to do or could only sleep alone. An hour later, he'd be on the internet, on a singles site posting ads for younger women. From then on, I recorded copious notes about his lies, infidelities, internet posts, and then for the next two years, I wrote a novel about a narcissistic diamond dealer who could only love very rich, very thin women under thirty. When I was on national TV, I talked about the diamond dealer's betrayals, obsessive internet requests to meet women under thirty, and that I thought he and most men were undeveloped and mentally ill. Women from all over the world called in to the shows ranting that they too had a

Marv Rothstein in their lives and were sick of men getting away with age infidelity.

I see my pattern—even though I change the names, just as I've done with my blog selling out the networks and the industry, I question if I'm unconsciously using Oliver for a future novel.

The past is always with you. Every moment stays in your unconscious. Every day I write a memory, hoping that eventually, like a tapestry, I'll face the moments I buried, and then identify how each moment influenced the next. Then I can figure out my next journey and understand clearly and accept why I am the way I am and what I want.

I decide to apologize to Mel for hurting him in any way. I email: *I saw you today.* I *would love to have a drink with you? Call me, Bette.* I click send.

Immediately, he emails to meet him the next night at Harris Café. Six on the dot. That was the place we first met.

Exactly at six the next evening, I sit at a cocktail table in the back. I order a vodka shot, assuring myself that I'm doing the right thing. At a huge Steinway piano, a man with high silver hair plays a medley of Cole Porter songs. I look up, and he's striding towards me, and as he'd always been, he's elegantly dressed, wearing a dark suit and perfect knotted blue silk tie. His silver hair gleams.

"Hello," I say. "Thank you for coming."

"You look wonderful, Bette." He kisses me on each cheek. He orders bourbon and soda, and another round for me. When our drinks come we click the edge of our glasses and drink.

"Well, it's been a while," I say after a tense silence. "...When I saw you the other day I..."

"Why did you do it, Bette?"

"You knew I was a writer. You never acknowledged me beyond a sexual possession. After great sex you'd drop me off and be online posting ads to meet a woman not over thirty. You dismissed me. Hurt me."

"You wanted too much, Bette. You used me for a story. You wanted everything."

"I wanted respect. You treated me like I was some perversion. You hid me from your friends and never included me in anything. You made me feel like I was some odd bug you'd picked up."

"You were different," he says. "I never knew what to expect."

"Well, I guess we both felt used. If I hurt you, I apologize."

After a tense silence, he takes my hand. "Bette...I've thought about you, more than you know. I've missed you...terribly. I'm sorry too, if I hurt you." He pauses. "Let's have dinner."

During dinner, I lavish in his attentions, his old way of looking at me, touching my hand, whispering that he desires me. Losing myself in his attentions and desire, wanting to feel what it's like again, and drinking too much, I go with him back to his penthouse.

To go back in time is like going into a familiar nightmare—everything is the same: the spot on the Persian rug where his bulldog Harry had peed, the same unread books, designer magazines shrink-wrapped and displayed.

In his beige bedroom, we undress, and fall into his huge beige Tempur-Pedic king-size bed. Without foreplay, he plops on top of me and though the feel of his thin, fit body feels familiar, the soapy smell of his skin suddenly repulses me. Sucking my breasts like a hungry infant, he's whispering how much he missed the *girls*. "My *girls*," he repeats. "Coming...I'm coming," he shouts as to the sky. "Are you? Are you? Are you?"

Then it's quiet. Dead quiet. He's lying still, exhaling deep breaths as if he'd run a race and is coming back to consciousness.

Was this all? I think. What I'd considered sexy? What I'd felt so passionate about? Written about in *The Viagra Diaries*? I realize that my decision to sell him out in *The Viagra Diaries* was never because he had other women, or that I'd decided early on to use him for a story. It was that I made choices that were based on what, deep down, I thought I deserved, men who disapproved of me or didn't want to know I was. This is a man who has no emotional capacity to go deeper.

So why am I here? To recapture something that I'd wanted and never had? I feel displaced and I want to leave. Quickly, I get up and start dressing.

"What's wrong?" he asks, his voice thin in the dark.

"It's late. I have to go. I'm sorry."

"It was wonderful. Was it for you?"

"I have to go," I repeat. I get up and quickly dress.

He aims his jumbo-sized remote at the flat screen TV the length of a wall. The sudden noise of canned laughter invades the sticky silence.

"Take care," I say.

"Thank you for the great sex," he calls out. He turns up the sound on his giant plasma TV.

At home I sit in the dark, admiring the moon fading to pale yellow, thinking about the night and why I had been there. I had gone back into time, with some fantasy of love that I see in movies and had once dreamed about. Not that I don't admire the day-to-day fifty-years-together love, but deep down I always knew it didn't belong to me. You can't go back and change the story. This one tonight had already been told.

Sometimes revelations hurt. Even though knowing what I don't want is a relief, the death of a fantasy hurts. Until dawn I watch the dark transition into daylight, and then I sleep.

* * *

Oliver and I spend days and weeks going over scenes, Oliver polishing and re-polishing. We spend hours discussing an image, a scene, the look of the film that spans from 1960 to current times. Though he's attentive I notice that around me he's often distant, and often I see him with Rain or Joe.

Before we leave for Hawaii, Oliver decides to reshoot the deposition scene. He wants me to meet him at the shoot and make sure he has it right.

I arrive downtown, at the high-rise office building, and hurry into a fancy office with glass walls that overlook San Francisco. Exactly as I'd written it in the novel.

The actors, including the one who is playing the celebrity lawyer, are in their places. Oliver greets me with a hug, and we're happy to see each other.

I'm sitting in the back, watching Oliver, Joe, and the lighting technicians take their places.

"Action!" Oliver shouts.

Dianne, wearing dark glasses, sits at a table, her lawyer next to her, watching Charley whispering with his swank celebrity divorce lawyer. A court reporter at the end of the conference table types slowly, her face expressionless. The camera is close up on Charley's taut face as he draws doodles on a yellow legal notepad.

"Isn't it true that you refused intercourse?" Charley's lawyer screams. "That you made all this up to get Charley's fortune? Answer yes or no!"

Dressed in a dark navy suit, Dianne's pageboy hair is set perfectly. She answers in a prim, faint voice. "No sir."

"No, what?" the lawyer shouts. "That you wouldn't let him penetrate?"

"He's the one who wouldn't!"

"Yes, or no!" the lawyer shouts.

As I watch the actors rehearse this scene, I detest Dianne's meekness. But the scene is perfect, just as I'd written it, and the superb acting and dialogue set up Charley's betrayal. The scene is so real that I'm back there, and when the scene is over I feel drained and like my skin is on fire. Rage, I feel rage. He'd stolen my innocence, and I see clearly now that he planned it and knew that he was going to do this. I imagine his face when I surprise him with a gun.

"Are you all right?" Oliver stands before me.

"I'm...fine. It's a good scene, Oliver."

"You're crying, Bette."

"No, I'm fine. It's beautifully written—elegantly shot."

He kisses my forehead. "I'll be editing all night. I'll call before I leave for Hawaii and I'll see you there next week. I miss you, Bette."

When I leave, wanting to shake off the past, I decide to walk. As I admire the light shimmering over the city, I stop and watch a white bird with long ridged wings soar in and out of the clouds, confident about its destination. I love this bird, its beauty, solitude, and confidence. I hold out my hand wanting to touch it. It flies higher and higher, just missing the rooftops. But I can't stop thinking about the gun hidden in the wooden box on my closet shelf.

25

"So Satan Bernstein Productions is salivating for *The Viagra Diaries,"* Edwina says from her car phone. "Satan has a shitload of money. Now that WC released the rights, he can't wait to get it on air. He'll pay double."

"The Viagra Diaries is dead, done, and I no longer care to have my work ruined again." I hear Amen breathing on the extension.

"Satan wants to take a meeting," she says in her sweetest tone, as if she didn't hear me. "Can you be here tomorrow? The sooner the better, before the network sewer rats make a deal with Bitterman."

"Bitterman never paid me," I protest. "They're all scumbags."

"Honeybun," she sighs. "Satan Bernstein is a chance to make buck-a-rooneys. Go for it."

"I'm busy with my film and I'm leaving for Hawaii in a few days. Oliver is already in Hawaii shooting the last scene."

"No one cares about a wimpy virgin who gets stood up!" she shouts. "Your Jewish Princess novel didn't sell! And no one watches Oliver Abbot films except arty farty vegan freaks."

"Oliver has literary credibility," I say. "He's an artist, not a hack. He's made films on Margot Fonteyn and other artists."

She sniffs. "...Bette, I have to pay Lester alimony. I have IBS, I'm on Xanax and four anti-depressants a day!" She pauses. "... It's been so long since I've had a show on air. Even the Jewish pinhead boy executives in Armani don't take my calls. Don't let me down. Satan is willing to put six figures on the line. Straight to series."

"I want authenticity."

"Just hear what Satan has to say. Please, Bette. For me. I'll set up a Skype call for early tomorrow. You can get the drift."

I hesitate, reminding myself of all the years she's been trying to sell my books, the near misses, and her disappointments, that I owe her something. Then again, I'm broke and you never know, I remind myself. "Well, just a meeting. For you," I say.

"Amen! Pronto!" she screams. "Set up a Skype call for tomorrow! Honeybun, be ready. Amen's assistant India will let you know the time."

The next morning I'm on Skype. Satan Bernstein is a very thin man, about forty, with huge, over-styled puffy hair and dressed like a mafia don. In a smoker's gravelly voice he raves about *The Viagra Diaries,* while his team of assistants, no more than twenty-five, record his every word on their MacBooks.

"You're a fucking Goddess, Bettina! I'll make this series into an Emmy."

"Bette," I correct.

"Bette, Bettina, okay," Satan shrugs. "I'm bonded to your project."

"Bonded," the team repeats.

"Talk to me, Bette," he croons. "How do you see Anny Applebaum?"

"Not as a cartoon," I reply. "As a sixty-five-year-old authentic woman. A real person."

He snaps his fingers. "I got Damian Moon to write the series! He loves the title." The team high-five each other.

"I care more about the story than the title," I say. "Damian Moon writes about trolls and Nazis," I protest.

"He can write anything. He got Lindsay Lohan to commit to play Anny Applebaum."

"She's too young. No, I won't let you ruin my project like WC did. I want authentic."

"Fuck authentic! No one wants authentic!" he shouts unpleasantly. "We want a hit! Hey team, thoughts?" He snaps his fingers.

"Anny is transgender?" says Epic, with a tiny, valley girl voice. She has a stone-white face and dyed black hair.

"Bi is very…in?" says Jersey, this obese boy with a shaved head and white skin.

"So is Asperger syndrome," says Cedar, a tall girl with a giraffe-like neck.

"I don't like the name Anny Applebaum. I like the name Lucy Morgan," Epic says. "Anny Applebaum is too…"

"Ethnic?" Christmas finishes in a high tone, like she got the right answer.

"Lucy Morgan is a WASP name! Anny is Jewish," I say. "I don't want the name changed."

"Anny transitions to a man?" Faith is as thin as Gumby. She has very red lips.

"Great twist," they chime, all typing.

"Anny is a zombie?" Epic shouts like she won a prize "...*The Walking Dead* is..."

"Anny kills the zombie? Goes to prison?" interrupts Chance, a thin boy wearing a baseball cap.

"Enough!" I shout, holding up my hand. My face is pressed close to the computer screen. "Thank you, but this isn't working for me. I pass. Good luck."

Twenty minutes later, Edwina calls. "You blew it! Satan is insulted. I want you to apologize."

"He wanted to change everything! He's worse than Bitterman. Apologize for what?"

"He says you were rude and that you only want your characters and your story and that you don't know what you're doing. He doesn't like your book. He's trying to help you."

"If he doesn't like it why is he so hot on it?" I reply. "I'm sick of these divas."

"He has more money than God. He has three shows on air and everything he touches is gold. You fucked it up."

"Edwina, I'm sorry. But I don't care to work on mediocre scripts with imbeciles. I'm not interested in the money, I'm interested in making something artistic and memorable. If my Jewish Princess film is successful, I'll see that you make money on the back end too."

"Unfortunately, Jewish Princesses have no market. Call me when you return from Hawaii."

I awake at dawn. My plane leaves early for Hawaii and I can't wait. I put on my glasses. A butterfly dropped on my windowsill. It's beautiful, its wings like stained glass.

Barbara Rose Brooker

My orchid suddenly blooms tiny yellow petals. I love this time of day, when silence has a thousand whispers.

26

Late morning, I arrive in Hawaii. The air is balmy and smells like scented flowers. As the airport van drives up the winding road, the sun shining on the Royal Hawaiian Hotel pink and tiered like a wedding cake, hardly breathing, I'm remembering the day in June 1960, when Charley and I arrived at this very same hotel. On the plane after our disastrous wedding night, he hadn't spoken to me, but I'd assured myself that he was just tired, and that we'd have three glorious honeymoon weeks of sex and passion.

As I get out of the van, beautiful Hawaiian girls with waist-length hair like black satin drop white and yellow orchid leis around my neck.

Struck by the lobby, exactly as it was in 1960, I feel I'm back in time—the same emerald green plush carpets, wooden ceiling fans, lit wicker lamps, and velvet loveseats. French doors open to lush gardens, marble fountains spray streams of rainbow-colored water.

At the desk where I check in, the bellman informs me that Mr. Oliver Abbot had left a message to meet him at the Terrace Café at noon.

Upstairs, I freshen up. My pink floral wallpapered room faces the beach surrounding the expansive turquoise ocean. Doors open to the terrace, and the warm breeze smells of the ocean and the sun.

As I unpack a few things, I have a flashback of arriving in the wedding suite. Wearing a white linen suit, white high heel pumps, a white rose tucked into my huge bouffant styled hair, Charley had announced he had to meet a client. Assuring myself that he was busy, I unpacked, carefully hanging the dozens of pastel sundresses and dyed-to-match pumps, telling myself that everything was fine, ignoring that some tragedy had occurred.

Excited to see Oliver, I change from my wrinkled jeans to white jeans and a black halter top. I brush my hair loose, tuck a lily into the side of my hair, my heart beating fast in anticipation of seeing Oliver, and hurry downstairs.

The hotel is the same as I remember it and I feel a sudden queasiness like when I'm standing on the edge of a high cliff and can't look down. Even the Terrace Café is the same as it was in 1960—yellow silk umbrellas floating over oval glass tables and glass bud vases filled with sprays of orchid petals. Sipping hibiscus tea, I'm remembering sitting alone on the beach, ordering two towels and pretending that my husband of one day had emergency business and would be back soon.

Oliver appears. As I watch him hurry toward me, I feel breathless. Wearing a blue Hawaiian shirt, snug worn jeans, and a necklace of shells, he looks beautiful and magical and graceful and I know that I love him forever. I rush into his arms, and not caring that people are looking, we kiss and hug, murmuring how glad we are to see each other. "I've missed you," I say, feeling suddenly shy.

Over pineapple salads, Oliver high on the gorgeous island locations, he animatedly explains that the beauty of Hawaii juxtaposes perfectly with Charley's betrayal and the suspense as why he brought Dianne to this paradise for one day. But money is running out, he confides gloomily. If he doesn't finish the film soon, he will have to shut it down. "I can't pay the bills."

"You'll do it," I say, believing it.

He shrugs. "You always say if you don't take risk, nothing great happens."

"Yes, I believe this to be true."

Oliver informs me that later this evening when the sun goes down he is shooting the wedding suite scene, when Charley tells her he wants out. Afterwards, to celebrate finishing the film, there's a luau planned in the hotel dining room.

"...Is Rain here? The gang?"

He grins. "It isn't Rain. It's us."

"What does that mean?"

"In time we'll know."

After lunch, barefoot and holding hands we take a walk along the beach, admiring the ocean's myriad of colors and the surfers skimming the waves like birds and the water so clear you can see through it. A warm wind blows and the air smells like the sea and scented flowers. I stop and look at a pink starfish splayed on the edge of the water. It's so still and I think it's dead. "Poor starfish," I say.

"It's trying to get back into the sea," Oliver says, gently holding the starfish, his long fingers stroking it.

"A beautiful creature," I say.

He smiles. "The starfish symbolizes infinite divine love." Oliver drops the starfish gently by the edge of the sea, and while the water swirls around our feet, our hands locked, we watch the waves slowly drag the starfish back into the sea.

At the edge of the sea, I hold my arms out imagining I'm moving across the water. "See, I'm flying, Oliver."

Suddenly he holds me in his arms and we embrace for a long time. After we pull away, we resume walking along the edge of the water and the sun slips beyond its edge. Silently, we walk back to the hotel.

"I'll see you at the shoot," he says, leaving me in the lobby and going in a different direction, our kiss still lingering between us. Something changed today.

Upstairs, after bathing in gardenia bath oil, I remember the sweetness of Oliver's embrace and wonder what he meant by saying "in time we'll know." Know what?

Carefully, I dress in a white off-the-shoulder dress and high heel white leather sandals. I poke a fresh gardenia into the side of my hair and apply pale lip-gloss on my lips, and when it's dark I go upstairs to the shoot at the same wedding suite that Charley and I had been in.

When I enter the set, once again I'm back in time and for a second I can't breathe. The set is bustling with cameramen, actors huddled together, the usual activity. I sit next to Rain and several other crewmembers, bracing myself for the pain I know that I'm going to feel.

The wedding suite is large, with French doors that face the ocean. Moonlight drapes the room in a golden glow. From the beach below, sounds of bongo drums and trade winds rustling contrast with the eerie silence between the actors playing Charley and Dianne. Sprays of orchids cover the large king-size bed set on a high, on a platform, like an altar.

"Action!" Oliver calls. The set is quiet.

Charley, wearing a white dinner jacket, and Dianne, wearing a pink strapless organza dress and matching satin pumps, have just returned from the honeymooners Luau in the dining room. Dianne's dark hair is arranged in a French twist and an orchid lei drapes around her long, slender neck. Her pale face is strained. The camera pans the room as Charley drops coins and keys on the high wooden dresser, the sudden clanging sounds jarring the silence. He removes his jacket and undresses for bed. Dianne closes the drapes, her back to the camera.

"Dianne, I made a mistake," Charley says. "I don't love you. We're going home tomorrow."

Slowly, her hand still clutches the drapes.

"Did you hear me? I made a mistake," Charley says.

Dianne lets go of the cord and the drapes slowly close. She turns and faces him. He stands hesitantly by the bed.

"Home? I can't go home," she says. "We took wedding vows a day ago. Till death do us part, we vowed. I can't go home."

"Be ready early in the morning. I'm taking you home." He gets into bed and turns off the light.

Standing in the middle of the room, in the dark, Dianne drops her clothes on the floor and gets into bed. The moonlight fades and bongo drums rise from the beach and the scene goes dark.

"Cut!" Oliver shouts.

There is silence. Then all at once everyone is talking, congratulating Oliver on the power of the scene. Fighting back tears, I'm moved by the scene's emotional power—the sounds of the sea, bongo drums, waves ascending and retreating. I think back on all the times Oliver and I discussed this scene as the catalyst to Dianne's rise from despair to redemption.

The crew joins us for dinner and I'm sitting near Oliver and Joe. Over mahi mahi fish and martinis, everyone happily discusses the end of filming. I'm feeling happy until I see the tender way Joe touches Oliver's hand, a lover's touch. So it was never Rain, it was Joe.

Quickly I excuse myself and hurry to my room.

It's two a.m. Lying in bed, I'm thinking about Oliver, playing back the many times I saw Joe and Oliver together. Was I imagining that Joe was looking at Oliver in a way that only lovers look—a quick glance, slight movement of the mouth as if a kiss, touching, laughing at anything he said? Exhausted, I slip into sleep.

Somewhere near dawn, I get up. Wearing my trench coat over my naked body, I hurry along the darkened hallway to Oliver's room. I knock on the door. It's silent. Is he sleeping? I knock three times, my heart beating faster. After impatient footsteps, he opens the door. He's wearing a blue cotton robe half-open, his mane of hair tousled, his face flushed.

"Bette? Are you all right?"

"I…love you, Oliver. I want to make love to you." I stand there, burning from desire.

"I…it's late, dear. Let's talk tomorrow."

"Honey! Who's there?" Joe calls.

I wake with a jolt. I'm shaking. Did this happen? I get out of bed and am relieved when I see that my trench coat is hanging in the closet. But dreams don't lie.

On the terrace, I sit on a lounge chair, watching the sky turn to half-light. Soon morning arrives. Yesterday, Oliver and I planned to hike today and spend the day together.

After I have breakfast, trying to balance my thoughts, I dress for the day. Oliver said to meet him in his room at ten.

He's dressed in a white T-shirt, shorts, and sandals. "I have to make a couple of calls," he says enthusiastically. "I ordered your favorite tea. It's on the terrace. I'll be with you in a few minutes."

I notice his bed is made and I wonder if he slept here. At a table on the terrace, I drink hibiscus tea, and notice Oliver's leather notebook, the one he always carries and writes notes in. It's open. I read: *Notes: Dianne transitions from a fragile victimized girl, to an impassioned, confident woman. She redeems herself. She has the gift of vulnerability, but Bette refuses to be vulnerable. She's amazing in many ways...creative, unconventional, odd, ageless, and helps people. A great inferiority complex. Men are prey for her material and she waits for any sign of rejection and then she strikes. Destruction nurtures her talent. Until Bette lets go of the Charley trauma she's emotionally...*

Oliver stands in front of me, a stricken expression on his face.

"Am I...all those things?"

"Bette, we're all many things. I studied you for the film. There's so much about you I want to know, and so much I love."

"Are we only a story?"

"A good story lives forever, Bette. I'm your story too."

"What about...Joe?"

He smiles. "I love him differently. You have my heart." He pauses. "Bette, I love who I love. Love has nothing to do with sexuality." He looks at me tenderly, like a parent looks at a too-exuberant child. He pulls me up from the chair. "C'mon, let's see the most beautiful gardens in the world."

Oliver rents an open jeep and we drive miles past rows of pineapple fields and lush foliage damp from the layers of mist. Nothing matters but this moment, and I feel contented in a way I never have. An hour later, on a flat ridge, Oliver stops his jeep. Tourists wearing backpacks and cameras around their necks prepare with their guides for their hike up the mountain.

Wearing hats and dark glasses and small backpacks, we begin our hike along a path overlooking the entire valley, Oliver often stopping to photograph the breathtaking views, trees, and waterfalls spraying the air like mashed crystals.

After an hour, thirsty and hungry, we descend the path, and in a tiny village below we stop at a café. At a wooden table, we sip iced pineapple juice, enjoying fruit salads and admiring the peacocks wandering about the gardens with colorful exotic birds hiding in misty trees. "It's so beautiful here, there must be a God," I say.

Oliver smiles, sunlight dappling on his face. "There is. God is this moment, the air, the flowers, and the beauty. Us. In your haunting art." He looks reflective.

Pleased by his compliment, he listens intently as I talk eagerly about my painting. How I love the light in a Caravaggio painting, the deep emotions in a van Gogh painting, the subtle romance in a Manet.

After lunch, we explore the tiny village and buy shells and necklaces from bins. The air smells of flowers and the stalls display rows of pineapples. As we walk to Oliver's car, I feel this overwhelming urge in the middle of the street and I place my arms around Oliver's neck and kiss him deeply, whispering, "You're special. Very special. I love you forever and with all my heart. I want to make love to you."

"I would love to," he says, tenderly.

Back at the hotel, a light dusk floats along the gardens. Wordlessly, without discussion, we return to my suite. Shadows make shapes along the room and a rising breeze blows from the open doors. Fresh gardenias are strewn about the silk pillows.

I undress, watch as Oliver quickly undresses, and think how beautiful his body is. Feeling slightly shy and self-conscious about my pale body, I follow him into bed. Without talk or explanations we embrace, pressing our naked bodies so close they're one. Oh my God, I'm in ecstasy. I love him. I can't feel enough of him. I love him inside me, and he's so gentle, so loving.

When it's over we lie still, our bodies pressed together. You can hear the waves crashing along the beach mixed with the faint sounds of bongo drums from the other end of the beach. Never have I felt so emotionally and sexually fulfilled. It wasn't just the sex that felt so pure and romantic and tender, it was the release of our love for each other. There were no blubbery prostrations of lust, or unnecessary words. Just us.

We continue to lie quietly, my body on top of his, kissing and hugging and whispering. I am leaving the next day and Oliver is staying a little longer to scout other locations for background scenes.

"Is Joe staying?" My voice sounds anxious and I regret asking.

"Of course," Oliver replies. "He's an excellent videographer. I need him."

"Is sex with him..."

After a long pause, he says, "What we have Bette, isn't about sex. Sex is sex. Love is something else."

"I'm jealous of your other men," I say after a long silence.

"And I'm jealous of yours." He kisses my lips tenderly.

"I'd rather have love sometimes with you then love all the time with someone I don't have intimacy with."

* * *

When I return to San Francisco, I need money, so I concentrate on my writing workshops. I continue to work hard in my therapy, diving into my subconscious, identifying pieces from my life—conversations with my mother, daughters, incidents that traumatized me. Sometimes this process is so painful I can't breathe. "Post-Traumatic Stress," Dr. T. murmurs. Amazing how every second, every incident of our lives stays alive.

Often, I take a day off to walk along the edge of the ocean, admiring the light, the waves rising and crashing, wondering what we are, and if our deceased loved ones are somewhere out there. I feel they are. As I walk to the end of the beach, I feel Ricky, feel his sorrows, and hope he's at peace. When I think of the past years, my wishes for fame, financial riches, the dreams feel worn and no longer interesting, like old clothes sometimes do.

Oliver returns from Hawaii, and he disappears into his work, living for days in the editing room. Often, we roam the museums, go to concerts, or watch films, eagerly discussing if the film holds up the storyline.

We spend nights together, making love and whispering secrets, confessions, insights, exploring ideas, until he has to leave. Happily, I resume my work, deciding to write a novel about love. Never have I felt so present within my life.

"You love him, don't you, Mom," Lisa says on the phone.

"Yes."

"Even though he lives a separate life? Has men and women in his life?"

"Yes. I don't need him to complete me. I feel completed. I love him completely and dearly. I love who he is."

She sighs. "When a woman says he completes me, I feel bad for her. Love doesn't need anyone to complete it. It is what it is. You are who you are. Our choices reflect who we are."

Tonight, a mist covers the city in gray. It's been several days since I've seen Oliver. Remembering Hawaii, the feel of his body on mine, the beauty of the Hawaiian mist, I write Oliver a poem.

I arrange white roses in a glass vase,
Each rose a kiss.
In the night I sing songs to you
On high octaves, as I float to the moon.
Love carries me to destinations
You don't know.
Wait for me to show you eternity.
My heart is you.
Love, sometimes, Bette.

I email the poem.

The next morning, I awake early. I check my emails. Near dawn, Oliver had emailed me a poem.

You turn pink, my darling,
In the shape of a rose.
I kiss your heart.

I saw you last night in your dream,
Did you see me watching?
You danced intricate steps,
As if you drew them in the air.
Watch for me in your dreams.
I'm always there.
Take me to your soul.
Love, sometimes forever. Oliver.

I print out his poem and place it in the wooden box along with his former notes, shells, rocks, and feathers he purchased in Hawaii.

27

The end of summer, Larry and Nanny bring home their beautiful three-month daughter Annabelle. Never had I yearned for a child, but as soon as I held Annabelle everything changed. Like an angel stuck to my heart, all I think about is Annabelle...every night I call Nanny wondering what Annabelle is doing, what she's eating, and what sounds is she making and if she's happy. With each tiny change Nanny tells me about—a sound, her laughter, and the blue musical ball she loves—I'm enchanted. Everything I hadn't allowed myself to feel when my daughters were born, I feel for this little being. Just looking at her I feel overwhelmed by love, wanting to show her love, keep her safe, guide her with everything I know is right and good.

Today at noon, Nanny is having a Meet Annabelle Party so friends and relatives can meet the baby.

At Nanny and Larry's house, pink helium balloons float on the ceiling, matching the baby pink roses in vases all over the house. Nanny, wearing a pink leotard and pink T-shirt with Annabelle's face printed on the front, greets everyone. Larry, wearing a T-shirt printed DAD is in the open kitchen making pink martinis. Nanny's dogs observe everything, plopped in on the center of the room. Poor Annabelle is sitting in this bouncy rubber chair, and relatives taking pictures surround her. She's a beautiful child, with dark curly hair, wide black eyes, dark skin, and when she smiles, dimples indent her fat cheeks.

"Isn't she adorable?"

"They had to adopt an Arab. An ISIS kid," Crystal says loudly with an irritated shrug.

"Stop it!" Larry frowns and gives her a glaring look.

"You couldn't adopt a Jew?" Crystal shouts.

"She needs a blessing," says Imani, who specializes in voodoo healings. She makes these hideous goat sounds in Annabelle's face and poor Annabelle is screaming and the dogs are barking.

After Nanny puts Annabelle in her bouncy with a fresh pacifier in her mouth, she announces that lunch is ready.

Sitting around the room, balancing their plastic plates on their laps, the relatives pig out on the array of rice dishes, lamb, cauliflower, and hummus.

"So now Nanny cooks Muslim? Chicken soup isn't good enough?" persists Crystal.

"She's *Syrian*!" Larry shouts.

"What difference what she is!" shouts Nanny.

"Send the kid back! Next, she'll be praying on a rug, you watch," Crystal continues. "So Bette. I read your TV series was pulled?" Crystal smiles.

Larry quickly interjects, "Bette has a film coming out, and it's based on her Jewish Princess novel."

"Charley? The rat?" Aunt Zoe says, laughing like it's a joke.

Larry is aiming his humongous video camera at Annabelle who is slumped and sleeping in her bouncy, amid everyone comparing pictures of their grandchildren while Aunt Zoe tells ISIS horror stories.

After everyone leaves, Nanny gets Annabelle ready for bed. For a while, I rock Annabelle in my arms. She smells like summer grass. I feel so much love I'm going to burst.

In Annabelle's nursery, I watch her sleep peacefully in the crib, her cloth doll next to her, the mobile of stars spinning gently. Weeks ago, I'd painted blown pink roses on the nursery wall, with squiggly green stems. Nanny pasted decals of animals on her toy box, and Lisa knitted beautiful caps and blankets. I was blown away to see, in a white lacquer bookcase that Larry made, my published novels displayed. Next to the books sits a photograph of me at a book signing. "We want Annabelle to know you, Mom."

Full circle. Yes, like branches on a tree, we're one, growing from the same roots. At this moment I realize that my daughters and my granddaughter, not fame and fortune, are my legacy.

* * *

And things do change when you least expect it. It's a windy afternoon and after a long walk I stop at a café in North Beach where I sip my latte and edit some new poems. Opera arias play from overhead speakers and glass cases display homemade Italian cakes like perfumes, wrapped in transparent pastel colored papers. I love these times, typing on my laptop, enjoying the music, the coffee and the crowd. Then, Edwina calls from her car.

Quickly, in her fast voice, she informs me that Satan Bernstein wants to re-option *The Viagra Diaries* and also the blog for a sequel, and promises to put in writing that I have complete creative input. "Could you die and go to heaven!" she says, her voice rising. "This is unheard of. Honeybun, it's a fucking win-win."

"How did he read the blog?" I ask.

"Evan Allen pitched it to him a while back."

"Well...I don't want to work with Evan Allen. Biggie Delano represents the blog."

She shouts. "You don't want 400K? Evan Allen got Lee Nancy Clark. She read the blog and even though she thought it was poorly written, she likes the narrator and will play you. A major star! Just her name and it's an Emmy!"

"I don't want to work with Evan Allen again."

She screams, "Take a Xanax! I'll call you tomorrow!"

Not twenty minutes later, Evan Allen calls. Edwina called him and told him about Satan's offer. In his patronizing voice, he rants that Satan Bernstein is the perfect network producer for *The Viagra Diaries* and that he'll sell the blog over the phone.

"Biggie Delano is representing the blog. It's his," I say.

"Biggie Delano is a whore!" he screams.

"But you'd said that you didn't want it," I protest. "You only sent the blog to a few publishers!" I argue, trying to sound calm. "I told you I was sending it to Biggie Delano and you said to go ahead."

He continues a diatribe about how much work he's done for me and how sick he is of narcissistic authors who can't write. "You can't write. You're all whores!"

"Well, sorry you feel this way," I say, but he's already ended the call.

Concerned about Evan Allen's threats, immediately, I contact Marci Feldstein. It's been a while since we talked.

Quickly, I tell her about the blog, that Biggie Delano is representing it, and I relay Evan Allen's threats. She goes ballistic. "So what the fuck do you want me to do? I haven't been paid a penny by you! You people are crazy. All the same! How dare you! That nasty blog makes fun of Hollywood and you think I'm on your side? You idiot.'"

* * *

Biggie Delano calls. "Your sales figures on *The Viagra Diaries* are so bad, it's going to be a hard sell. And also you trash the industry. A hard sell, but I'll do it." He sighs. "I've received a nasty letter from Evan Allen's lawyer who is threatening to sue if I sell *Blast.* He claims he worked hard trying to sell it and that he has claim to your work. And he's a rat and a whore."

"But I have no deal with him, Biggie. I signed nothing. He never even read the blog, and at that time I didn't have the book. He sent a log line that he wrote. Talk about fame whores."

He sighs, as if exasperated. "Let me make a few calls, figure this out, and I'll be in touch."

After he hangs up, I call Lisa and tell her about Biggie's call, obsessing about Evan Allen's threats. She listens intently and then she advises me to sit back.

"It is what it is, Mom. Stop obsessing. My therapist says I have ulcers over your projects. I'm not an agent anymore, I'm a therapist, and you need to tell Dr. T. about your anxiety."

"I'm just saying..."

"Don't just say, do...I have a gender fluid meeting. Gotta go."

28

Evan Allen is suing Biggie Delano, claiming Biggie stole Blast from him. Unfortunately, he's holding a possible sale. But Biggie is used to the "rats," he says, and assures me not to worry. "If anything, his law suit promotes interest. As soon as the publishers hear Evan Allen is fighting over the book, I'll sell it."

Oliver finishes the film, but he's way over budget and in trouble with his investors, the banks, and his castle in Australia is in foreclosure.

To celebrate finishing the film, Oliver has a loft party and we have a great time eating pizza, drinking wine, and dancing to Michael Jackson music. Not even the presence of Joe, Rain, and many beautiful artists concerns me. I'm so thrilled about the film and love Oliver so much that nothing else matters.

But problems begin. Oliver has trouble distributing the film into theaters and spends weeks trying to book the film without success, until he finally books a small San Francisco art house theater, right after Thanksgiving. Excited, he and his team send digital copies to film critics. A well-known Bay Area film critic from the *San Francisco Chronicle* writes: "*A compelling film that holds up for all the generations. Don't miss it.*" Another critic from the *Berkeley Express* writes: "*The story of emotional violence, and a young woman's struggle to have her voice heard and her rise to artistic heights.*" Rain sends Evites to the opening, to distributors, editors, artists, and friends, and we start getting RSVPs.

"This is going to be a happening," Moo Moo says on the phone. "Eddie Samson, a billionaire, wants to meet you. He said he'd invest in the film. He invests in the arts—Broadway shows, films, and documentaries. He lost his wife and doesn't know what to do with this money. I talked up the film. Meet him."

"Sure," I say, thinking of Oliver's debt.

Eddie Samson calls. We chat about meeting. "What about Ethiopian food?" he demands in his New York accent.

"I can't eat that."

"Japanese?"

"Can't have raw fish."

"Indian?"

"Can't."

"Hey! Moo Moo says you're the arty type and open to anything."

"So let's meet at the North Beach Café," I suggest.

"Six?"

"Sure. I'm easy. You'll find me. They say I look like Clint."

"Who?" I ask.

"Eastwood," he replies impatiently.

Decked out in my slinky black dress and tiny black hat with a tiny black veil, I arrive at the North Beach restaurant, a landmark authentic Italian restaurant. It's festive and elegant. Waiters wear tuxedo jackets and framed celebrity photographs hang from the wood-paneled walls, and there's this great mirrored bar.

Sitting at the bar, I order a vodka shot. I'm enjoying the drink, praying that I raise money to save Oliver's film.

"Bette? I'm Clint."

I turn and face this small man bent over like question mark, with critical blue eyes behind black-rimmed glasses and a few tufts of curly gray hair. A nice face actually, but taut and humorless. In a pompous tone, he instructs the bartender exactly how to make it, exactly what measurements of gin and exclusive spices. He wears an expensive gold Apple watch.

He clicks his glass on mine. "Moo Moo says you're the arty type. I can see that...very post hippie. As I said I don't care if you're older."

"Uh huh. Thanks."

"You're not my usual type, but I like artists. Moo Moo says a film based on your Jewish Princess novel is about to debut. She said I should invest."

"Yes, it would be good," I say.

He purses his small lips. "I was married to a Jewish Princess. She shopped. Spent a fortune with my money."

"Uh huh."

He brags about his companies and how he exports and imports nuts, and how wealthy he is, how hydrated. "That's why I look young."

"For sure," I say.

"Everyone loves my nuts," he says, drolly, then chuckles, as if he's told this great joke. His watch buzzes. "Whoops. Hold it. Blood pressure pills." He places his thumbs on either side of the watch and closes his eyes. When he opens them he says, "Ah.

My heart rate is that of a kid." He opens a gold pillbox and lays three pills on the bar. Then he takes them one by one, closing his eyes and sighing heavily. "At least they're not Viagra. Something I don't need."

"Wow."

"Wow is right. The last woman I had sex with had a heart attack. She was overcome with lust. Put that in your *Viagra Diaries.*"

"Uh huh. Well, Moo Moo said you'd be interested in investing in my film. Oliver Abbot is a fabulous writer and director. The film could be an Academy Award-winning best film—"

He looks at me intently, as if evaluating a stain. "Every artist and her brother wants me to invest. I've invested and invested and ended up with dogs and lost fortunes." He starts complaining that women artists are always after his money. "I invested in a painter and now I use her paintings for toilet paper. I bring the women beautiful bags of my imported nuts, but do you think that's enough? By the second date they've got a son, a nephew, a grandson who needs money for some cockamamie film that they're making."

"Well, Moo Moo said..."

"Moo Moo talks out of her ass," he snaps unpleasantly, blowing his bad breath on my face.

"So when did your wife die?" I ask, wondering how to get out of here.

"Three days ago."

"How did your wife die?"

"She choked on a nut."

He tells me what a "klutz" she was, that she was bipolar and hysterical, and that he put in his time for thirty-two years.

I look at my watch. "Unfortunately, I have to go, I have deadlines and have to work early in the morning."

I run out of there and taxi it home.

As I slip into my dream, I'm wearing a black chiffon dress with no back, and my hair is wound with tiny white roses. Oliver and I dance the tango, and even though I step on his feet and lean too far forward, he leads me beautifully, and he bends me back and then up and bubbles are floating all around us and...

* * *

On Google, I locate Charley's office telephone number. I call and ask to speak to Charles Berkowitz Jr.

"Who's calling?" asks a woman with a crisp voice.

"Bette Roseman. Tell him that I was married to him once."

"Just a minute," she says in a slightly amused voice.

Quickly, he comes to the phone, his feathery light voice exactly the same. He greets me as if I'm a long-lost relative, repeating how many years have passed and how sorry he was when he'd read my father had died. "Lou was a great guy. A man's man," he says. "I remember when I asked him for your hand and promised I'd take care of you. A man's man," he repeats.

"Yes, my father was special."

He sighs. "Bette, so many times I've thought about you." He pauses. "I've seen you on TV and wow, you're an author. I'm impressed."

"Uh huh."

"Who would ever know you had that kind of talent?"

"I was nineteen. You didn't know me. Know anything about me. Anyway, I'm calling because I need closure."

"Are you…is your health…?"

"Not that kind of closure," I say irritated by his ignorance. "I need to see you. To ask you something."

He remains silent, as if thinking about it. "Tonight, meet me at six?"

"Yes."

"At Ruth's Chris Steak House. At the bar," he says.

I dress carefully in my black pantsuit and black ankle strap high heels. I wear the silver earrings to my shoulders that Oliver bought me in Hawaii. I apply deep red lipstick, gray eye shadow, and brush my wavy hair past my shoulders. I'm ready.

In the crisp cold night, I walk to the restaurant not far from my apartment. On the way, the fog curling my hair, I'm remembering the fancy expensive French five-star restaurants where Charley used to take me, so different from a steak house. Probably a place to hide me. He never did anything randomly.

I cross the intersection and approach the restaurant, remembering clearly the day I met him. I'd been working at Saks, saving money to go to night school and study art. I'd modeled the Grace Kelly-style wedding gown at the Saks Fundraiser for big donors. He sat in the front row and all the women were whispering about him. He was almost thirty, handsome as a movie star, and already a multi-millionaire, he was always featured in the columns with beautiful socialites. After the show, he introduced himself and asked if he could call. It was the only time I pleased my mother. Every weekend for a year, he'd wine and dine me on Friday and Saturday nights. At the Fairmont Hotel we'd dance to the Mills Brothers singing "Up The Lazy River." In his Jaguar, we'd make out, but when I wanted to do more, he'd say *no you're my princess, let's wait.* "Men like Charley only marry virgins. Play your cards right," Mother preached.

I go inside the restaurant. It's so dark I blink several times to get my bearings. The long, mahogany-mirrored bar is in the front. So I can watch him as he arrives, I sit at a table in the back, where it's dark and I can see the bar and the front door.

I order a vodka shot, enjoying its quick warmth. I order another, remembering dressing for dates with Charley—my hair set in a bouffant, wearing matching outfits with white kid gloves and carrying a beaded envelope-shape purse. Sipping my drink, I watch couples at the bar playing liars dice. It's almost six. Charley was always on time, "on the dot," he'd say proudly. He was precise about everything—his clothes, the order of things. "I'm a neat freak," he'd laugh.

Exactly at six p.m., I watch him walk in and hurry to the bar with the same indolent strut, the same puff of jet-black hair now banded with silver. As always, he's impeccably dressed in a dark, expensive suit with a pale blue silk tie.

He sits at the end of the bar next to an empty chair reserved for me. He looks at his watch, and, as if the bartender knows what Charley drinks, he gives Charley his drink. Charley shakes the glass twice, making sure the ice settles exactly the way he wants—"I like three ice cubes melting," he used to say. He glances at his watch again, looks towards the door, and then continues to chat with the bartender, smiling and raising his glass for another. "A man about town. A catch," Mother had raved. At the expensive restaurants he'd taken me to he always knew the bartenders, parking valets, headwaiters, slipped them wads of cash.

I finish my drink. "*A man's man*," he said about my father. He didn't care that my father mortgaged his house to pay for the wedding, or that he stuck my father with all the bills and demanded the wedding gifts returned to him by court order, demanded that I return the square-cut large diamond engagement ring, that he told a reporter how my family only wanted his money.

I open my purse and freshen my lipstick in the gold heart-shaped compact Nanny gave me.

Clutching my leather envelope purse, I hurry to the bar. I tap Charley on the shoulder. Slowly, he turns and faces me. Relief spreads across his slightly bloated, vain face. "Bette—you look... beautiful. I'm glad to see you. I..."

I open my purse and quickly aim the small black gun at his face, enjoying his shock. "For my father," I say. I pull the trigger.

He slumps to the ground and there's pandemonium. I shoot again to make sure he's dead. Then again. Again. Again.

Sirens.

People.

His eyes are open. Blood everywhere.

It's over. Finally, over.

At last, it's over.

"Another round Miss?" the waiter asks.

I open my eyes, shaking myself from the reverie. "...No, thank you. Just a check please."

After I pay the bill, I hurry past Charley still talking to the bartender and outside into the night.

I walk fast, following the moon all the way home.

I dream that I'm walking on the edge of a long beach alongside of the ocean. Billie Holiday sings a medley of songs and the waves crash like thunder and then slowly recede back into place. The air is crisp and beautiful. I hurry to the pale gray cottage with the small garden. The front door is painted blue and surrounded by rose bushes. It is my house, serene. A place to enjoy solitude and work.

I knock on the door but no one answers. I knock again, and just then I awake.

29

As the leaves parch yellow and blow along the hills, Thanksgiving arrives. Lisa, Hank, and the family are at Nanny and Larry's house. In a few days, the film is opening its debut. Oliver is in London trying to make distribution deals in Europe.

Nanny prepared a traditional dinner. All of us, even Annabelle in a high chair, growing so beautiful, sit at Nanny's long wooden dining room table decorated with tiny vases of red roses and paper turkeys. Platters of turkey and mashed potatoes, roasted vegetables, and koogles are set along the buffet.

Wearing a strapless red tube dress, her hair tied with red roses, Nanny serves her homemade, still-warm popovers and everyone claps. Lisa, wearing pink, sits next to me, and I love having her here. Not only was she always there for me—always sending little cards with cash inside, a lipstick, perfume, a book, and always helping with my career—but she's achieved so much in her life, and with no help and much hardship. Even though we don't see each other a lot, she lives deeply in my heart.

Mozart plays from an overhead speaker, and everyone is eating and talking at once, either about how fast the years have gone, "time flies," they murmur, or about who died, who had gallbladder surgery, cancer, and other diseases. "Here one minute, gone the next," they lament. Between eating, Hank explains his work with artificial intelligence and claims that in the future robots will take over.

"Oy. Bette needs a man not a robot," Aunt Zoe says.

"I have a man I love," I say. "And I'm fine anyway."

"The fairy ballet dancer?" Crystal says, her sequin sweater bursting over her fake breasts.

"He's a genius," I say. "A gorgeous man."

"I agree," Lisa says. "It's wrong to label people. People are people."

"Mom loves Oliver," Nanny says, glaring at Crystal.

"Can't she get a straight man?" Aunt Zoe persists. "A normal man?"

"There's is no such thing as normal," Lisa says.

Annabelle is crying now. Uncle Benny is choking and gagging from eating too fast and Aunt Zoe slams his back with her fists.

"I think she has a poo poo," Larry says, lifting the crying Annabelle from her high chair.

Aunt Zoe yells. "You couldn't find a Jewish child. You had to find a Muslim. Next she'll be wearing a rag on her head."

"Shut up Ma!" Her son yells.

"Who wants pumpkin pie?" Nanny says. She sets her beautiful homemade pumpkin, apple, and cherry pies along the center of the table.

Soon the evening is over. Crystal pops out the Tupperware containers from her humongous purse and fills them with the leftovers from everyone's plates. Zoe stuffs the turkey centerpieces into her huge, plastic floral-print tote bag.

After I hug the kids and everyone good night, everyone promising to see me at the film debut, I take an Uber home. Driving across the bridge, I admire the clusters of stars like diamond brooches pinned to the dark. The stars clustered in groups and the mist floating over the baby bay bridge shaped like a harp with strings is so beautiful, and I thank my higher power for all my blessings, for my grandchild and my daughters and for family and for it all and suddenly I know that I'm firmly on my path of dreams.

When I return home, there's a long box by my door. It's a bouquet of pale orange roses—the color of the roses I'd admired in Hawaii. And the card reads *Love sometimes, Oliver.*

30

The night of the film debut, Oliver and I are at the Mission Theater. Even though it's still early, there's a crowd. The lobby smells of dust and popcorn popping in an old-fashioned machine behind a faded wood counter. Worn red Chinese-patterned carpet seems incongruous to the intricate moldings and dusty crystal chandeliers. Built in the early twenties, the theater has framed posters of old movies and stars that hang from the walls—Betty Davis, Carol Lombard, Charlie Chaplin.

Lisa and Hank, along with Larry and Nanny give me a bouquet of white roses. I give one to each of them and one to Oliver, who places it in his jacket lapel. Majestic in his fitted black velvet jacket, turtleneck, and high boots, he's charming and gentle with the girls. "Your mother's work is extraordinary. She's the world's best keep secret."

"We think so," they say graciously.

"He's something," Nanny whispers. "Lisa says so too."

Along with local press, the *San Francisco Times* art critic arrives. He's a scruffy, slight man with humorless eyes. Men and women of all ages, races, sexualities, many of my students, neighbors, family, stand in groups, talking.

"My God you look arty farty!" Moo Moo, surrounded by two very young boys, says. "I love the hat—the feathers. Very..."

"Jezebel," lisps her latest boyfriend, an Italian waiter she met at her favorite restaurant. After I introduce her to Oliver, she whispers. "I get it. Straight men don't look like this."

"I don't care how he looks or what he is or isn't. He's just fabulous."

"He looks...Middle Eastern."

"No, he's part African American."

"Oh my God. You're so...*liberal*."

Then there's an announcement that the film is beginning and for those who can't get seats, there'll be an extra showing the next day.

I sit with Lisa and Nanny, their husbands, Oliver, and the crew.

The lights dim and the theater is dark.

It's so strange how when a dream comes true, you think you're dreaming. After the title, the film opens to the wedding night at the Airport Motel. The camera moves to a wedding bouquet on the wooden dresser, a white nightgown on the floor by the bed. "Blue Moon" plays from the radio and the story begins. Dianne and Charley's naked bodies are pale silhouettes as they kiss, but as Charley stops, the camera moves to Dianne's face as she says "Do it now. Please, now."

"Not tonight," he says. He moves away to light a cigarette, and as the smoke rings rise slowly to the ceiling, the camera moves close to Dianne's dazed, shocked face.

As the movie progresses, each scene so clear, so beautiful, you can hear a pin drop. Nanny and Lisa clutch my hands, and Lisa is crying.

Almost two hours pass. The film's sheer beauty and artistry, Oliver's insights, talent, and deep sensitive artistic judgments overwhelm me. Skillfully, he combined technique with emotion. He transformed my commercial novel into art. For the first time I feel artistically validated and realize that each life has its own path and fate and that I followed mine. Oliver is my redemption. I feel released from my past, like I was just born. At last Charley is over. Only a story now.

When the film ends, at first it's quiet, but then everyone stands and applauds and the lights go on. Oliver looks radiant. Joe whispers something in Oliver's ear, and a beautiful young boy gives Oliver a huge bouquet of red roses.

"Mom, It's wonderful. I never knew. I understand you better now," Lisa says, hugging me. Tears are in her eyes, and we hold each other tight.

"Oliver did a great job," Nanny says sincerely. "It's wonderful, Mom."

Then, like dreams do, it all goes so fast. In the lobby I'm crushed by people I haven't seen for years asking to get together, exclaiming that they want to read the Jewish Princess novel and congratulating me. Moo Moo and Myra and women I know from the past who had shunned me, are exclaiming that they always believed in me and knew that I was a star.

The lights shut off, and my girls and their husbands and Oliver and his crew go to North Beach to dinner.

Dinner is merry. Over spaghetti and singing waiters, Oliver toasts the crew, and then the crew toasts Oliver, and then everyone is toasting everyone in the happiest night of my life. Oliver raises his glass and toasts me, as I watch his intense, emotional face and listen to his beautiful words: "Without Bette's insights, talent, beautiful novel, this would not be possible..."

By the time we finish dinner it's very late and Lisa and Hank go to Berkeley to stay with Nanny and Larry.

Maybe it's near dawn. I can tell because stripes of light shimmer along the wall. I'm at Oliver's loft and in his bed. The room smells of roses. We'd quietly celebrated—had a glass of champagne and then made love. Quiet, sweet love.

I whisper, "Do you like sex with me? I love it with you."

"This isn't about sex. It's about love, Bette. I love you." We kiss a long, tender kiss. "I'm leaving for Australia soon," Oliver says after a long moment. "I need to get back to my work...find another project."

"What will I do without you?"

"Great things, Bette. Live happily. Write another novel. That's what will keep you in love."

"But love isn't only a story."

"It's our story. Write about it. We'll make another film."

"I want to be with you forever. You were the catalyst to my authentic self, to my art, and I'll never love anyone like I love you. I know this. You entered my heart and I became the way I'm supposed to be. You're part of me. I want to be with you, live with you."

"After the first week you'd be bored. I know. So would I."

"But why? We love each other."

"We love our work more," he says gently. "It's our work that binds us. We're the same that way. Love, sometimes is perfect for us. It gives us time to breathe, to explore our souls, to gather more material. It's the way we are, Bette. Love isn't one size fits all. Our love is in our fate. You always say that one's fate is not seen, but felt. You have to follow it."

"Is...Joe going to Australia?" I hold my breath. There, I said it. But why? Instantly, I regret asking him about Joe. We've already been through all that. Once again, my old fear of rejection has activated.

"Darling, don't," he says softly. "You know the answers. You also know that I love you deeply, and we'll always find ways to be together."

"...Oliver, I dream that I'll someday be able to buy a cottage by the sea and you will stay with me and we'll collaborate on another film then another and explore art and love and life."

We kiss a long, slow kiss, our bodies pressed close, whispering endearments. Oliver closes his eyes and sleeps. Only the wind rattling the windows invades our silence. There is nothing more to say. Nothing that can intrude on this special love, this connection we have, and I'd rather have what we have sometimes than live all the time without this love I feel.

It's time to sleep.

When morning spreads and Oliver is still sleeping, I dress and take a taxi home. Everything is different now.

The next day the *San Francisco Times* film critic writes a rave review: Not only does he write that this is *"an important film to see, brilliantly produced, directed and written,"* but he goes on to write about Oliver and about how he started as a journalist, had made award winning documentaries in England and in Australia, and found *The Rise and Fall of a Jewish American Princess* in a used book store and loved the story so much he decided to make a film. On a low budget with little backing, he spent the past two and a half years making this film.

Several days later, Oliver is returning to Australia. Joe will run his San Francisco production company. But he needs to return to his home. Totally, I understand, but at the same time, I feel like I do when standing at the edge of the sea and imagine it's pulling me out and then suddenly stops. Not knowing when I'll see him again, I wonder if we won't be together until we have a project to work on.

At the airport, I walk him to the gate. So far, we haven't said a word. I'm feeling a mixture of panic and love and sadness, a feeling you feel when you're running after something you want and it keeps getting away from you.

"Don't be sad my love," Oliver says, gently holding me.

I bury my face in his neck so he won't see the tears. When I regain my composure, I look up and see that he's feeling sad too. "Soon, Bette, we'll be together. I promise. It's not goodbye. It's time to rejuvenate, time to work. For both of us."

I nod, trying to smile. "I love you, Oliver."

He smiles. "A rose blooms and then stops. The seasons arrive and the rose rests, and then it blooms again."

We embrace and I watch him walk to the plane, his feet extended, his black coat disappearing as he enters the plane. I stand by the window until the plane soars into the air.

* * *

It's amazing. Even if a film doesn't have commercial appeal, if it's authentic, you get an audience. Dozens of local and national film critics write glowing reviews about the film and it's held over for months. It is thrilling. Oliver calls and informs me that a well-known Australian producer is pitching our film to Netflix. So far, any money coming in is paying off Oliver's film debts. But we're very optimistic that soon we'll receive royalties.

"Everyone is talking about the film," Edwina says on the phone. "Bitterman and his new story developer Glo want to re-option *The Viagra Diaries*. They heard that Evan Allen is suing Delano for the blog. They're interested."

"Well, I'm not."

"Honeybun, I'm talking six figures."

"I'm no longer interested in *The Viagra Diaries*. I'm busy with our film. Things are going great."

"Honeybun, don't blow this. Your little film will be here and gone, and you're lucky if you make a dime on it. Films like yours don't make money."

"Well, I'd rather have a good film than a stupid avatar."

"Art doesn't cash in," she snaps. "Your film will end up at art house, dusty theaters and old ladies with senior discounts will go to the matinee specials."

"At least it's not commercial, dumbed-down work."

The jarring sound of her blender invades the sudden silence. "Honeybun, you owe me." After a long moment, her voice suddenly vulnerable, she confides that Amen got into her bank account and ran off with her money. "Plus, my fucking idiot husband won alimony. So now I have to pay the dick idiot a fortune."

"I'm sorry, Edwina. I really am. You deserve better."

"Please, honeybun, Bitterman is sorry. He'll do what you want. He's groveling, he'll pay you anything and probably will let you write the whole damn thing. Just take Bitterman's Skype call."

"He hasn't paid me the fine or released the rights."

"Marci Feldstein *assured* me WC will release the rights immediately. Please, honeybun, just listen to what Bitterman has to say? His tail is between his legs. I'll tell him you'll talk with him pronto, if he emails you the rights."

As she continues to rant how broke she is, I feel sorry for her, remembering all the years she'd worked for me and had close calls and that maybe making a lot of money will help Oliver's production company and together we'll make more films.

"Well, for you, I will," I say after a pause. "But if I don't like what he says, this will be over and I'll forget it forever."

An hour later, Edwina and I receive the rights.

The next morning, I'm on Skype talking to Bitterman. He looks like the Godfather, wearing a pinstripe suit with huge, dark glasses and slicked-back hair. Sleaze City. He's got this spray tan personality, and as if he hadn't pursued in court, called me names, betrayed me, he's acting like he's a best friend. After working with Oliver, this project feels like it happened in another lifetime.

"...So congratulations, Bette on the film. *The Fall of a Jewish American Princess* is phenomenal!"

"The *Rise and Fall*," I correct.

"The public is clamoring for *The Viagra Diaries*."

"I'm really busy now with my film."

"Unfortunately, films don't make money. After a few senior special tickets, it's over."

"They said that about Van Gogh."

He snorts.

"We *salivate* over Nanny," says Glo. "The book is a masterpiece."

"It's Anny," I correct. "Nanny is my daughter."

"Oh yes. Anyway, *The Viagra Diaries* is my favorite book."

"Uh huh. Have you read it?"

"I read the synopsis. It's...radiant?"

Bitterman lights a cigar. "Bette, let's put the drama to rest and get a hell of a TV series on air before the fucking vultures and whores want in. Satan Bernstein will try to steal your projects. He's a whore, so be careful. I'll re-option *The Viagra Diaries.* Resurrect my script. Straight to series. Fifteen episodes. Glo has lots of ideas. Go, Glo."

"We think that *we* should change the title to *Diary of an Avatar*?" Glo says hesitantly.

"Then the vultures won't sue for *The Viagra* shit!" Bitterman explains.

Glo looks perplexed. "I'm thinking Kris Jenner? Maybe..."

I say, "Thank you both very much, but I've decided to pass."

"Pass what?" Bitterman shouts.

"On both projects. I'm not interested. I'm going to concentrate on art."

After I hang up, I'm relieved that I finally let it go.

Not two minutes later, Edwina calls and shouts that I just fucked up my career.

"No, I just started it," I say.

"*The Diary of an Avatar* is a win," she insists. "Your reputation is mush."

I say. "No longer do I want idiots to smash my work, and the money doesn't mean that much to me. But thank you Edwina, for all you've tried to do. You're my forever friend."

* * *

The roses are almost in bloom. The days and the weeks pass quickly, and everything feels different. At times I feel as though I've transitioned to another life—one so full, rich with nature and beauty and infinite challenges.

Yes, truth matters. You can't stay on your path of dreams if you don't take risk and know your truths. It's a miracle; day and night, the Mission Theater is packed and good reviews spread to notable film journals, online newspapers, and magazines. When there are demands for my out-of-print Jewish Princess novel, Avalon calls and wants to reprint the novel, but I'm going with the small press in Florida, the only publisher who took a chance on it.

Edwina leaves constant messages that she has sure deals on *The Diary of an Avatar.* "I'm talking mafia money," she says, excitedly. "Everyone wants *The Viagra Diaries*. My phone is ringing off the hook. I'll be in touch, honeybun."

Fate takes over and my other published books that had been dormant on Amazon are suddenly selling, not a lot, but there's movement. Also, what blows my mind is that publishers and agents who dismissed me are suddenly texting that they'd like to publish my other books. Is this for real? Soon I'm receiving royalty checks, not huge but I'm able to open saving accounts, and for the first time in years I have credit.

It's strange with dreams, once they come true, they don't matter because you've moved on to other things and new dreams. When a dream comes true, it feels different from what you'd expected. If anything, I retreat into solitude, loving the days alone, walking and taking pictures of the hills, the view of the surrounding ocean, the mist draping the Golden Gate Bridge, and birds swooping low.

Spring arrives. The roses are opening and the trees are full of buds. Evan Allen lost the suit. Plus, my new novel is going well. Taking my time, I write every day, but not like I used to, with the exclusion of life.

Often, I go to Oakland and spend nights with Nanny, Larry, and my granddaughter. I love going with Nanny to the dog park, pushing Annabelle in a stroller, Nanny's dogs she rescued from the slaughter trucks in China running happily alongside us. Strange with life. You think that you're not happy, or that you're not living as well as others, or that you should be doing other things, but each life has a texture, and its shape is exactly as it should be. What you do with it and how you live it and the choices you make are up to you. Never did I think I'd say this, but I love my life. I'm in love in a way I'd never thought possible.

To keep my creativity alive and to process my thoughts, I paint women in gorgeous dresses, with wild hair and in love on ten-foot sheets of butcher paper.

* * *

"Good news. I sold *Blast,*" Biggie Delano says on the phone.

"Oh my God!" I'm standing on a street corner, waiting to cross an intersection.

"A small advance though. Your sales figures were too terrible, and all the bad publicity, lawsuits, bad press. But once the blog is published, I'm sure it'll take off. Wait till they read it."

We talk a while, enjoying gossiping about Bitterman, the manifesto, and the film.

He laughs. "I've seen Oliver Abbot's picture. Gorgeous. I love that he's gay."

"Obviously, he's bi."

"Bi, gay, it's all the same." He sighs impatiently. "Bring Oliver to New York with you."

"No, you'll flirt with him."

We laugh.

"Seriously, you and Lisa plan to come to New York. We'll celebrate."

* * *

"So let's go to New York," I say to Lisa on her car phone.

"You think I can just pick up and go? That I don't have suicidal patients?"

"I know."

"You don't know!" she shouts. "You go, Mom. It's your work."

"I'd love to be with you," I continue. "It's not just about the work, it's about being together. We'll go to the ballet, the theater, do things."

"Maybe Nanny can get a sitter and she can go too? The three of us for the first time will be together?"

"I agree. We'll be a family."

Nanny agrees, and we plan a trip to New York in the fall. We want to see the leaves change color and attend a Van Gogh exhibit and be together.

I'm living a dream and dreams last only a short time, and it's important that the girls and I create a memory they'll never forget. I'm happy that they see how if you stay on your path of dreams, though the path sometimes gets bumpy, if you stay firm, stay true to who you are, dreams come true.

* * *

Winter has a special light. The dark is blue, and the daylight is sometimes pink. It's time for renewal. I love winter. It's a time for introspection. I go deeper and find more revelations and regrets and memories and as the trees retreat until spring, I prepare for renewal.

Nanny and I and the baby spend weeks looking at cottages in Half Moon Bay, by the ocean. I want the little cottage I've seen so many times in my dreams. Most of the cottages by the sea are too expensive but I know that fate will find mine. I'm planning on using the advance money from the sale of the blog, and hope to pay cash.

But if you believe in your dreams and can improvise, your dream will come true. One windy afternoon, by the edge of the sea, I find and buy a small wooden cottage, a fixer upper cottage almost touching the edge of the roaring sea. In foreclosure, it was a good value and I bought it. With Larry's encouragement and help, we begin fixing it up. I know exactly what I want and we spend days in little dusty antique shops, IKEA, and furniture shops, picking out paint colors.

I hired students who painted the cottage a pale ice gray with white trim, and sanded and stained the old wood floors a pale apricot color with a high gloss. Larry and his contractor friends put in a new kitchen with white counters and white tile floors. Tall oval windows face the sea and overlook the garden where I planted rosebushes.

Though I'm far from my grandchild and Lisa, several months ago I gave up my apartment in San Francisco and live in the cottage full-time. This is the first place I paid for and own. I love living alone. Solitude is not the same as loneliness; it's a celebration and communication with the self, nature, and things that you love. After a lifetime of hiding my feelings so deeply that I couldn't feel anything, and then the years facing my past and eventually my truths, I have revealed who I really am and not who I'd thought I was. Every day is a new discovery. I feel joy for the simplest things—a walk, the myriad of light that falls along the sea at different times of the day and night, the shopkeepers and their rituals, the little grocery store at the end of a mile-long path.

Even the tastes I'd thought I had have changed, and the cottage reveals new parts of me. I haunt small galleries and flea markets, and decorate my cottage with sapphire blue velvet chairs, and contemporary throw rugs. I hang my paintings of women next to African masks and photographs of women writers from the nineteenth century. Floor-to-ceiling bookcases overflow with my art books and collections of first edition poets I love. On tables and shelves are the ceramic bowls I find at flea markets and art fairs. Framed photographs of my brother Rick, my granddaughter, Nanny's dogs, my daughters, and Oliver lean against the walls or are perched on tables. My life surrounds me. Strange you think your life should be one way, even fantasize how it should be, while the whole time you already have so much. At last I feel whole.

My desk where I write sits by the window where I can see the ocean. The pink seashell my mother bought me is next to my computer. Sometimes I hold it next to my ear, remembering that day with my mother when she was sweet and happy and full of love. My father's photograph and screenplays which I had bound are always beside me.

I love the cottage, writing all day and then walking along the sea, exploring the past and contemplating the future. I'm halfway finished drafting a new novel about art and love, questioning what love is. I think like the mutations of a rose, love has so many ways, sides, and complications. It isn't one thing. Nor is there one way to love. I really feel that our culture has turned love into a commodity, into a religion, into a manifesto of rules and into a one size fits all. I love the idea of living forever with a great love, but not with the rules of marriage, which I find ancient and emotionally barbaric. Not that I don't admire those couples who can sit in silence, are bonded, and live all their lives together. It's a beautiful thing, but it should not be taught as the only way to love.

Why do two people want to be one? I ponder. Why can't two people be individuals who come together in their own ways? Just have their own love?

Yes, change is necessary to exhume the past, the darkness that lives in unresolved souls.

Still, Edwina calls, still she's working on *The Viagra Diaries*. "Honey, as we talk CBS is salivating. Are you ready for the great news? Bitterman wants back. He promises that he'll work with you. He'll make *The Viagra Diaries* sexy and glam."

"Not interested," I assure her.

"Think about it."

"I already have."

"Honey, you're hot now. I'll be in touch. Think about it." she says.

But there's nothing to think about. Nothing ever again. Nothing about Bitterman or Hollywood entices me. I don't care about the money and the money I'm making from the film is enough, more than enough. I'm used to budgeting and getting along on little and I feel content. Everything has changed since the film. My former dreams of fame and fortune seem tawdry and so fragile. Until Oliver, I'd needed the dream of fame and fortune to fill the hole in me. But now I'm interested in making art, investigating and knowing my inner life. Which to me is recording the underneath of feelings, observations, insights, and so many things. Wanting to reach my essence, I continue to excavate images and feelings I often discover in my dreams, when I'm writing poetry or walking along the edge of the sea, or watching my granddaughter play.

Sometimes my soul feels heavy, like an extra organ in my body. Like a magical jellyfish, I imagine the soul transparent and stuffed with incidents, regrets and feelings I haven't yet identified.

I turn off the lights and leave the white wooden shutters open. While I sleep, I like to know the sea and the stars and the moon are near me. Tonight, it's windy and the sea is turbulent and I love the sound of the wind. My parents' wedding photograph is on top of the piano I recently purchased. Also a framed photograph of Ricky and I standing by the ocean and our arms are around each other. I am tall and he is small. We are smiling. Various photographs of my daughters, and also one of my father at Universal. He stands proud, his sad somber eyes open wide, his hands folded.

I dream that I'm inside a huge glass egg and I dive through the opening on top, into the sea, soaring to the bottom where I lie flat on my back. My arms fall beside me and bubbles float from my mouth, my eyes, my hair.

I float to the top and I watch Ricky on roller skates skate past me, the wind blowing his bright red hair. He doesn't know his past or his future, he just skates and is free. I call out to him but he doesn't answer. He can't hear me.

I watch my mother arrange peonies into metal frogs, making sure that each stem is secure in each tiny hole. She doesn't like anything out of order. As she works, she hums a symphony. She sits at her grand Steinway piano now. She begins playing Chopin, her listless fingers float along the ivory keys, her heavy hooded eyes half-closed.

There is my father as usual, dressed in his custom gray silk suit, his thinning silver hair combed neatly back from his high, intelligent forehead. He doesn't smile. He looks tired. "Daddy! I love you! Daddy, I'm you. Do you hear me?"

He wanders away. My words are still bubbles and soon I will wake. I can hear the ocean in my dream. It is outside my window and it's beautiful.

* * *

Spring and summer have passed. Winter is so beautiful, the sky silver, the fog like cold lace, and it feels like everything is beginning.

It's past twilight now. I stand by the sea and wait for the dark. I slip into my past. You can't ignore the past. It's there to examine, to find truths and misplaced events. The sea is wild and turbulent and beautiful and as the tide rushes under my feet, I close my eyes and imagine that I'm diving off a cliff, spinning in the air before I touch the water. Dizzy from the beauty, I open my eyes. The wind blows the waves high, crashing them thundering along the edge of the beach. I watch the waves slowly recede and think there is nothing as mysterious, as elegant as the laws of nature. I begin my walk back to the cottage. Holding a basket filled with poems and shells, I walk faster along the edge of the sea, my bare feet making imprints in the sand. I feel exhilarated, in awe of life, of nature, its infinite questions and mysteries.

Night falls. The sky is suddenly dark and full of stars, and they're so beautiful I want to reach up and touch them.

I rush up the twisty path, past the roses, and even in the dark, as if during the day they'd swallowed all the sunlight, they glow.

My new rescue dog Dianne, a beautiful sheep dog, is running towards me, happily barking, and as I look up at the cottage, I wave to Oliver waving from the window. I hurry faster.

The story has been told. A new one begins.

Acknowledgments

To my daughter Suzy Unger who never gives up helping me to reach my dreams. She is my muse, and producer. My daughter Bonny Osterman for her loving support, cakes, chicken soup, and endless help. My sons-in-law Henry Unger, Gary Osterman for their help in so many extra ways. To Florence Osterman. To my late brother Robert Rose, my brother Richard Rose, and to Patti Rose. Special love to Candeice Milford for her devoted support, and cherished friendship, and special gifts. To John Milford, for putting me on stage. To the talented Janet Gallin for her consistent support, cards, cheers, and friendship.

Special gratitude to my literary agent David Vigliano for his support. Enormous thanks to Post Hill Press' Allie Woodlee for her insightful and honest editing. Special thanks to Post Hill Press' Maddie Sturgeon for her precise, detailed editing, patience, and kindness. To the Post Hill design team for their diligence and expertise. To Bill Bowker for fixing my computers and for his friendship. Always to my wonderful friend, writer, TV host, Eileen Williams, and to my oldest friend Norma Kaufman, and to her late husband David Kaufman. Special love to all my students at San Francisco State University/Olli. Especially to writers

Marsha Michaels, Michael Gordon, Francee Covington, Cathy Fiorella, Vivian Zielin, Lucy Sweeney. To Ernie McNabb for his generosity, Riki for our morning phone calls, and for her PR help. To Patty Axelrod for her courage.

Always to my adored cousin Linda Diller, my beautiful friend Kelly Eder, my brilliant soulmate and playwright Mira Pasikov, Dr. Janine Canan my favorite poet, James Bostwick, a terrific writer and friend. Love to my fabulous talented niece, Keran Davison.

Special thanks to the fabulous writer/producer/agent Tony Krantz for his help and support, and to Patti Felker, the best entertainment lawyer in LA. Also thanks to Erwin More for his help and to Marilyn Atlas for her friendship.

Special thanks to Risa MaKabe for her friendship and generosity and fabulous style. To the late Barbara Brenner for listening every week and who I will miss forever. Dennis Beckman, Takiyah Smith, Richard Ayoub, Bradly Bessey, Suzanne Spitz, Michelle Spitz, and Marilyn Schneider who reads all my books. To Barbara Babin for all her dinners, and Patty McPeak for her laughter.

To Kathy Lerner, love, forever and my BFF until eternity. Jerry Astrove, Donald Alex, and forever love to Barry Miller and David Weiner. To Dr. Michael Mayer for the trip below. Nancy Klein Green, Diane Rosenberg, Toby Tover, Joanne Abel, and all the friends I didn't mention because of space. Thank you.

Fred Holub, Geoff McNalley who live upstairs and I couldn't do without. Audrey Lavin for her support of my paintings and books. Always for Tara Cortez-Cayton and her help and friendship. Everyone at Shanti—especially Susan Zavado, Barbara Manzanares, Luisa Palaban, Lily Tsen, Judith Harkins, Deanna Gibbons, Janet Sipos, Tasia Bartell, Myrna Aronoff, my students and staff at SFSU/OLLI, Sandra, Stella Elert for the cards and support and always, Susan Savage.

Jeb Wright, a writer to watch, Olivia Barbee, the best neighbor, and special love to Delilah Sharp.

Gratitude and love to the late Bob Brooker. My late cousin Nancy Rosenthal. To the late Marlene Levinson.

Always special thanks to Book Passage, Corte Madera, SFSU, the SF Commonwealth Club, *JWeekly*, and to the SF Age Institute.

About the Author

Barbara Rose Brooker, MA, age activist, teacher, painter, and poet, has published eleven books of fiction and won a National Library Award for her poetry. She has appeared often on *The Today Show, The Talk, ET, Andy Cohen,* and *Watch What Happens Live*. Also a columnist, she has published *Boomer in the City* for the *JWeekly* and the *Huffington Post*. Currently she teaches writing at San Francisco State/OLLI, and other venues. She is the founder of *agemarch.org, the* first march in history to celebrate age pride! She believes that anyone at any age can write and publish a book. She lives in San Francisco, has two daughters, and loves dogs. She is at work on a book of short stories about aging with glamour and never giving up on dreams.